ABORTION STORIES
FICTION ON FIRE

Edited by Rick Lawler

MinRef Press

For Tang Kung

who was there when we really needed him.

Deepest thanks to *Carol Lynn* for her comments, suggestions, and encouragement.

Acknowledgements

Introduction and Afterwords Copyright © 1992 by Rick Lawler.
Foreword, "Abortion and the Failure of Consensus" Copyright © 1992 by David Brin
"Silver Stars" Copyright © 1992 by Alan Bryden
"Still Life" Copyright © 1992 by Ron Dee
"Crackland" Copyright © 1992 by Molly Gallagher
"Abortion Is Life" Copyright © 1992 by William Campbell
"Healing Hands" Copyright © 1992 by Esther C. Gropper
"Bait and Switch" Copyright © 1992 by Barry Hoffman
"Khellie" Copyright © 1992 by Mike Hurley
"The Days of Babies" Copyright © 1992 by Joyce Hunt
"Rock-A-Bye" Copyright © 1992 by Edward Lodi
"We Are Flesh, We Are Flame" Copyright © 1992 by P. Willis Pitts
"Factors" Copyright © 1992 by Gregory Nyman
"Dr. Pak's Preschool" Copyright © 1989 by David Brin, originally published by Cheap Street Press, 1989, reprinted in *The Magazine of Fantasy and Science Fiction*, 1990; Reprinted by *Pulphouse Publishing Short Story Paperbacks* series, 1991
"TLC" copyright © 1992 by Virginia Orphant
"RUI-480 In the Cosmic Circus" Copyright © 1992 by Wendy Corrina Leadbeater
"Rabbit Hole" Copyright © 1992 by Ginny Sanders
"GP Venture" Copyright © 1992 by L. Crittenden
"Fetuscam" Copyright © 1990 by James S. Dorr, originally published in the Spring, 1990 issue of *Pandora*
"New Moon" Copyright © 1992 by Nowick Gray
"Feed Us" Copyright © 1992 by Wayne Allen Sallee
"Ask Dr. Schund" Copyright © 1992 by Alan M. Schwartz
"Seventh Son of A Seventh Son" Copyright © 1992 by T. Diane Slatton
"Order of the Virgin Mothers" Copyright © 1992 by Lois June Wickstrom
"Miscarriage" Copyright © 1992 by A.M. Friedson

MinRef Press
8379 Langtree Way
Sacramento, CA 95823

CONTENTS

Foreword   i
    David Brin
Introduction   v
    Rick Lawler
Silver Stars   11
    Alan Bryden
Still Life   15
    Ron Dee
Crackland   31
    Molly Gallagher
Abortion Is Life   37
    William Campbell
Healing Hands   51
    Esther C. Gropper
Bait and Switch   57
    Barry Hoffman
Khellie   77
    Mike Hurley
The Days of Babies   83
    Joyce Hunt
Rock-A-Bye   91
    Edward Lodi
We Are Flesh, We Are Flame   95
    P. Willis Pitts

Factors   103
  Gregory Nyman
Dr. Pak's Preschool   107
  David Brin
TLC   135
  Virginia Orphant
RUI-480 in the Cosmic Circus   141
  Wendy Corrina Leadbeater
Rabbit Hole   149
  Ginny Sanders
GP Venture   159
  L. Crittenden
Fetuscam   167
  James S. Dorr
New Moon   173
  Nowick Gray
Feed Us   187
  Wayne Allen Sallee
Ask Dr. Schund   195
  Alan M. Schwartz
Seventh Son of A Seventh Son   199
  T. Diane Slatton
Order of the Virgin Mothers   209
  Lois June Wickstrom
Miscarriage   245
  A.M. Friedson

Foreword—
Abortion and the Failure
of Consensus

David Brin, Ph.D.

Something akin to civil war awaits us, as the upcoming Battle over Abortion reaches full-pitch. With each side devoutly convinced of its moral high ground (and the vileness of its opposition) a spiral of self-righteousness and scorched earth spreads across the land.

One side appeals to a long-standing tradition of supporting the rights of individuals, especially to control their own lives. Americans look skeptically whenever the state (or some group) tries to impose a particular morality on everybody.

The other side has its own taproot to American sensibilities. Many consider abortion murder, while others see in it the start down a slippery slope toward euthanasia, forced sterilization, and a general collapse in the perceived sanctity of life.

Recently, a despairing pundit proclaimed our problem to be one of "binary laws for an analog world". In other words, people want everything neatly defined...what is human and what is not. When an embryo is living, when it isn't. But nature seems to prefer murky borders and intermediate stages. While extremists on both sides self-righteously over simplify a complicated issue, the rest of us have to wrestle with ambiguity. The names "pro-life" (as opposed to *"anti*-life?") and "pro-choice" are self-chosen terms which reflect the art of propaganda far more than any effort to persuade with reason.

What ever happened to the American genius for compromise? We are not, by native inclination, creatures of ideology, who give absolute loyalty to "party lines." We're a nation of ticket-splitters, who expect and demand that a Republican president find *modus vivendi* with a Democratic Congress.

"Pragmatism" and "consensus" are venerable terms in U.S. politics. Today one sees liberals agreeing to experiment with workfare and "Choice in Schools," formerly anathema to the left. Meanwhile, oldline conservatives are admitting, at long last, that right-wing dictators are just as bad as the socialist kind, and that human rights can be a valid basis for foreign policy. There has even been movement on gun control, with a large majority agreeing that assault rifles don't qualify under any definition of "sportsmanship."

If ideologues can adjust and re-adapt on so many other issues, why has there been so little progress on abortion? Radicals on both sides persist in painting the situation in stark black and white, a choice between two moral extremes. Human life starts at conception and all abortion is murder. Or whatever goes on inside a woman's body is her business and nobody may interfere.

In fact, neither extremist position represents the views of average Americans. Public opinion polls show a substantial majority of Americans feel abortion is unpalatable and undesirable. But just as many also agree that a woman's control over her own reproductive life should include abortion as a last resort option.

This uncomfortable ambivalence has so far seen few ideas for compromise. So the arena has been left to the radicals. Pro-Choice activists accuse Pro-Lifers of hypocrisy. "How many poor black babies have *you* adopted, lately?" they ask. Why aren't Pro-Life groups at the forefront, demanding better healthcare, paid maternity leave, and education for the poor children they sponsor into existence? Why do so many Pro-Lifers also oppose sex education in the schools, where kids might learn to avoid unwanted pregnancies in the first place?

These are telling indictments, but Pro-Choice radicals aren't immune from criticism, either. Why are they so unwilling to admit that abortion is dangerous, invasive and offensive to most Americans? Why do they respond so shrilly and unreasonably to the modest suggestion that *restraint* and *self-control* may be worthy elements in a workable sex-education curriculum? In so doing, the left only ruins its credibility with common-sense Americans. Only those wearing ideological blinkers cannot see that character-building and patience are even better defenses against unwanted pregnancy and disease than free condoms.

This would be a refreshing sight—a third type of picket sign, raised at those ghastly rallies. Signs saying—"Will you people on both sides please SHUT UP?"

I would like to see a national conference, to which only moderates are invited, along with educators, philosophers, medical specialists, and religious leaders. The discussion would focus on how we might achieve what the majority clearly wants—a step-by-step *diminution* of abortion—by eliminating the need for it in the first place—while continuing to secure a woman's right of choice over the long run.

Such a compromise might begin with moderate Pro-Choice people admitting the benefits of a vigorous campaign to persuade young people to a less frenetic view of sexuality. No so much abstinence as *care*. So long as no religious content is dealt out, why shouldn't health classes teach girls to respect themselves, and boys to be patient? This can be promoted without necessarily binding teenagers in a straight-jacket of puritanism. Moderate Pro-Lifers might find it easier to accept what they now find loathsome, the teaching of contraception, if restraint were part of the curriculum.

(On the other hand, it can be pointed out that the Bible actually contains not a single mention of pre-marital sex, let alone a declaration that it is a sin.)

The gag order on federally-funded health clinics even mentioning, or offering referral, to abortion centers, should be withdrawn as the shame that it is. On the other hand however, why should it be anathema when Pro-Lifers ask for access to clients at clinics, to offer them alternatives? Of course, this should exclude poor women being subjected to shrill, gory propaganda. But could not rules be set down, so that intimidation is replaced by a window of time in which alternatives might be sincerely presented? Each side seems patronizingly dedicated to *protecting* newly-pregnant women from full access to information. Perhaps a better way would be to agree on a morally neutral, non-coercive video that clinics might show, offering *all* choices, and sources of help and aid during a time of confusion and fear.

Of course no compromise will ever be acceptable to radicals of either side. But a national consensus might push the screamers back to the fringes, where they belong. It might also begin to achieve something the rest of us desire: a diminishment of the rate of abortion, not by suppression but by eliminating some of its unfortunate root causes.

In this way, we just might be spared a grisly, crippling, noisome civil war we never wanted in the first place.

So we come to this volume, an attempt to break loose the logjam of ideas by applying the pry-bar of *art*. Specifically, fiction. The stories written for this volume represent the fantasies, nightmares, and hopes of two-dozen gifted individuals, all of whom have been—like the rest of us—disturbed by the national debate...the national agony...over this terrible issue. Each of these writers has, in her or his own way, tried to convey some sense of what the word, and the act, "abortion" means to them.

Art often consists of exaggeration, and if some of these tales seem daring, challenging, absurd, eerie, disgusting or dismaying, then that comes with the territory. Not all art is good, but there are always pearls to be found amid dross, when bright people probe the limits of shocking reality.

These artists, at least, are trying. If there's to be any hope for moving the discussion away from sloganeering toward meaningful solutions, then we *all* had better start trying a lot harder.

David Brin is the bestselling Hugo- and Nebula-award winning author of Startide Rising and the Uplift War, Earth, The Postman, and other novels. This is the first of his two appearances in this book.

Introduction—
Blessed Assurance

Rick Lawler

How come I haven't seen any books with short stories about abortion? Whenever you ask a question like that, you've got potential for a book. So when I asked the question during the summer of 1991, I knew what the possible result might be.

I'd asked the question, "What's the address for the Premier of China?" back in 1989, and that ended up in a two-year ordeal—putting together a book of names and addresses for the leaders of earth's nations. **How to Write to World Leaders** is available from Avon Books. Buy copies for everybody you know, and I'll retire.

This, however, was an entirely different kettle of fish. Abortion is a controversial subject. Was I going to get my head chopped off for even suggesting such a thing? After all, I'm not female. I've never had an abortion. I've never been pregnant. I reasoned, however, that one did not have to be a boxer to make an adequate referee.

What is it about abortion that causes such controversy?

Simple. It's the absolute, total, immovable assurance that each side is right.

For the pro-life candidate, abortion is murder. It's worse than murder, it's legal killing of babies—unborn helpless babies.

The pro-choice candidate just as firmly believes that a woman has the right to choose what happens to her body. An unwanted baby is better off terminated while it's still the size of a tadpole.

Pro-life: It ought to be illegal to murder babies.

Pro-choice: You can't legislate morality.

Pro-life: Every life born into this world is a new hope.

Pro-choice: Making abortions illegal would only promote illegal abortions. Dark alleys and coat hangers. Dead mothers *and* babies.

Pro-life: A baby is a baby; it's our duty as human beings to protect babies, not kill them.

Pro-choice: A first trimester fetus is *not* a living human being.

Pro-life: A first trimester fetus is *absolutely* a living human being.

And on it goes.

Even the common ground is looked at differently. A group of pro-choicers may admit that legal, easily available abortion promotes abortion of convenience. It's just too much trouble to be pregnant, so get rid of it. Most pro-choicers will freely admit they are pro-life; many are anti-abortion. But they feel the right of choice takes precedence over their personal beliefs. And once you mention that word "choice", you're automatically pro-choice.

Pro-lifers are much more likely to be uncompromising. Every conception ought to result in a birth. Of course, these people are less likely to concern themselves with the living conditions in which these babies find themselves after leaving the hospital.

If the mother's addicted to cocaine, throw the bitch in jail. If she's on welfare, make her go to work. If the pregnancy was the result of lack of sex education, that's too bad. Abstinence is the answer.

Right.

Isn't it strange that the majority of pro-choicers are liberal, and these people tend to oppose the death penalty. It's okay to kill 'em before they're born, but not after, huh?

Pro-lifers are more conservative; these are the same people who overwhelmingly support the death penalty. Go figure.

I guess that once you're born, the pro-choicers will do everything they can to make sure you stay around as long as you want. Once you're born, the pro-lifers could give a rat's ass what happens to you, but if you screw up, they'll be more than happy to do away with you.

Both sides seem to have forgotten that there are over 5.5 billion humans on earth today, and each day brings another 240,000 new mouths to feed, bodies to clothe, minds to educate. That's the net daily increase of earth's human population.

Neither side seems to have any answers to that.

Needless to say, this argument could go on for pages. I find it curious that I can argue with myself, take both sides, and believe every word while I'm doing it. I guess I'm the last person to come to for answers.

Introduction

But if you've come here for some great stories, you've come to the right place. I doubt you'll find any answers; but I guarantee you'll have something to think about.

Someone who has their mind made up, and doesn't want their opinion to be altered by facts, might be more willing to explore other ideas if presented as fiction. Fiction provides an emotional distancing that non-fiction can't.

There are the strong stories. Check out Edward Lodi's chilling story and see what the cat dragged home, or the one by Gregory Nyman (which scared the editor so bad he was afraid to reject it). William Campbell has provided what could only be termed a pro-life horror story. T. Diane Slatton offers an emotionally-charged excursion into the pain of procreation.

You'll find well-known writers here. David Brin, of course, is the bestselling S-F author of Hugo- and Nebula-Award-winning novels. His story is about a fetus that performs its own abortion. Ron Dee is just emerging as a prolific novelist. His work tells the gentle story of a woman who made a choice a long time ago. Barry Hoffman, the editor of the critically acclaimed annual magazine *Gauntlet*, tells a story about an abortion clinic with a difference. P. Willis Pitts, well-known British playwright, offers a science fictional view of a returning life-form that seeks a physical body in which to return to earth.

Idea people tell tales that range from a story based on gnostic mythology to one that proposes the use of crack-addicted babies for entertainment purposes to one that proposes a man's right to choose.

Some of these stories are not for the weak of heart (or mind). For instance, well-known horror writer Wayne Allen Sallee gives us a frightening look at a hell for serial killers, and asks, "where do babies go when aborted?"

There are other stories, by Esther C. Gropper, by Nowick Gray, by Alan Bryden, and others, each and every one worthy of mention in this introduction. Twenty-two short stories and one poem, all but two seeing print for the first time.

But enough; I could go on and on. It's time to take the plunge. Dive in and enjoy an outstanding collection of fiction—a collection that's as relevant as today's headlines.

— *Rick Lawler*, April 1992, Sacramento, CA

ABORTION STORIES
FICTION ON FIRE

Silver Stars

Alan Bryden

Dear Ms. Jones,

I read your poem "Silver Stars" in *Vision-ings* magazine. I really liked it alot. I thought of it when my boss yelled at me yesterday, and it made me feel better instead of getting mad like I always do.

I've read alot of your stuff before. It's all great. I love you. Can you print a book soon? I'd really like to meet you.

Sincerely,

Sam Linebarger

He wants to meet me. God.

Flickering lights ran the length of the crowded ward Patty Jones lay in. Trying to read under those had made her eyes burn again. And for what? Just some stupid fanboy letter. She moved her withered hand over the bed's railing and let it drop. Let the janitor have it.

God only knows how much time that letter had wasted. The way the doctors spoke, Patty wouldn't even see her twenty-first birthday. And the effort wasted on the letter most likely shortened that even further. No, Sam Lineburger, I'm not going to write you a damn book.

Just the exertion of moving her hand had sent shudders through her body. Patty could never remember a time without pain—but she never got used to it. Since before she was born, cocaine and heroin and God only knows what else had saturated her body. Medical science could create a plastic heart, or cut out cancer with a laser. But an addict was still an addict. And Patty was an addict.

If the police had only found out about her mother's pregnancy earlier, they could have forced her to have an abortion. The woman was already under court-ordered contraceptives—that was back when there was just the pill, not this Norplant that courts can order on irresponsible mothers. And in this case, "irresponsible" was an understatement. With four children already, drug addictions, confessions of child abuse—the judge's decision must have been pretty easy.

Maybe the contraceptives had failed. Maybe the bitch had palmed them. Hell, she could have gotten an abortion! The government would have paid for it.

Now Patty had to pay the price. If only the pill had worked. If only she'd been aborted. If only the fucking whore had ODd or something! God damn her!

That outburst must have triggered an alarm on the nurse's monitor. Roly-poly Nurse Winter stood over Patty's bed now, giving her something. Ow. But after the injection, a little relief did creep in.

Every day of her life, Patty had expected death. Always. She'd been told about her problem—why she couldn't be like everyone else.

But she'd stumbled along. First on crutches, then in a wheelchair—it was hard, but every day, she'd seen the sun set. And she'd actually excelled, selling poems, winning a few prizes. Best of all, writing had let her forget the pain for a moment, letting her feel truly alive.

Still, it all caught up with her. Piece by piece, she had disintegrated, faster and faster. Her voice, her hands—the tools she'd used to live—now were nearly useless.

Darkness hovered nearer now, closing in. The world was a blur of painkillers and dull aches. Maybe with money from a book, with halfway decent treatment, she could survive.

There was so much to do! A hundred books to write, just so this Sam Limburger could stand up to his stupid boss. Did I really help him? Is he really stronger? I only wrote the things for myself, my own pain.

He really liked it a lot. Alot. He'd said. It really was a good poem, wasn't it? Her weakness spilt onto the page had strengthened him. Now he loves me. He wants to meet me. Take me out on a date, to a show and dinner and dancing and living and loving and living. I want to write books. For him. To help him and love him.

I died so much and lived so much, shooting my silver stars across little scraps of paper, riding on them and flying and burning with it all so alive.

It was good to be alive, Patty thought. As she died.

This is Alan Bryden's first professional sale, although he has been writing since 1987. He has, he says, "a handsome stack of rejection slips." I chose this as the lead-off story because it evokes the dual emotions of the abortion controversy. If Patty had never been born, she would have been spared the pain and suffering. But the short life she had affected for the better those who read her works. The inner fight Patty had with herself is the same one we all wrestle with.

Still Life

Ron Dee

Sometimes, late at night, the frustration came.

Kat looked at Bobby—she still called him Bobby even though he was the vice-president of the investment company now. But no one else did. His closest friends didn't dare to refer to him as less than Robert. Sometimes she would stare at him, wondering why she was here, lying in his bed.

She looked at him like that now.

But he was asleep, his eyes trembling under closed lids.

She thought...hoped...that he felt the frustration, too.

But he wouldn't talk about it anymore.

Why should *he* feel the frustration?

Kat sat up, throwing her sheets aside, and stood. She was awake now, but the dream was closer instead of fading. Kat walked to the long hallway of their home, finding her way through the shadows that seemed to grope for her the way Bobby still tried to. The shadows were her past, holding the promise of a life that always seemed to be within her grasp...

But not quite.

The hallway became the living room. Another hallway...the kitchen...into her work room at the back of the house. Her studio.

The curtains were open and the light of a crescent moon lit the walls.

Kat sat down at her desk, staring at her unfinished layout for the department store ad. It was like her life, except tomorrow, she would complete the draft, wait for approval, and then finish it. The ad would be viewed by millions in a Sunday paper supplement...admired for the prices it displayed instead of for her artwork.

"Why?" she asked the twitching shadow of a treelimb on the wall.

The limb grew still.

Kat woke up in bed. Bobby was gone. The shadows were gone. She remembered them for only a moment, took a shower, dressed and made herself breakfast. Pancakes with a strawberry topping. She smiled and added chocolate syrup and a layer of cheese gratings. *Pregnant.*

Yes. This was her craving when she was pregnant.

It was funny she remembered that so well. Twenty-one years had passed since that singular event clouded her life. She remembered taking a test in class that day and passing the college infirmary. She took Bobby's hand and they walked inside...and the doctor smiled as he gave her the news.

Bobby didn't smile, and her own smile faded quickly without his. They had a long talk about purpose...about life. Bobby had two more years before he could get his degree, and she had three. Neither of them were well off...with a baby their degrees might as well be a thousand years away. Bobby didn't even offer to get a job...only to pay for the abortion.

Kat had gone back to her dorm room and cried. She had looked at her paintings...a watercolor and two oils that had been exhibited during a local art show.

He wasn't ready for a family, and he convinced her that she wasn't, either. They both had their whole lives ahead of them...

She wanted a baby, but not so soon.

It was a difficult decision, but that wasn't when the shadows began.

Finishing the department store layout, Kat bundled it up and looked at the painting on her wall. It was her best work: The still life with a robin, but she had painted it so long ago...back before her life had turned dark. Before—

She forced an artificial smile and went to her car. She had to drop the package off downtown. She steered the car from the residential district to the main streets until tall business buildings surrounded her with their shadows. Still caught up in her own gloom, Kat parked and went inside one of those buildings, hardly speaking to the receptionist as she left her folder. The woman told her they would call her, and Kat nodded, walking out. She looked at her watch and got back in her *Toyota*, then drove to the TU campus. At one o'clock she was scheduled for a guest lecture on commercial art.

Commercial art. Was there such a thing?

At least it pays, Bobby always said. He always thought of success in terms of decimal points.

But it wasn't what she wanted. It wasn't part of her dream. She had lived for that dream, but it was always just beyond her...part of that dream already gone forever: She had gotten her abortion, but the doctor had made a mistake. Not an obvious or dangerous one, but a mistake nonetheless. When she and Bobby finally married three years later and set up housekeeping, she learned that the infection the operation gave her had made her sterile.

That ensuing lawsuit was ruled in their favor, but the knowledge she would always be barren was what brought on the shadows, and the sorrow grew deeper each year—

Suddenly the university buildings seemed to take shape through the windshield, and Kat sighed, pushing memories aside. Time, like Bobby, had no pity for her reflections.

Kat parked near the stadium on a streetful of apartments, picked up her briefcase, and slammed the door shut. She walked away from her car and past a large number of students going to or returning from lunch. She steered past the library and entered a massive, stone building, thinking of how badly she had wanted to adopt a child, but each one only reminded her that she could never have one that would truly be her own.

She could never have a child. Not her *own*.

Even as she found the lecture room and set up her drawings while students filed in, she could not forget the shadows.

"Is there much chance for your commercial stuff to help you get into real art?"

Kat's gut flinched. "Of course there is," she spoke slowly. "Just as much so as getting a promotion with any other job. Still, years can pass before you get the chance you want. You might never get it."

A tall woman who looked twenty spoke up: "Do you do anything serious? Oils and watercolors... Are you waiting for your chance?"

Kat blushed. "I have tried," she managed.

"Any luck?" asked the tall woman, tugging her long brown hair.

Kat shook her head briefly, not allowing her emotion to show. She opened her mouth, then pressed her teeth tight, and finally opened her mouth again. "It's all a gamble," she spoke finally.

The tall girl raised an eyebrow, keeping her smile. "Just like life?"

The question was innocent, but Kat flinched. Before she could speak, someone else raised his hand. A young man about the same age. His face was very serious. "Do you recommend commercial art for someone who is trying to break into other forms of art?"

The blond boy became a shadow as his words echoed in her head. Kat swallowed hard. "You have do something to survive," she told him. "To survive, you have to do whatever you can."

He nodded and wrote something down, then cocked his head. "From the looks of your mohair suit, you've survived pretty well, haven't you?"

Kat barely smiled and pointed at another student.

Gathering up her materials and replacing them in her briefcase, Kat left the course instructor, sighed and walked toward the doorway. The students had gathered around her after the lecture and she had answered their further queries, but was glad it was over.

"You don't seem happy," spoke a soft voice at Kat's shoulder.

Turning quickly, Kat saw the tall woman who asked her questions during the lecture. "I'm just tired," Kat replied.

The woman nodded. "I have trouble sleeping, too, sometimes. It gets so I feel that life has just passed me by, and even though I can't do anything about it, it bugs me."

Looking at the woman's youth, Kat shook her head. "At your age, life is just beginning."

"Is it?"

Something about the woman drew Kat's sympathy. She smiled at her. "What's your name?"

"Robin...like a bird."

Kat narrowed her gaze. "Interesting name."

The woman's slender face built into cheery laughter. "I like it. It makes me feel free."

"Like a bird?" asked Kat.

Robin's smiled wobbled. "It just makes me feel free. Real. A name makes you *real*."

The tone of Robin's voice was hopeful but uncertain. Kat made a noise of lazy amusement. "Is that so? It's an interesting theory. Maybe you should be taking a course in Humanities or Philosophy."

They walked together through the doorway and into the wide hall of hurrying students. Robin shook her head. "Not me. I mean, it's like when you first start class. No one knows your name and they could be talking to anyone when they're speaking to you. A name makes you somebody. It makes you *real*." Her eyes seemed to light up. "*It makes you part of the outside world*."

Kat glanced at her briefly. "It takes more than a name."

"You're right, of course," the younger woman nodded agreeably. "Names are only the beginning. They're kind of like hopes and promises. If those hopes disappear, the name is only a memory of what never came true."

"Maybe a poetry class..." Kat stopped as they came to the exit doors, staring into the woman's dark eyes. Sad eyes. Kat felt a stirring inside herself of an excitement she hadn't known for too many months, imagining how she might capture those eyes and the disguised mournful texture in them on canvas.

"Are you okay?" Robin asked.

The words didn't even break her concentration and the sudden desire to paint the portrait. Kat felt possibilities of freedom, of escaping from her own shadows by releasing the shadows in Robin's eyes with her artistic ability. With the way she was suddenly identifying her life inside those deep pupils, Kat knew it would be her best work... another still life with a *Robin*.

"Do you—"

Kat sighed deeply, hiding the tremble rousing inside her. "I'm okay," she whispered.

"Well, I guess you have to go, huh? Thanks for talking with me."

Robin started to turn away and Kat reached out her free hand to stop her. "Please..."

"Are you sure you're okay?"

Kat shook her head tightly. "You. Your eyes."

Robin tilted her head uncertainly.

"Have...have you ever posed before?"

Those strange eyes blinked nervously. "Posed?"

"Like a model...for a painting?"

Robin's face flushed bright pink. "You mean like...*nude*?"

Kat nodded her head up and down, then stopped and felt her own face becoming hot. "Uh...not exactly. I mean..." She took a long, deep breath. "I mean, yes—*like* posing nude, but not *nude*. I want to paint you...your face, I mean. Your *eyes*."

A pair of students passed them, laughing at some joke, but Kat barely heard the interruption. Already, she was selecting peach and blush from her palette, imagining them stroked carefully onto a newly stretched canvas.

"My face," Robin whispered, and touched each cheek with a hand. She pulled back a lengthy strand of hair. "You really mean it? *You* want to paint my face?"

Kat swallowed.

"Sure," Robin spoke, still quietly. "I mean...it's like what I was saying about names, isn't it? A name is hope, but when someone puts your image down on canvas, that's really real, isn't it? Like Jan VerMeer's *Head of a Young Girl*. She was painted over 300 years ago, but she's still alive, kind of."

Her sudden enthusiasm made Kat giggle. "I'm no VerMeer," she replied.

"When? When do you want to do it?"

"Whenever it's convenient for you," Kat shrugged. "I'll pay you, of course."

Robin was shaking her head. "I ought to pay you. This will be great. I can hardly believe it! Can we start tonight?"

Surprised, Kat stared at her bubbling, happy features with brief hesitation, then shrugged again. "If you like. It will probably be better for me with the inspiration so fresh."

"Yes!" Robin blurted gleefully. "Do you have a studio?"

Hesitation again. Kat felt icy prickles raise the invisible hair on her arms, but managed to open her purse with one hand and gave Robin her card. "Can you come over about seven?"

Robin nodded quickly, grabbing the card like it was a pass to the stars. "That'll be great. I don't have any class tomorrow, either. You can work as late as you want!"

Kat came home and ate alone. Again. Bobby left a note that he was having dinner with some clients. For once, she didn't mind. Her urge to create was blossoming inside. Strong, too, like it once had been.

Like when she was young.

After putting the dishes in the sink and throwing out the food she'd barely touched, Kat changed into her painting clothes, a long shapeless kimono with bizarre patterns of dark and bright smears—so many it would be difficult to be sure which had come from her own carelessness and which were intended. She went to her studio and selected a fresh canvas, setting it on the easel. Then she began arranging lights and choosing between her pastels for a background, although she knew she would do it again after Robin arrived. Her lower belly burned with stimulation like it had when she and Bobby had once made love, but she ignored the thought of sexuality. She knew it wasn't sex. It was the anticipation of beginning her life again. Of *painting...*

Of painting Robin.

Kat's eyes strayed to the still life of the bird, the first robin, that had been her greatest achievement so far.

So long ago.

She had painted since then. Often at first, but each attempt seemed more lackluster than the ones that preceded it. Something about the robin that had posed so patiently for her outside her dorm window those years before had impelled her to immortalize it. When she hadn't finished that afternoon and it flew off, she had only hoped she could finish it by memory.

But the next day, it was back, as though by her invitation, and she worked again furiously, finishing before it left again at dusk. She put out bread crumbs for it the next day, intending to thank it, but it never returned.

Weird. Still, she had forgotten how weird it had been a week later, after that visit to the college doctor.

Now that another Robin had come into her life, she remembered.

Weird again. Robin and robin.

Weird.

The doorbell rang.

Clopping noisily in her house slippers, Kat gave a last look at the studio and then went into the front hall. Her heart was thudding hard even before she touched the doorknob, like on that night when she made plans to lose her virginity. As then, warmth again flooded her face and abdomen.

The doorknob was firm and hard, and her fingers lingered around it like it was alive, and then she twisted it slowly, deftly, and opened the barrier that had closed her away from herself so long.

Robin was smiling behind the outer glass, and Kat opened that door, too, moving her eyes over the woman's lithe shape in her silky, long dress. Robin's hair was brushed back, hiding the length behind her shoulders, and those eyes glowed with the awakening Kat felt in her own soul.

But still, behind that light, the darkness dwelt.

"Come in, Robin," Kat greeted her breathlessly, holding the door open as the woman walked into the hallway. "I'm glad you could make it."

Robin turned her eyes through the dimness with a sense of wonder. "I wouldn't have missed it. I feel really privileged to be here."

Kat laughed. "You really are very polite. Thanks. Do you want something to drink maybe...something to eat?"

Bunching her fine shoulders, Robin was quiet.

"Wine and cheese maybe?"

Finally, the tall woman nodded. "That would be nice."

Taking Robin's hand, Kat led her to the studio. The warmth of arousal tickled her again, more powerfully this time, in the touch of the girl's flesh. But not really arousal like it had been with Bobby. A release. She held to that.

A *release*.

"This is wonderful!" Robin exclaimed when they entered the room. "I love it. This place looks just like I want *my* studio to look."

"Really?" Kat murmured, pleased but also accustomed to the admiration of younger, budding artists. The intrusion of that reality tempered her excitement a bit and she left Robin to study the paintings and ad trophies on her wall as she went to the kitchen. Opening the refrigerator door, Kat pulled out an opened bottle of *Korbel*. She twisted off the stopper and poured it into two clean glasses, found a block of Colby mixed with Monterey Jack, and cut off some slices. Putting it all on a silver tray, she added crackers and canned cheese spread, and carried it back. Robin was at the far wall, staring at her older paintings intently.

"Did you do all these?"

Kat just grinned. "A long time ago. That's some of my best stuff. My newer paintings don't really measure up. Hopefully, though, my portrait of you *will*. I want this to be the best thing I've ever done."

"So do I," blushed Robin. "I want it to be something everyone will take notice of, and I know it will be with these other things you've done. You're really talented."

It sounded like one of the millions of lame compliments other novices had given her. The words at least, but the tone in her voice was anything but. Timid, maybe. Hopeful. Kat felt warm again. Hopeful, just like a name.

"All I have to do," Kat chuckled, handing Robin a glass and leading her to a chair, "is capture you as exactly as I can. You'll do the rest. Those eyes of yours will do the rest."

"Like Vermeer's *Head of a Girl?*"

Sipping her wine, Kat grinned back and began to position Robin's face, not giving her time for her own drink. Robin let her, putting the glass down. "We'll have time for munchies later," Kat apologized, "if you don't mind. I really want to get started."

Robin's smile was small, but not sad, as if she had not expected refreshment first.

"Just hold still, okay? I'll get everything set and then you can relax a bit."

Robin nodded and then didn't move. Kat smiled to herself, then went to the lights and changed the shadows on Robin's face. But they would draw attention away from the eyes, and those were what Kat most truly wanted to emulate. She finally fixed it to take away any hint of the artificiality lighting would create at all. Those eyes contained all the shadows any painting needed.

A half hour passed like it had never existed, and finally Kat was ready to pick her colors. The brushes she had already chosen. An aqua haze, she decided, to keep the image dreamy, with a hint of reality beyond. That was the truth of the girl. A face lost in dreams...with the eyes nearly nightmarish.

A nightmare of shadows.

At last she sketched in the likeness of the mild face three feet away, plainly, no embellishment, and began the first brushstroke.

Hours passed. Three. Unaccustomed to sitting, Robin grew tired and her eyelids drooped. Though Kat hated to admit it, that signalled the end of this session. Robin apologized and agreed to meet her the next afternoon, and Kat saw her to the door, then hurried back to study what she'd accomplished.

There, before her, was Robin's still eager countenance, unblemished by the wrinkles of time and turmoil, almost completed. The eyes were just begun, nearly blank in their expressionlessness. Tomorrow, she would fill them in and try to recreate that particular powerful quality that so touched her own soul.

Kat put down the brush and turned to the still life she completed all those years before, then picked up a slice of cheese, munching it. The smell of her paints and thinner made the air pungent; made the snack sour with the guilt that she had brought this food in for her guest, and Robin had not had the opportunity to accept the offering. But like that little bird, Robin would come back tomorrow, and when they finished, tomorrow, or maybe the next day, Kat would offer her a better thanks then. She owed her that much at least, because she knew right now that this was the masterpiece that had built inside her for these many years: The masterpiece that would shut away the shadows of torment. By expressing her own sorrow and loss through the eyes of Robin, Kat's uneasy past would be removed, transferred by some mysterious artistic power from her deepest emotions onto canvas, to be wondered at by others and perhaps never understood.

Like *Mona Lisa's* smile or the *Head of a Young Girl.*

Kat began cleaning her brushes, not daring to go on now with her perfect model gone.

The front door clattered open, then shut again.

Kat barely noticed.

The front closet opened and closed.

"*Kat?*"

She looked up, seeing Bobby in his rumpled suit and loose tie, his shirt open at the collar. Without a word, she put the caps on her tubes and covered the canvas.

"Are you painting *again?*"

She began turning off the bright lights.

"I wish you'd forget that crap and stick to the ads, you know? Everytime you try to paint something you freak out and go frigid. Paintings don't make money, anyhow. Ads *do.*"

"We've got enough money," Kat said.

"Never enough," Bobby muttered, walking to the easel laboriously. He reeled a bit, but she didn't need to ask if he'd been drinking, she could smell it on his clothes and breath.

"Did you make us some money tonight then?"

"Maybe I did," laughed Bobby. "I got Dick Gunter and his bitch so dizzy they were laughing at everything I said. They want to make a deal. The deal we want."

"You should have made it tonight, then," Kat told him stiffly. "No one makes the deals you want when they're sober."

He opened his coat and drew out a folded bunch of papers, opened them and studied them. "As a matter of fact, he *did* sign it."

Bobby chuckled and reached out to her, dropping a sweaty, hot hand on her neck. "Congratulations are in order, huh?"

His sticky flesh felt like acid against her. Why did he always throw his success at her like this? *Always!* Kat didn't even try to stifle the budding aggravation and shoved him back, showing the agitation. *"Leave me alone*—why don't you go jerk off if you want congratulations? You ought to get your praise from the one who appreciates you *most!"*

Her force had knocked him back against the coffee table and some of the crackers fell to the carpet. He staggered, nearly falling, but caught himself.

"Son-of-a-bitch," he grunted again, surprised. "Should of known better after all this time, shouldn't I? You get to painting, and you're someone else all over again. Not the way you used to be—not even what you became—just...*someone. Someone I've never known."*

Kat stood in front of the easel, flanked by her older paintings and the brushes. "It's your own fault."

Bobby flinched. "Yeah. That's right. Everything is my fault. I do everything wrong, don't I? I mucked up your life. I made it *bad.* I took away the power of your art... *I* made you get a job..."

"You *did.*"

"I *helped* you get a job," Bobby shot back. "Because you were pissing your life and everything else *away.* You had to do something and be something. I married a woman, not a basket case. If I had wanted to sleep with a *Frigidaire* I would have bought one for the bedroom."

"All you think about anymore is *sex.* You think that's all there is—"

"With you, *yes.*" He sneered as they lapsed into familiar fighting stances. "You've changed so much, Kat. I've tried to love you. I've talked with you late into the nights. I've bought you everything you wanted—"

"You can't buy my talent back!"

He faced her and his features were ghastly red and furious—vermillion almost.

"I wasn't the one who sold your precious talent," he breathed. "I hoped your commercial art would bring it back, but you putter around in here every couple of months, starting something new each time, but never finishing—"

She slapped him.

The dark red imprint of her palm was a fiery outline on his paling complexion, and Kat wondered at how quickly the tones could change. Like the way her life had changed... She sniffed, and saw herself reflected in his pupils...like she were the shadows in his eyes as much as the abortion and her sterility were shadows in hers. Kat flinched. "You...you won't ever talk to me about the *baby* anymore!"

The anger in his features twisted in confusion. "The *what?*" Then he touched the flame on his cheek like it was a hot coal, and backed a step. "The baby. *Our* baby?"

She squeezed her eyes tight, shutting him out, like he had so often shut her out.

"The *abortion?*" he asked more softly.

Her hands clutched each other.

"It's too late to talk about it, Kat. We talked about it until I couldn't think of anything else. How do you think I feel that we can't have kids now. But how were we to know then? It was a one in a million chance, and neither of us knew—we were just trying to survive!" His brow was furrowed deeply with the lines of his life...their life.

"Survival of the fittest, huh?" she spat, unable to stop herself and pleased that he did feel something—that he *did* know something of her pain.

"Maybe," he whispered. "But whether it was right or wrong, it's *done*. It was done long ago. You made me face up to that years back, and I really hurt about it. Why the hell do you think I've put up with your crazy moods so long? You've just got to face up to it and go on." He held out his arms to her.

"It was your fault," she whispered coldly. "You told me you'd leave me."

The room was silent and Bobby slowly dropped his hands. He shook his head. "I was wrong." He walked to her and she stiffened, then he passed her and she held her arms tight around her middle, not trusting him. A long minute passed.

"This is pretty good," he spoke again at last. "Who is it—she looks kind of familiar..."

Kat turned slowly, her throat dry as she saw him holding up the cloth she used to cover the wet canvas. His face was thoughtful now, bemused, the imprint from her slap fading fast.

"This really is fine, Kat. Are you going to finish—"

A bubble of fury exploded inside her and she slapped him again...harder, wanting her mark to last on him this time, branding him with the pain she felt forever so he could not dismiss it by merely changing the subject.

His face darkened with a frown and he slapped her back, pulling the punch at the last second so that it only stung. He was backing away already, towards the hallway. His eyes bore into hers, and then she saw the shadows there in his pupils, too. Deep shadows.

"Finish this one, Kat. Finish that painting or I think we *are* finished. You've got to do something with your life all by yourself for once, without anyone else to blame. I'm leaving for a few days to give you that chance, okay?"

Kat bent her fingers and made fists. "I knew you'd *leave!*"

"It's my choice," he said. "We all make our own choices. I could say you're making me leave, but I won't. I'm leaving of my own will, and I'll come back of my own will...soon. We all make our own choices, okay? You've *got* to own up to that—"

"You bastard!"

He disappeared and his steps were in the front hall again, and then, the front door opened, and slammed shut.

The doorbell rang.

Kat was still in her kimono. She felt the divan's harsh fabric against her face and winced, pushing herself up and staring around the shadowed room. The unfinished portrait of Robin stared down at her with empty eye sockets and she sat up, transfixed by the emptiness, dropping her bare feet onto the crackers littering the carpet.

Maybe she should just leave it that way. Eyes full of emptiness. Eyes that didn't really exist. Maybe that would destroy the shadows. By not painting them, maybe she could deny them. If she actually painted them, wouldn't that only be affirming that they *did* exist?

Like a name. Robin had said a name promised hope...or maybe, dread. *Fear.*

Ring.

Kat stood, crumpling the saltines under her toes as she caught a breath and remembered the rage she felt last night...moving faster now...into the front hall...

But maybe empty eyes were worse than eyes full of shadows; a life begun, but never experienced.

Like an aborted baby.

"I...I'm coming," she called as she neared the door.

Long ago, on those carefree college nights, she was filled with pleasure...had never really contemplated she might be creating a life...and Bobby hadn't either. They had merged, painting empty eyes on the canvas of her womb.

Ring.

She pulled the door to her like she had welcomed Bobby, but the door only opened to blind her with sunlight. She stared into it blankly, blinking and trembling. The sound of the outer door swinging open filled her ears, and then a calm hand pressed into her wrist.

"Are you okay?"

It was Robin. Already Kat recognized her quiet tones as if she had known them for years. As the glare left, she saw the tall woman's face and those concerned eyes stroking her, still not quite masking their shadows.

Kat leaned against the wall and breathed deeply, almost guiltily. Inhaling...exhaling...filled anew by the excitement and peculiar dread of creation. "I'm...okay."

"Are you sure?" Robin asked, not shutting the door. "We could do this tomorrow."

"No." She was surprised that her voice was so firm. "I've...got to finish this." She moved her fingers around Robin's elbow and pushed the front door closed by herself. "Come on."

It didn't take as long today to adjust the lighting. Only the eyes were left, and Kat could see those shadows clearly reflecting her own soul. She was glad she had cleaned the brushes last night and now squirted daubs of zinc oxide, mixing it into the shades of amber, mahogany and other colors with speedy caution and without preamble. Flat black, too, but with a texture of gray.

Then she began to paint the world within those eyes...a world of unspeakable sorrow and pain...of something unfulfilled, but holding a lingering hope.

Hope barely realized.

Kat lost herself in those eyes, transmitting them onto the canvas as perfectly as she could into a truth that contained her own self. She looked from the canvas eyes into the reality, and back, until she could not distinguish one from the other, and then stared into the shadows of her own self, timeless, not understanding that the hours were passing...

The phone rang ten times before Kat heard it. The answering machine wasn't on. It jarred her out of her trance and she got up, staggering through the room to the coffee table.

When she picked it up, she heard the dead tone of disconnection. *Disconnected.* The way she felt. It brought back the glaring operating table lights above her, hard steel cold under her back.

Shaking her head, Kat tried to orient herself, and felt the thirst of her dry tongue...the gnawing ache in her belly. Her heel crushed a cracker and she bent down to it, feeding the crumbs past her cracked lips—

"Robin?"

Kat heard her own dry crackle and swung around, staring at the empty chair where her patient subject had stayed seated for so many hours...hours without intermission or refreshment...

"Robin?"

Gone.

Just like the little bird outside her window so many years before.

Dazed with exhaustion and thirst, Kat faltered steps to the hall...into the kitchen, and poured herself the last of the *Korbel,* sipping it and munching on the bar of cheese until she felt the life she had virtually transposed from inside herself, into the paints, reviving. She dropped the empty bottle on the tile and it made a hollow sound, not breaking, and then she returned to the studio...to the painting.

To those eyes.

The sky was dark now beyond the window curtains and no shadow crept in through their crevices. The only shadows were in those eyes: Shadows of regret and broken dreams.

Kat's lifetime echoed in the painting.

"My God," she blurted tiredly, stumbling back to the divan and lying atop it, no longer held by the eyes and then closing her own, drifting into a peaceful, resting sleep.

When Kat awoke, she first saw the still life with the robin on the wall. A memory of her past more truthfully than any photograph, because it contained her own feelings.

Then *Robin.* A thousand memories. A billion memories that never were.

Kat felt a solace in those eyes now, viewing the shadows that had once been her own.

She waited for Robin to come back. Waited all afternoon, then she picked up the phone and dialed a number.

"*University of Tulsa,*" answered a woman's voice.

Kat nodded, anxious, biting her lip. "Yes. Could you check for a dormitory or class listing for a woman named Robin?"

"Last name?"

Kat hesitated, then swallowed hard. "Uh—"

"I'm sorry, I'll need a last name."

"I'm sorry. Uh...I'll call back."

Dropping the receiver into its cradle, Kat stared back at the portrait.

The robin had flown away.

Kat studied the portrait closely, but beyond the eyes this time. She saw its familiarity that had escaped her before because of those eyes: The button nose so like Bobby's, the narrow chin like her own, the medium forehead, the tiny ears, the hairline, the lips...a mixture of her ancestry and of Bobby's that she couldn't deny.

Moving to the mirror on the far wall, Kat looked at her own eyes that were so like Robin's, but bright in new hope, shining with the light of rebirth.

Robin had flown away. Free...

And then Kat cried, remembering how the robin had never come back.

Ron Dee's published credits include five novels (with a sixth to be released by Pocket Books within the next few months); Boundaries (Ashley Books, 1979), Brain Fever (Pinnacle, 1989), Blood Lust (Dell, 1990), Dusk (Dell Abyss, 1991) and Descent (Dell Abyss, 1991). The Ultimate Dracula anthology (Dell, 1991) contains his short story "A Matter of Style", and another short story "Genderella", will be published in the Hottest Blood anthology by Pocket Books. His short story, "The Turning" is being published in a chapbook by Simulacran Press. Now that you've read "Still Life" and know how good he is, you'll no doubt want to pick up his novels.

Crackland

Molly Gallagher

"I think it is agreed by all parties...whoever could find out a fair, cheap, and easy method of making these Children sound and useful Members of the common-wealth would deserve so well of the public as to have his statue set up for a preserver of the Nation."

Jonathan Swift, *A Modest Proposal*, 1729

Notice: The management of MindLink Entertainment Centers, Inc., and its subsidiary, Hospice Centers of America, is not responsible for any physical, mental, or psychological damage incurred by its customers. Underage children who take part in the activities of this Center are wards of the court and hence are protected under Public Law A473.1B and by extension under the Drug Liability Act of 1993, Subsection 5j.

TWIST .. SHIVER .. SNAP .. BURN

"Well hi. Are you going to be hooking me up today? Great. Oh no, this isn't my first time. I've been coming here, well almost since you opened. I feel it's the least I can do—for the babies I mean.

"Of course I'm concerned. I'm deeply concerned. Those poor babies. Addicted from birth. And not even their fault—not really. Parental rights? Absolutely not. Any woman who would indulge in cocaine when she is pregnant has no rights. It's the rights of the child I care about. If they have to be born—and I'm not sure that isn't a mistake right there—then get them away from the parents as soon as possible and into a caring environment. Well yes, I know they're hard to place. I'm not saying it's going to be a normal family environment. That may not be possible. But even an institution has to be better than having a drug addict for a mother. If the mother can be gotten into some sort of rehab program, fine, but save the child first. Of course, it's taxpayers like you and me that will end up paying for it all."

CRACKLE .. BRIGHT .. BRIGHT .. SIZZLE

"I want to help, do my part, whatever. Time? Well, time really is hard. I'd like to, but there's my work. Tom, my husband, and I both work. My job is very demanding, and I adore it. It's not unusual for me to put in a fifty- or even a sixty-hour week. Unfortunately, that doesn't leave me much leisure time."

COLD .. SNAP .. TWIST .. SHIVER SHIVER

"Money though, well that can usually be managed. I know it's not the same as actually doing something, but you can't tell me that money isn't welcome. Although once you give to one, everybody's got their hand out. I must get twenty begging letters a week. Not that Tom and I have that much left over at the end of the month. Together, yes, we do make a lot, gross though you know, not net. What we shelled out in taxes last year would probably pay your salary for a year. It would buy a lot of diapers for these babies. The little we have left after taxes, well, most of Tom's goes for the two mortgages and the maintenance fees, things like that, oh and utilities. Last month's phone bill, my god.

"My take-home goes for things like food—I'm not much of a cook so we eat out a lot—dry cleaning, different membership fees, oh and of course our vacation fund. That is one thing I insist on. We only take two vacations a year, real vacations I mean. Ski weekends and things like that don't count. And boy do I need those vacations. If I couldn't get away at least every six months, I'd go crazy. The stress you know."

CURL .. SIZZLE .. BURN BURN .. SHIVER

"Adoption? Yes, I suppose it is best if you can find real homes for them. I know there are people who do adopt them. I honestly don't think I could handle it right now. It wouldn't be fair to the child. If I had more time of course. But right now, no. And they say, you know, that they aren't like normal babies—I mean what kind of baby doesn't want to be held or kissed or rocked to sleep?"

COLD .. SHIVER SHIVER .. BRIGHT

"No, I think this is the best way for me to help out. Tom doesn't think so because it's not deductible, for taxes I mean. I don't understand that, but I guess you know all about it since you work here. Are you about done hooking me up? Yes, the pads are comfortable. I can barely feel them. Just don't get my hair caught. And by the way, the girl last time didn't get all the gel stuff she put under the pads off my temples. It gave me a terrible rash for days. I was about ready to call our lawyers when it finally cleared up.

"Anyway, I told Tom that I didn't care about the tax deduction, and if I was willing to spend what should be my 'fun' money on this, he shouldn't complain. I mean he can't deduct my hairstyling or facials either, and they're practically a business expense. So I give up a few luxuries to come here. I mean, what's a chipped nail compared to the life of a child?"

POP .. TWIST TWIST .. SNAP .. SHIVER

"Hey, this one isn't too young is it? Last month, the girl talked me into trying a real young one, seven or eight months I think. What a waste. Nothing. Dark and cold and empty, with just a shiver or two. Like being hooked up to a lump of coal. Fourteen months? Yes, that sounds good. I don't want to try one too old either. Anything over eighteen months is more than I care to handle. I know their development is a lot slower—than a real baby's I mean. But I don't want to take the chance of there being a mind there, you know, thinking or something—you don't know how it might react to all this. Who knows what damage the drugs have done. I prefer not to get involved in anything messy. Yes, I know some people get off on that sort of thing, but I don't.

"At least thanks to people like me these children have a way of giving something back to the society that supports them. Sometimes I think the mandatory abortion law everyone was talking about—you know, for the crack mothers—might have been a better solution. I know Tom voted for it, but well I couldn't make up my mind and then I never did find the time to get out and vote. Besides this is better isn't it?"

COLD COLD .. TWIST .. SNAP SNAP .. BRIGHT

"Okay, I'm ready. Is the baby? Just out of curiosity, is it a boy or a girl? Don't tell me any names. Oh, just numbers. I guess that's easier for you. Ready? Okay, let me just compose myself. *Relax... relax...deep breath...focus...sun...palm trees...river...sand...beach... relax.* Okay, go ahead."

BUZZ .. SHIVER SHIVER .. BURN .. POP

"I feel it. Oh god, yes, I feel it—SHIVER-BURN-POP—yes, oh."

TWIST .. CRACKLE CRACKLE .. BURN .. SNAP

"It's so strong. Ahh—CRACKLE-CRACKLE—and it's so bright, it's like—BURN-SNAP—it's like I'm being, oh."

DOWN .. DOWN .. SIZZLE .. BURN BURN BURN

"Oh—DOWN—yes again yes—DOWN—I'm falling, I'm burning —BURN—I can't, the heat, oh, the pain, oh yes—BURN-BURN—I feel, I can touch, I..., it's..."

WHISPER .. WHISPER .. SOFT .. HUSH

"What? I—WHISPER—What? HUSH—No. Come on. Louder. Come on. Go, go, burn, burn, burn."

BURN .. SNAP

"Ah. Yes—BURN-SNAP—yes."

BURN .. CRACKLE .. CRACKLE .. TWIST

"Yes. I feel—CRACKLE CRAC— What? Oh, time already? It's always over so quickly, like a roller coaster. I don't see why they can't increase the connection time. It's not like I'm hurting it or anything. What I mean is, it's not like the babies can—yes, I know the rules are for my protection too. Yes, thank you, I did enjoy myself. It was great, really great. Uplifting, almost spiritual. Like giving birth. Definitely worth the price of admission. And doesn't that show Tom was wrong, about the mandatory abortions I mean. I feel so good about doing what I can to help these poor sick babies. Maybe, just maybe, thanks to people like me, their lives won't be a total loss.

"Are you done unhooking me. Great. Did you get all the gel off? Great. You've been a treasure. Here's a little something for you. Do you have a card? I'll be sure and ask for you next time."

Molly Gallagher is a technical editor/writer living and working in Albuquerque, New Mexico. She has a Master's in English literature and originally intended to teach Shakespeare and Jacobean drama, but got sidetracked into technical writing and has been there ever since (approximately 15 years). She has done everything from proofreading, through editing and quality assurance, to managing a publications department for a software house. This is her first professional sale. She has been a member of HWA for about a year.

Abortion is Life

William Campbell

I lay back on the long, green bed, and feel the white paper sheet crumbling beneath me. It feels sterile and cold against the bare of my back not covered by the blue smock I'm wearing. The nurse slides fluffy pink stockings over the raised stirrups at the end of the bed. I place my bare feet on them. The stockings provide little comfort, little warmth. I think of my father.

"Dr. Benard will be with you in just a moment," the nurse says, moving back and forth making preparations. She moves slowly and deliberately, as though motivated by a great loss. The nurse and I exchange looks. She smiles at me, but I can tell it's insincere, for her eyes are colorless and empty. I can't bring myself to smile back at her. Her half-smile turns into a frown as she turns away from me, cheek-bones dragging. I get the impression she doesn't like me. That, or she simply doesn't like what she does for a living. Can't blame her; I wouldn't like it either.

The windowless room is larger than most doctors' examining rooms, but smaller than an operating room. Posters illustrating various cervix sizes and stages of fetal development throughout a pregnancy are hung on the far wall near a system of cabinets. They make me wonder what stage I'm in, how big my baby is. The nurse goes into one of two doors at the back of the room and comes out pushing an innocent-looking machine. I see the bottles on top of it and know that it is *the* machine. The nurse stops it by my feet and attaches a long, hollow tube. I bite my bottom lip.

"This isn't going to hurt, is it?" I ask.

The nurse looks up at me, startled. "Well that depends. You see, the fetus will be evacuated through this hose. Most say that the fetus doesn't feel a thing, but *I* think it's murder."

I stare at her with a dull, horrified look. Did she just accuse me of being a murderer?

"But if you're wondering if it'll hurt you any, there's not much to worry about. Maybe a few cramps...of course *you'll* be under anesthetic."

The doctor, a large man of Mediterranean appearance—dark complexioned, deep brown eyes, and a soft beard with only the fewest of gray hairs—comes in. "And who is this beautiful young lady?" he asks, scanning my medical chart.

"Her name is Amy," the nurse answers.

"Uhm-humm. And how old are you, Amy?"

I'm sure the answer is right in front of him on my chart, but figure he's just making small talk, trying to make me feel more comfortable. His accent is soothing, and somehow I feel safe with him. "Fifteen," I say.

"This is Amy's first time here, doctor," offers the nurse.

Dr. Benard sighs. "Thank you, nurse. Don't you have some preparations left to do?"

"Not really, just about everything's rea—" I notice the doctor's stern look, one of discipline and authority. "Yes, doctor," the nurse says, backing away.

Dr. Benard smiles at me. "Do you have any children, Amy?"

"No."

"I see," the doctor says, smiling again. "Grandchildren then, any of those?"

I can't help but giggle. The man seems pleasant and gentle; not like Daddy. "Sorry, no grandchildren."

"Ah," the doctor says, stepping between my legs. He starts to examine me. I feel one hand on my belly and the other inside me. He moves his hands softly and gently, providing neither pleasure nor pain. "When was your last period, Amy?"

"About nine weeks ago...I think. They've been pretty crazy ever since...I bite my bottom lip. Hard. I almost let out a secret.

"...Since I started high school," I say, repeating the story that Daddy had me rehearse over and over last night.

The doctor continues with the examination. "Have you ever had an abortion before, Amy?"

"No," I whisper, inhaling deeply.

"I see," Dr. Benard says. "So, you want to have kids someday?"

I think about this for a long time. If it were my choice I'd keep this one, or at least give it up for adoption. But Daddy says it's a bad thing; his little girl being pregnant. He says that my mother even had one before I was born. I cringe with the thought of my crippled mother having an abortion. I hate her, and I *don't* want to be like *her*. I realize that I've been toying with the string to my smock. "I dunno, maybe someday," I say, voice trembling. Already I feel too much like her.

"Good," the doctor says, continuing the examination. "Now I need you to try and relax. Good. You're doing very good. Any recent medical problems?"

"No." I suddenly wonder if there's something wrong; if I'm too late. Daddy would be furious. "What's wrong?"

"Nothing, you're doing fine," the doctor says, removing his gloves. "Everything looks fine. I don't think we'll have any problems at all."

"Oh, thank God."

The nurse returns with a tray filled with various medical instruments. She takes a needle and squirts out a few drops. "This is the anesthetic I told you about earlier," she says, lifting my arm and massaging the inside of my elbow.

I watch the doctor stretch out and smooth on a new pair of gloves. He takes an instrument from the tray. "Amy, you're going to feel a little pressure, nothing to worry about." He inserts it inside me and I can feel it open me up. It doesn't hurt much, though.

The nurse suddenly injects the needle in my arm. I close my eyes and try not to think about it. "Ow, ow." The needle slides out. "Is that it?"

"Not quite," the nurse says, "there's still a couple more." She takes a new syringe, squirts out a few drops from that one, then, smiling at me, hands it to the doctor.

"Now this is going to numb you, Amy. When I inject it you'll feel a little pinch, nothing more than a mosquito bite," the doctor says in that comfortable accent of his.

I grind my teeth and clench my fist, refusing to cry out again. I try not to think about the pain. I concentrate on my mother. I wonder how bad her abortion hurt her.

"Okay, Amy, you're doing fine. Just try to relax.." The doctor takes something else from the tray. "Just two more pinches. You ready?"

"Tell me when it's going to hurt."

"You'll feel a few cramps, Amy. Then it will be all over."

There's a sudden knock on the door. I hear it open. "Dr. Benard, we need you outside," a new voice says.

"I'm in the middle of a procedure," the doctor replies without looking at the speaker.

"But doctor, it's an emergency." Then I hear the speaker whisper, "it's another bomb threat!"

"Damn!" I hear the doctor say under his breath, slamming his fist on the tray. Instruments rattle. "Please excuse me," he says, then, in a more firm tone to the nurse, "don't break her down until we confirm the threat. I want to finish her today if we can."

"Yes, doctor," the nurse says. Dr. Benard leaves. The nurse leans over me, strands of her dark hair fall from her thin white cap. "Don't worry, everything's going to be fine," she says, smiling with that false grin of hers.

I try to grin back. "Did I hear him say something about a bomb threat?" I ask

"Relax, it's nothing to worry about. We get them every day."

"But shouldn't we clear the building?" I try to sit up, but the anesthetic has kicked in. I'm feeling a little dizzy.

"No, no need for that," she says, easing me back down on the bed. "You see, I know the kind of people who make these calls. They're interested in *saving* lives, not *destroying* them."

I wish Dr. Benard was back. I don't like this nurse; she seems to be implying that *I'm* destroying a life. I want to tell her about Daddy, how he's making me do this. But Daddy told me not to tell anybody about our little secret.

"You see, I used to be one of them; protesting, making calls, writing letters to members of Congress," the nurse is saying, "but then I finally wised up.

"You know the old saying, 'fight fire with fire,' well that's what I'm doing. I became an abortion nurse so I can *save* lives."

That's absurd. I almost laugh out loud.

The nurse walks over and stands between my legs. I don't feel like laughing any more. "Wh-what are you doing?"

"Nothing, dear, just relax," she says. I feel her remove the device that the doctor left in me. "I've learned that once an abortion is canceled, most women won't try again. You see, I'm saving your child's life."

I hear the device fall to the floor with a metal pang. I try to convince myself that she's merely breaking me down so we can clear the building, yet I somehow know that the nurse has other intentions. Daddy is going to be so mad. I let my feet fall from the stirrups. That feels *so* much better.

The nurse goes to the back of the room and opens the other door back there. She goes inside and I hear the metal sound of a heavy bar being removed. Another door creaks open and now I can hear the sounds and smell the smells of the city outside. The nurse must have opened an emergency exit.

"Nurse, are we leaving?" I ask. She doesn't answer. I manage to sit up on my own, bracing myself on the bed. I still feel too light-headed to walk.

I can see into the room that the nurse entered. It's brightly lit and full of canning jars, like some sort of pantry. I can see outside into the back alley. A white van is backing up to the exit. The nurse hops out and opens the van's rear doors. There's a cot set up in the van. Good. She must be planning on evacuating me. Perhaps the van is to take me to another clinic.

I'm expecting the nurse to come and help me out, but she's busy in the pantry, loading several boxes into the back of the van. I'm tempted to call out to her again, but her hurried expression tells me not to bother her.

I realize that I'm breathing hard, as though I'm caught up in her mad rush. I think about the bomb. Maybe it's not a threat. Maybe it's for real. I need to get outside. I swing my feet off the bed and hold myself steady. The little pantry isn't far, but I can really feel the anesthetic now, and it's making me feel kind of sleepy. I didn't think it would be so strong.

Somehow I manage to stumble to the pantry. I lean against the door frame and call, "Nurse...we gotta...get...out of here..."

The nurse stops what she's doing. She sets the box that she's carrying on the floor and removes a large jar from it. "We got to get them all out," she says. "Got to save all of God's little children so they can grow strong and healthy. See?"

She hands me a jar.

I hold it up and peer into it. It's full of a clear fluid with some sort of dark mass swishing inside it. I'm still feeling lightheaded. Hard to focus. Somehow I force my eyes into clarity, and I can distinguish the shape: a fetus, its humanness clearly recognizable. So this is where they put all the aborted fetuses. I've always wondered about that.

"See," the nurse says, "isn't he a healthy one."

I look at it again, my eyes focusing better now. I see dozens of tiny tracks of stitches holding it together, and I suddenly understand the nurse's crazy rambling. I'm holding a baby, aborted, yet by some miracle of surgery, sewn back together. An operation done so crudely that some of the stitches are already coming undone. It flounders in the liquid like an old Raggedy Ann doll. It's lidless eyes swing toward me.

"Oh my God, it's still alive!" I scream, throwing the concoction down. I hear it smash against the sterile floor, and feel tiny pieces of glass and flesh splatter my feet as I turn and run.

I don't even make it past the front of the van when a lightheaded, dizzy feeling comes over me. I'm about to collapse. I begin to fall, but something catches me. Even though my eyes are closed, I can tell that I'm in the arms of the nurse.

A nurse, thank God! She'll take care of me. I let myself fall into her. Her body is warm. I feel like a little girl in my mother's arms. I feel...*safe*.

I wake up in a strange bed, in a strange room. It's a child's room, a young girl's. There's a pink canopy above the bed that I'm in, and stuffed animals of all shapes and sizes are lined on shelves along the wall. The lighting—a small lamp on the table beside me—is low and blue, giving the room a comfortable feel.

Then I see the large, hospital machine on the other side of the bed. There's a small monitor on the front of it, and it has dozens of different colored wires coming out of it. The screen is blank. None of the wires are hooked up.

I throw the sheets off me and stand up, examining the bed. Folded down at the foot of the bed are some stirrups, and under the bed I can see the mechanical device that raises and lowers it, just like the beds at the hospital. Once I saw a show on PBS that talked about modern childbirth services. The lady on the show said that nowadays hospitals try to make it comfortable and relaxing for the expecting mother. She showed what the new, comfortable rooms looked like. She called them birthing rooms. I realize that's what this room is...a birthing room.

Suddenly a flash of memories comes to me: Daddy taking me to the clinic, Dr. Benard, the bomb threat, the attempted abortion...The abortion! I didn't go through with it! Daddy is going to be so angry. I got to find him, make him understand that it wasn't my fault. It was that nurse, the one with the fetuses...

The nurse.

I stare at the machine, the birthing bed, and try to tell myself that I'm not where I think I am. *Please, please, don't let me be there.*

There's a door at the other end of the room. The knob begins to turn. It opens.

"Good afternoon, Amy. I thought you'd be waking up soon," the nurse says as she enters, pushing a small cart. "Here, I thought you might be hungry, too. Hope you don't mind a late lunch."

She sets the cart beside my bed and removes a silver dome, revealing a bowl of soup and a grilled cheese sandwich. There's a tall glass of grape juice beside it. God it smells *so* good. My stomach roars. I can't help but sit down and dig in.

I've finished most of my plate and I'm taking a drink of my juice when the nurse asks me if I like it. I nod as I drink. Through the curve of my glass, I can see the nurse standing and watching me eat. She's wearing a white uniform and a motherly smile. That gives me the creeps. I tilt the glass and take another gulp.

The glass.

I recognize the glass's design. It's not a glass at all, but a jar, just like the ones on the top of the suction machine. My juice suddenly tastes like my period smell.

I set the juice down and jolt up. Grape juice is leaking from my mouth. I cover it with my hand, trying not to throw up. The nurse must've noticed what I'm about to do, for she has opened a door. "The bathroom's in there," she shouts. "Hurry!"

I hurry. I make it to the stool just in time to empty my stomach. Sticky globs of chicken noodles and thick, cheesy chunks of toast float in purple stool water. It stinks. I flush it and barf again.

"Are you okay, Amy?" The nurse asks. She's staring at me. I give her a go-to-hell look, the kind that I often give my mother. The nurse gets the message and closes the door. I wipe my mouth with a long strip of toilet paper.

The bathroom is small but nicely decorated; cozy. There's a large, old-fashioned style bathtub, and a sink. By the ceiling there's a thin window that I recognize as the type you find in basements. The window is just barely big enough for me to crawl through, maybe.

"Oh, Amy, you're going to just love it here," the nurse is saying through the closed door. "You'll have all the comforts of home."

I'm standing on the closed stool, and my fingers can just barely touch the bottom of the window. I get on my tippy-toes. I can reach the handle. I turn it and pull the window open. It makes a loud creaking noise.

"Amy? Amy, what are you doing?" I hear the nurse say, a panic in her voice. The door opens. I try to scramble up, but it's too high. I feel a small prick on my bottom. The nurse grabs me and pulls me back down. She takes me back into the bedroom, lays me down on the bed. I try to struggle, but I'm feeling too weak. I manage to knock over the food tray, though. Blood-colored grape juice spills on my hospital gown as my mind begins to swim in blackness. I hear the fetus jar shatter. It echoes...

　　　again...echoes...again...

　　　　　　echo.

I'm lying on the birthing bed with my feet propped up on stirrups. The hospital machine is turned on, screen beeping. I'm breathing heavily. Labor. I have a contraction. The nurse is between my legs. "This is it, this is it. Push!" she's telling me. I push. I feel the baby slide out from me. I feel relieved. The nurse is holding the baby. "It's a girl!" she says, handing her to me. "She looks just as beautiful as her mother...except for one *small* flaw."

I fold back the blanket that my daughter is wrapped in. The nurse is right; she does look like me...except for one minor flaw: my little girl came out chopped to pieces...

I wake up in the middle of a dry, silent scream. I sit up and thank God it was only a dream. My eyes adjust to the dim light, and I realize that I'm still *here*, still in this crazy room.

The birthing room.

Without thinking that the nurse might be on the other side, without even considering that the door might be locked, I rush to the door and work the handle. I need my Daddy.

Good, the door isn't locked. I throw it open.

The nurse is standing at a small, multi-shelved table that I recognize as a baby's changing table. Above the table is a round, chrome-backed lamp, like the ones doctors use in surgical rooms. The nurse is bent over and looking through a wide magnifying glass. She's working a needle and thread through a tiny piece of bloody meat. Blood is splattered on her white uniform. She looks up at me, smiles.

"Hello, Amy. I'm glad you're here. This child of God needs your prayer." I take the only exit I can find. I dart upstairs.

The nurse's house is a maze. I come up from the basement and into the kitchen. The kitchen is dark except for the small lights coming from several incubation machines. I run into the living room, where there are even more incubators, dozens of them, all with tiny, sewn-up fetuses inside. There's a yellow light flashing above one of them. I stop and stare into it.

Under the yellow glow is a small infant, a boy. He stretches his thin arms and legs. I think about my mother's abortion, whether I would have had an older brother or sister.

"That's Elvis," the nurse says, standing beside me. "He's almost ready. Should be born any time now."

Even though the child is less than perfect—flat, hairy head, misshapen nose, an eye so lopsided it's almost vertical, no top lip—I find myself staring at it fondly. I know I'm too young, but part of me really *wants* to be a mother.

I turn and look at the nurse. Her arms are folded across her chest, and she's moving back and forth ever so slightly, as though in a trance. Her expression is calm and peaceful. My nightmare of the birthing room has disappeared.

The yellow light suddenly changes to red as a loud beeping noise goes off. The nurse starts hitting buttons and switching switches. The incubator's clear dome rises. "Happy birthday, Elvis," the nurse says, disconnecting the child from the machine. She lifts him out. "Would you like to hold him, Amy?"

I can't help but accept the offer. I've just witnessed one of the most unusual childbirths in the history of time. Speechless, I somehow manage to say, "please."

The nurse chews her tongue as she delicately hands Elvis over to me. With both arms, I hold him to my chest. He smells warm and fresh as baby powder. He's breathing; I can see his stitched-up chest rising and falling with each breath. I decide here and now that I'll never have an abortion, no matter what my father does to me. Never.

The nurse smiles at me as I cradle the child. Now her smile is sincere. I can even see the color of her eyes; soft and warm and brown. I smile back. "He's wonderful," I say, making funny faces at Elvis.

I'm too busy fondling the child to realize that its stitches are coming undone as it breathes. The infant's head suddenly falls back, swinging back and forth by a few threads on its neck. His legs crumble next, then his torso splits open. Elvis falls through my arms.

I'm frozen for an instant, staring at the nurse as she picks up the bits and pieces, crying, "Oh, Elvis, I thought you'd be the one. You were growing so strong and healthy. I thought you'd *live*." I'm tempted to bend down and help her, but something makes me think of my father. This is what he wants to happen to...my...my...

...*our*...

I'm outside, mindlessly wandering under a sky full of stars, heavy streaks of tears flowing from my eyes. I stumble in the nurse's dirt driveway, past her white van. Behind her house is a sagging barn. I'm attracted to a flickering light inside.

The barn is set up like an old schoolroom with several rows of old-fashioned school desks. On each desk is a pair of ceramic prayer hands and a thick black Bible. At the far end is what appears to be an altar with a makeshift pulpit surrounded by dozens of candles. Behind the altar is a huge black drape with a white cross painted on it.

At first I'm hit by the same gentle, baby powder smell that I smelled on Elvis. But then I smell something else underneath it, something ugly. Once when I was little I had a cat named Cupcake that accidently got swiped by a car. Daddy helped me bury Cupcake that day—we had a backyard funeral service and everything—but I missed Cupcake. That night I went and dug him back up and brought him to bed with me. Cupcake stayed in my bed for three days before my mother complained about the smell. My mother washed the sheets at least eight times, but she could never get the odor out. She eventually had to throw them away. I realize that's what I smell now: Cupcake, three days dead.

As my eyes adjust to the dim light in the school/church, I notice that the folded prayer hands aren't ceramic, but real flesh and bone children's hands. I realize, too, that the Bibles aren't Bibles either. Lying face down on each and every desk is a child's head; thick, black hair matted with blood. Other bits and pieces of children's body parts are littered on the seats and floor. A chilly wind suddenly blows through the barn's thin, rotted wood. The candles wave and flicker.

Mommmmmmmmy, the wind howls. I tell myself that it's only the wind.

Mommmmmmmmy, the wind goes again. I back up a step.

Mommmmmmmmy. The candles dance and go out. Something cold creeps against my ankle. I jolt, knocking over a desk. I feel something small and soft squash and ooze under my foot. Cold, child-sized fingers wrap around my ankle, try to crawl up my leg.

Mommmmmmmmy, the wind cries again, its voice the strangled chalk-filled voice of a dead child. I scream and run.

MOMMMMMMMMMEEEEEEEEE!

Shortly after dawn, Daddy picks me up from the county sheriff's office and drives me home. We don't talk. The sheriff didn't believe my story and neither does my father. Just ramblings from a stressed-out teenaged girl. Mere delusions. *They* say; I don't have the energy to argue.

We don't talk during the long drive home. I watch my father drive. His jaw is set tight and his eyes carry a weight of seriousness to them. I wonder if he's the one who made my mother pregnant the first time; if he forced her to have the abortion.

He pulls the station wagon into the driveway, throws the car into park, engine still running. "What in the hell are you trying to do to me, Amy? What are you trying to pull?"

I look out the other way, staring blankly at our quiet brick house. I see my mother's face peering through the window.

"You're pregnant, Amy, *pregnant*! And I ask you to do something simple—an abortion, Amy, what could be simpler than that?—and what do you do, Amy? You run off! Next thing the police pick you up wandering around on some deserted road out in the middle of nowhere screaming some cockamamie story about broken children. Come on, Amy, what do you think you're pulling?"

Tears form at the corner of my eyes. I refuse to let them fall, refuse to let my father have the satisfaction; he's made me cry too many times before.

"Broken children!" Daddy shouts, slamming his fist on the dashboard. Then he suddenly turns to me, voice and face sober with fear. "You didn't tell anyone about our...our..."

"No!" I scream, almost wishing I did.

My father leans back in his seat, exhaling heavily with a sigh of relief. "Good, Amy, for a minute there I thought you might have done all of this just to get out of having the abortion. By the way, I talked to that doctor there. He said you could reschedule your appointment if you like. I made it for two o'clock tomorrow."

"No," I say again, this time my voice is nothing more than a whisper.

Daddy's face grows tense again, but I can tell he's holding back. "Amy...come here," he says, gesturing me toward him. I scoot across the station wagon's bench seat. He puts an arm around me, strokes my back.

"Amy, I understand if you're upset. You're pregnant, and I know you probably want to keep it, but you got to understand, Amy, it's *wrong*. We *can't* keep it. Understand?"

I understand. Daddy's right, and I know it...but...but. But. I just can't do it. Mother may have, but I can't. "No, Daddy," I say, my arms folded quietly and calmly in my lap, "I *can't*."

Daddy stops stroking my hair. His voice rises, "What do you mean you can't, Amy?"

I turn and face him square in the eye. "I can't—I will not—have an abortion."

Each of Daddy's eyes grow as big as his mouth, which is wide open. "Okay, young lady. I've been trying to make this easy for you, but I see I've been wrong."

Daddy grabs me by the arm and pulls me out from his side of the car. I clutch the trench coat that Daddy had me put over the blue smock. He pulls me inside the house.

"Neil, is something wrong?" My mother says from her wheelchair as we enter. Like most times, my father ignores her.

Daddy takes me back to the bathroom, stopping to get a hanger from the closet. "Get your clothes off, Amy," he says, bending the hanger.

"Neil, what are you doing?"

"It's none of your business," Daddy shouts at my mother. He closes the bathroom door. "Amy, take your clothes off now."

I back all the way up against the far wall. "No, Daddy...*please.*"

"Amy, I said get your clothes off now."

I pull the trench coat closer around me. Hold my legs tight together. "Daddy, please."

"Neil! Neil! What's going on in there? Open this door at once!" My father steps forward, holding the hanger high.

"Neil, open the door this second before I call the police. I mean it this time."

Daddy snarls. He knows Mom won't really call the police; she never does. But for some reason he stops. "We'll talk about *this* later," he says, then throws the hanger at me. It hits me in the cheek. I don't have to touch myself to know I'm bleeding.

"Damn girl thinks she's got a mind of her own. Won't listen to a thing I say," Daddy says to my mother. The front door slams, then I hear the car's starter grind. Daddy must've forgotten that he left it running. Tires squeal as he drives off.

The bathroom door is left open. My mother wheels herself to the doorway and stares at me. "Why don't you listen to your father?"

I stare back at her hopelessly. "Why don't you *do* something about him? Make him stop!" I scream.

"Your father was a good man until you were born...until you crippled me forever..." Her face is flush with hatred. I'm her filthy little girl. Dirty, dirty...

I slide down along the wall until I'm sitting beside the toilet. Somehow that seems appropriate. Mother grunts and wheels off. I hear the TV come on in the room next door.

Beside the toilet I cry and cry and cry. I cry until it hurts; until my abdomen cramps and screams with pain.

The miscarriage is quick and painless. I stand and stare at the bloody fetus in the stool. It's no bigger than a goldfish. A very *small* goldfish.

The nurse is inside me: *Poor child. Poor poor child. Never did anything to hurt anybody, and now this. God's poor poor child.*

On the counter there's a plastic bathroom cup. I grab it.

"Come on, little baby. I know someone who can help you." I say as I scoop the child into the small blue cup. I know just the place to go.

William Campbell, 27, with premature gray hair, works as a speech-language pathologist and writes fiction in his spare time. He has other works appearing in New Blood Magazine *and* Aberations. *He lives with his wife and three-year-old son in Edmond, Oklahoma.*

Healing Hands

Esther C. Gropper

With her eyes closed, Bella could trace every rose on the wallpaper. She had thought it beautiful once; cheerful red to wake up to; intertwining vines that made bowers around her bed. Now she could scream at the enduring vitality of the cabbage roses that defied time. It was not true of life.

Time had changed her nut-brown hair and stippled it with white-like birch bark. Her skin had lost its smoothness and showed age cracks. Raging inwardly at the enemy scourging her bones, she pulled at the covers and sought the undercover comfort of her bed. She wanted to hide her memories in the dark holes of the night. She wanted to do what Lorna suggested—dwell on the positive things, positive things of the past.

Bella couldn't recall exactly when her daughter Lorna revealed healing hands. Looking back, it was there at a very early age when playmates offered bruised elbows and knees for the soothing touch.

Bella yearned for those fingers flying like hummingbirds over her own aching limbs, but the sorrowing soul inside her wouldn't let her yield to the tender hands. The shadowy form of an unborn child came between them.

"I can't walk," cried Bella, bound to her bed. "I have too much pain."

"Will you try if I work with you?" Lorna, now a mature and dedicated therapist, looked for the faith, the trust she found in others' eyes.

Bella tried to move her legs but nudging in her coffined memories was the unanswered, unrecompensed remorse, so deeply pressing on her as to paralyze her, something she could not confide to the healer and so it was out of reach of the healing hands.

Bella shivered as Lorna's hands passed over her cramped, pain-ridden legs. "I want to touch you where it hurts, Mother. I know it hurts you here," she said as her feathery hands felt the knotted nerves, caressed the calves. "I want you to think of the love in my hands, strengthening love, powerful love."

Bella heard those words of love and was reminded of Lorna as a child. Bella had listened with a heart full of amazement as Lorna played with her friends, felt and traced the flow of blood hidden under layers of skin, hidden from vision but not from her intuition. Feeling a pulse, she whispered rhythms she felt: plumpety, plumpety, plumpety.... Nature centered in her its rhythms; and when she felt some irregularity, she quickly pronounced, "That's where the bad thing is." Where blood oozed, she stanched it with pressure and washed away offending stains. "You're going to grow up to be a doctor," was often said about Lorna.

Bending over her now, Bella saw the soft brown curls tied back and clearing Lorna's forehead. The white clinic coat, open at her chest, revealed a white scar, a weaving caduceus that Lorna would carry for life.

Bella recalled Lorna at seven, running alongside her palsied friend Joan, trying to teach her to ride a bike. Joan failed to keep her balance; her crippled limbs would not respond to her hopes. The bike tipped, and the handlebar ripped into Lorna's breast. The wound set an enduring scar.

Nature had endowed Lorna, but she had not been as benevolent when she betrayed Joan. Lorna befriended the child, tended her, taught the handicapped girl simple tasks in patient, methodical games and tunes:

> *This is the way you button your shirt,*
> *Hold your hands so they won't hurt.*
> *One hand steady,*
> *The other one ready*
> *To push it through your pretty shirt.*

When the street youngsters organized their games, unwilling to include Joan, Lorna interceded and won a place for her. She admonished the others because they teased or laughed at Joan's uncoordinated attempts to run after a ball or to gather scrambled jacks. Lorna set an example for them to follow with the clumsy child: "Some people are slower learners," a phrase she overheard from Bella's teaching experience.

When the children were learning to jump rope, an impossible function for Joan's uncoordinated body, Lorna slowed down the pace of the rope-turning and making up another tune, deliberately accentuated essential words:

> *When you hear me say "You jump!"*
> *Lift your body,*
> *Lift your rump,*
> *Now all set to make the jump!*

Befriending Joan ultimately cost her the companionship of other children, but Lorna showed indifference to the loss. Joan's smiles and hugs were recompense enough for her loyalty. Time would see Joan become self-sufficient, and justify Lorna's dedication. Lorna saved souls. Bella accused herself of losing them.

Bella saw dedication concentrated in every feature of her daughter's face and in every movement of her body. The concentration was fixed in her high cheekbones and the eyebrows that followed the upward angles. The eyelids opened fully to reveal fathomless sea-green eyes. Love was in the width and depth of them. A gentleness pervaded her expressions. It was as if her heart pulsed with sympathy for human sadness.

Bella realized that there had always been something different in her daughter because, for all of her tenderness, there was a remoteness. An emptiness. A hunger for what she had not had in her childhood: Her father's love. A sister's or a brother's love. Bella bore the burden of these deprivations.

Anguish spurted like a fountain and fell on stones Bella couldn't dislodge in her chest. She had done what she thought was right at the time. Her marriage was foundering. She was contending with a man who guarded himself against deep relationships. He needed people but couldn't spare a smile or a kind word to encourage them. Inept at loving, he simulated it, told her he cared for her, for Lorna, but the lie grew too big to hold in his arms. The lie exploded when she conceived another child. What could he scrape together to give a second child? His seeds, he told her, trapped him, robbed him of his choices. He wouldn't stay with her if she brought another child into the world.

Bella acquiesced. She thought it would hold them together, but it was self-delusion. In every small domestic crisis, he showed cowardice. He was restless, the kind of man who took up short term residences in other's lives. He thought nothing of breaking his lease.

To fill the emptiness for Lorna and herself, she contrived parties—"unbirthdays" and treasure hunts. She bought play gyms for the lawn, badminton nets and basketball hoops to attract the neighborhood children to her home, to lure her daughter to play, to join groups, to test the limits of laughter and agility.

She watched Lorna quickly master the sports, as if they were homework or chores to dispatch before going on to things that mattered to her. She hardly showed pleasure in her own prowess. Her performances were the fulfillments of others' expectations. She habitually stopped to instruct Joan, to help her friend coordinate her movements.

In those days, Bella often sat near an open window where she viewed the play and pondered the child's patience and devotion. She watched as deeper, furtive thoughts throbbed with recollections of her aborted child. The unborn child would not stay submerged. It might have had similar gifts, might have been a better playmate for Lorna than Joan. There would have been less than a year's difference in age.

Age was something of which Bella was aware. Her skin now looked like her rose-strewn wallpaper, beginning to show cracks and discolorations. Her body ached. Her bruised conscience took its revenge by reviving buried thoughts, making inferences about the special qualities she saw in Lorna. Too many demons assaulted her. Too many ghosts came back to haunt her.

Bella remembered her grandmother's old world tales of displaced souls, of dark ominous nights when souls roamed with the winds to find havens, sometimes hitching a piggy-back ride on the soul of another person, looking for those succumbing in drownings or falls, reclaiming the bodies, the survivors joyous with another chance at life, stunning in their born-again souls. Fortune, fame, power accounted for as the natural luck these people had was never recognized as the dowries of grateful surrogate souls.

That was how her grandmother explained "luck." That there were lost souls, with so much to bestow, begging for bodies out there in the universe. How she wanted to believe that the little soul was near Lorna and guiding her healing hands, for surely this girl, now a woman, had rare gifts of healing.

"Listen to me, Mother. The mind, body, heart and spirit, like air, water, fire and earth—the elements—have been aligned to heal. Let your spirit heal, Mother. Release it. Let it go."

"What do you want me to do?"

"Let spirit heal. Let it touch your body. It is the connection with God. Trust yourself to it."

"Help me do it, Lorna."

"Hold my hand and feel the flow of pure love."

Her daughter was offering her a way to carry her burden but her conscience wasn't free to follow. She needed forgiveness, faith in forgiveness, peace in forgiveness. She couldn't bear to think again about her grandmother's lost souls. If her aborted child's soul was still afloat, it was agonizing on the winds. It would not forgive. It was finding vengeance in Bella's body. It would claim her body when her eyes were sealed. If that were so, she would die now to have the soul restored.

"Look into yourself now, Mother." Lorna's voice lulled her to rest. "Find your way to help your spirit. Let out all the self-punishing energies and let in the healing energies. Think of God's healing, cleansing spirit. Let my love find its place in your wounds.

Bella watched Lorna dim the bedside light, felt her light kiss on her forehead. She visualized Lorna walking the hospital corridors, her light, floating steps on the waxed floors. This woman, lambent with life, touched others with it. Bella asked for that healing touch and reached into the clawing darkness to find it, to engage it in the unchartered regions of her world where souls wandered to reconcile the loss, only to discover no one faced her but herself, no contenders for her love but Lorna.

Bella felt the silence in the room, the darkness so immense it took total occupation of her body. She surrendered herself to the silence and darkness, wanting its solace, wanting to forgive herself.

Tears came easily, but they did not wash away the pain. Every turn sent sharp stabbing jabs to her legs. She clutched the pillow and smelled the delicate tea rose scent of Lorna's body hovering around it. She listened to the echoes of Lorna's voice as she tried to console her. She visualized others in their pain. In the grateful words of the patients, Bella knew Lorna had been given a gift to give to the world; healing hands, and that it is given to very few to endow the world with so great a gift. She had nurtured Lorna's gift. She had her fulfillment.

It was then that she felt the soft stir of air on her skin, as if shadowy eagle-feathered arms reached around her neck and embraced her shoulders, covering the length of her arms and her bosom for a tighter embrace. She felt a lighter-than-bird kiss on her cheek. She raised her head to return the kiss of the forgiving soul.

Esther C. Gropper taught high school English for 20 years. That, in itself, is worthy of several medals and combat pay. She has degrees in English and guidance. Her published credits include pieces in Your Life & Health, Woman Beautiful, Southwest Outdoors, Short Stories, Prime Years, California Senior Magazine, *and many others. She has won several awards for her short fiction, and she has recently published a collection of her short stories in a volume titled:* In Just A Moment. *Ms. Gropper conducts professional workshops in writing and she's an editorial consultant.*

Bait and Switch

Barry Hoffman

Lara tried to focus on the words of the young pregnant counselor, but she kept drifting. Her decision made, she cared little about the details. She just wanted to get the damn thing over.

"...we're a little unconventional..."

She'd liked Larry. *Really* liked Larry.

"...require you to stay the night after the procedure..."

She'd wanted to please him. Wasn't prepared, though, to go all the way. Obviously, he wasn't either.

"...not merely a name or number, Lara..."

Morning sickness. Her period playing coy; a week late, ten days, three weeks. The home pregnancy test. Positive. At fifteen. Ninth grade.

"...want you emotionally as well as physically healthy..."

She couldn't confide in her parents. Good Catholics that they were, there would be no room for discussion. *"You made your bed,"* they'd say, *"now you have to sleep in it."* Larry, on the other hand, had enthusiastically embraced the idea of an abortion, when she broached the subject. *Fuck him*, she thought and laughed at the irony. It's what had gotten her into this mess in the first place.

So, she'd gone to the Avondale Clinic, terribly confused; one moment confident an abortion was her *only* choice; the next terribly guilty about terminating the pregnancy with extreme prejudice. *No*, a portion of her mind screamed. *No euphemisms. Killing your child.*

"...lifelong decision..."

Only fifteen. Too young to have a baby. Too young to face the humiliation. Too young for the responsibility. Too young to give up her plans for college.

"...bail out anytime, if you change your mind. Actually we hope you do."

She'd be able to bear children...when *she* decided the time was right, she'd been assured.

"...*lifelong decision...* "

She really had no choice.

"...*bail out anytime...* "

Her decision made, she just wanted to get it over.

"*Actually we hope you do.* "

"Do? I'm sorry, I missed that," she said, trying to focus on what she was being told.

"You must decide what's best for you, Lara," the woman gently repeated. "But even a decision you make here and now is not cast in stone. If you change your mind anytime before the procedure begins, it's fine with us. And, while we perform abortions at Avondale and don't begrudge your right of choice, we actually hope you'll change your mind. Regardless, we'll abide by your wishes and try not to make this any more unpleasant than it already is."

The clinic never ceased to amaze her. While she'd hoped for understanding and compassion, this went beyond her wildest expectations. Avondale was a mammoth four story state-of-the-art facility, taking up a whole city block. She'd been surprised, and more than a little relieved, to find no ranting anti-abortion protesters hurling insults or blocking her entrance once she'd made her decision. She'd been a bit bewildered when the first counselor, a pregnant—*very pregnant*—light-skinned black, no more than 18, had told her she'd have to return for counselling twice more before the abortion.

"...*we're a little unconventional...* "

She been shocked to find her second counselor a priest; a quite elderly man with his long white hair tied in a pony tail. He hadn't preached, prodded or laid a guilt trip on her, though. He'd merely laid out her options—

"...*a lifelong decision...* "

—and answered her questions.

And now, a third counselor, Yvonne, she recalled, was explaining her alternatives yet again. Yvonne, like the first counselor, was pregnant. In her seventh month, she'd told Lara. Twenty years old. Her *second* child, she'd beamed. Lara didn't dwell on it. She had more pressing matters of her own to consider, after all. But, the sight of the pregnant woman tickled a memory. Some, no, *many* of the woman who worked at the clinic were pregnant. A contradiction? A paradox? Hell, a coincidence. She found herself staring at the cross that hung from the necklace around Yvonne's neck. Very much like the one she wore. Somehow out of place at an abortion clinic, she thought. And, hadn't the first counselor worn one as well? Lara couldn't be sure.

"*...we're a little unconventional...*"

"*...a little unconventional...*"

"*...unconventional...*"

***

Lara opened up her mother's letter. They seldom spoke anymore. She'd married outside her religion—a Jew no less—and moved out of Ridley; unlike her other three sisters who'd married good Catholics and stayed close to home. A gaggle of grandchildren visited each weekend. Another strike against her.

"Lara," the terse letter read. "Thought you'd be interested in the enclosed. Drop by if you wish." *I'm fine, Mother, and how are you,* she thought bitterly. Lara couldn't help conjuring up the image of a cold, unforgiving woman.

Inside was an invitation; Ridley High School's tenth reunion. Ten years, she thought to herself. It seemed like yesterday that she'd graduated, four months following the end of the Persian Gulf War. She crumbled paper into a ball and was about to trash it, but reconsidered. Her job as a legal secretary didn't normally allow her the luxury of taking a few days off on short notice. Her husband, Benjamin, a lawyer himself was in the midst of a complex anti-trust case. Leaving suddenly, even for a few days, might unsettle him. And, her high school experience had left her with few riveting memories. On the other hand...

Ben had actually encouraged her to go. They had no children, so he wouldn't be burdened. And what with his current case, he told her, he wouldn't feel guilty not being able to spend time with her.

"Go," he goaded. "Make peace with your mother. See your nieces and nephews before they're grown. And the reunion might be fun. You can tell me which of my teen heartthrobs have gone to flab, which of the jocks are bald, who's divorced and who's having an affair. It'll do you a world of good."

So she'd gone. She hadn't made peace with her mother, but she'd seen her sisters and had a good time with their children. She didn't look forward to the reunion itself, though. Dreaded it, in fact. Dreaded most of all her girlfriends showing pictures of their children. Dreaded the fact that there were none of her own to show.

Fortunately, Toni Stankowski spotted her as she checked her coat after entering the Log Cabin restaurant.

"Lara! You haven't changed a bit. Well, not for the worse, in any event," she said and they embraced. "Let me look at you."

Lara was happy to oblige. The years had treated her well. She'd been blessed with a firm athletic body, which she maintained with aerobics three times a week. Her angular face still had an undernourished look to it. She'd never had the need for much makeup and wore little now. Her thick brown hair, once shoulder-length was shorter now.

Toni was actually Antonia Stankowski, who'd moved to Ridley at the start of tenth grade. She'd made it quite clear from the get go she was *Toni*, and anyone who dared call her Antonia was looking for a fat lip. Sports had been her life in high school; volleyball, field hockey, basketball, swimming, softball and track. It was actually a necessity, as she loved to eat and without an outlet to melt the calories she'd have been a blimp. At 5 foot two inches, she was four inches shorter than Lara, a full-figured girl with a plain slightly chubby face and close-cropped black hair.

The Toni Lara now looked at hadn't changed all that much herself. She was maybe ten pounds overweight, but her body was near as well-chiseled as it had been in high school.

"You're looking good yourself," Lara said. For the next thirty minutes they swapped stories. Toni had moved from Ridley in twelfth grade; her father's job keeping them constantly on the go. She'd become a phys. ed. teacher.

"It's the only job I could get where I could eat to my heart's content and work out so I wouldn't become a Roseanne Barr look-a-like."

She'd been married twice; her current husband of three years was on a business trip. She had no children.

"You, too," Lara said. "I don't have any either."

"I know your job's important," Toni scolded, "but you really..."

"It's not for lack of trying, Toni." Lara interrupted. "I can't. But what about you? You worked at that day care center after school and swore you'd have enough kids to field your own basketball team."

Toni was silent for a moment, as if deliberating whether to answer truthfully or make some flip excuse and move onto another subject.

"I can't either...at least not now. I...I got pregnant in twelfth grade, just before we moved. I had an...an abortion. I didn't love the guy, the timing was bad; hell, you know the line. I wanted kids, you know, but not then. I got married two years later and I planned on getting pregnant immediately. I mean, it had been so easy the first time and I didn't *want* a kid then.

"It led, in part, to the breakup of my first marriage. I was sure it was him. I had been pregnant before, after all. His macho ego couldn't take the fact that *he* might not have what it took to get the job done. Anyway, he finally agreed to see a doctor and he passed with flying colors. So I went for an exam and the doctor said it was me. I'd never bear children."

"Was it the abortion?"

"She said no. There'd been an infection leading to a benign inoperable growth, but it had nothing to do with the abortion."

"Jesus, Toni. I've got the same problem. I mean *exactly* the same problem." Lara told her about the abortion, her marriage to Ben, her inability to conceive and the doctor telling her she'd never have children. "She told me I'd contracted an infection. I had a benign inoperable growth. And it had nothing to do with the abortion."

"Shit, girl," Toni finally said. "We didn't come here to make each other miserable. Let's mingle."

An hour later, three other women joined them at a table; Yvette James, a tall dark-skinned black woman, Christy Cochran, a trim blond who'd caused more than a few boys into cold showers in high school and Denise Slater, the most surprising of all. Denise had been a shy introverted girl, who'd spent most of her time in the library. She'd transferred, so everyone thought, in the middle of her senior year to live with her grandparents. She looked much the same as when they'd last seen her; chunky with a sallow cratered complexion and shoulder length red hair - her most redeeming feature. Denise seemed uncomfortable around others, just as when she was in high school.

None of the women had children; all had abortions; all infections and benign growths that precluded childbearing.

"With five of us unable to conceive, it's more than a coincidence," Lara said, when they'd sat down. She took out a small notepad. "Let's list the common denominators."

"Let's not," Denise said, abruptly. "I made a mistake when I was in high school and I'd rather not dredge up old memories."

"Look, Denise. Something may have happened to us...," Lara began.

"Spare me," Denise shot back. "We all had abortions and we were all wrong. That we can't conceive now is proof that abortion is wrong."

"I take it you now oppose abortion. Had one when you found it necessary, but now want to deny others. A bit hypocritical, isn't it?" Toni asked, hostility in her voice.

"Not necessary," Denise said, her eyes locked with Toni's. "Convenient. Abortion was the easy way out; a coward's way out."

"You came to this realization kind of late, at least for the baby you aborted," Toni said, not backing down.

"You're right. I was young and confused. And, my parents were humiliated and even suggested I have the abortion. They had such plans for me and, well, a baby would ruin it for all of us."

"And now?" Lara asked.

"Now, I think abortion should be a last resort and *only* for those who've been raped. We never received the proper guidance in school. Sex education consisted of telling us how to avoid getting pregnant, rather than abstinence until marriage. Values were thrown out the window for expediency. After all, wasn't *everybody* doing it? We should have been taught responsibility and accepting the consequences for our actions. Things are no different now. Kids are told 'Don't worry if you get pregnant. There's a remedy, a cure. Abortion.'"

"You don't seem to leave much room for debate," Lara said, without Toni's animosity.

"There is no room for debate. Abortion is wrong, there's no two ways about it. I killed a living being and I must accept my punishment."

"Bull," Toni said, her face contorted in anger. "*I* didn't kill a living being. I aborted a fetus. It was my decision, one I agonized over. Hell, the clinic forced me to look in a mirror not once, but *three* times. And *I* made an informed decision. Sure I was scared, but no one forced an abortion on me. And, I don't want to have choice taken away from other women who've been knocked up."

Denise got up. "Look, we could debate the issue all night and we'd both feel the same as we do now. It's kind of sad, though, to come to a reunion to compare notes on abortions we had." She looked directly at Toni. "Since you talk so much about choice, I've made mine and I'm leaving."

"Good riddance," Toni mumbled, as she left.

"Toni!" Lara scolded. "You're not being fair. I'm pro-choice, but at times I have doubts of my own. However, that's *not* what we're here to discuss. Yvette, Christy, are you willing to hear us out?"

They both nodded. Lara sighed in relief.

"All right, let's get down to business. We were looking for similarities in our experiences."

"Well, we all had abortions in high school," Yvette began.

"But our doctors said they weren't connected with the growths," Christy said in response.

"And we didn't have the abortions at the same clinic," Toni said. "Both Christy and I had left town."

"What was the name of your clinic?" Lara asked Toni.

"Avondale. They'd just opened up. It was more like a hospital than a damn clinic. A huge place."

"Avondale?" Christy looked stunned. "That was the name of the clinic I went to. But you'd moved to Jersey and I'd moved to Connecticut."

"I had mine at the Avondale Clinic here," Lara said. "Yvette?"

"Me, too. I didn't think I could afford it, but they said they'd been endowed with grants for those with financial need."

"I didn't know there was more than one Avondale Clinic," Christy said. "Could they be somehow connected? Affiliated with one another?"

Lara noted the question and then asked the other three to describe their experience at Avondale. With skills she'd honed as a legal secretary, she probed using her own experience at Avondale as a frame of reference. When they were done, she summarized, her face drawn and devoid of color.

"All of our female counselors and much of the clerical help were pregnant. We all had to stay overnight. I didn't think anything of it at the time, but that's not the way abortions usually work, if there are no complications. A priest counselled each of us. None of us encountered picketing by pro-life groups."

They all fell silent until Toni voiced what they were all thinking. "Abortion clinics run by anti-abortionists."

"And as penance for having the abortion, they infected us so we'd never be able to conceive again," Christy finished.

"A lifelong decision," Lara said.

"What?" Toni asked.

"The counselors repeated it over and over again. 'A lifelong decision.' I thought they meant the fetus, but they meant *us*.

"There's something wrong," Yvette said. "I can buy almost everything you've said, but I don't believe a pro-life group would condone, much less take part in, abortions. It goes against everything they believe."

"Shit. You're right, Yvette, it doesn't make sense," Toni said dispiritedly.

"The counselors were all pregnant. Most of the clerical help, too," Lara mused aloud.

They all looked at her without comprehension.

"What if they didn't perform abortions?" she went on.

"Well, I didn't have no baby, honey," Yvette answered.

"What if they transferred the fetuses to other women. That would explain all the pregnant women at the clinic."

"Is it possible?" Christy asked.

"I think we've got to find out," Lara said.

"Pray tell how?" Toni asked.

"What if we picket the clinic?" Lara answered.

"Say what?" Toni said as she and the others stared at Lara incredulously.

She explained.

***

The next day, before the clinic opened, the four of them, each with a hand-made anti-abortion placard, picketed outside Avondale. They berated the help and cajoled the steady influx of young women seeking abortions to reconsider.

Most of the staff looked bewildered, as if this had been their first confrontation with pickets, yet passed without comment. At 9:45, though, one young woman, no more than 17 or 18 and looking ready to give birth any day, couldn't contain herself.

"Why are you doing this?" she asked, fingering the cross around her neck.

"How can *you* work here, carrying your child, knowing others will be killed with *your* help?" Yvette countered, glaring at her.

"You don't understand."

"Please, what is there not to understand?" Christy, asked sarcastically. "This is an abortion clinic, after all, or have we missed something."

The woman was clearly uncomfortable, seemingly torn between saying something to assuage the four protesters or accepting their presence. Finally, choosing her words carefully, she pleaded for understanding. "We're not all we appear. We really are concerned with the unborn."

"Concerned how quickly you can rid the world of them," Christy responded tersely.

"No, we don't..."

At that moment, a young priest intervened. He'd come from the clinic. "Catherine, why don't you go inside. I'll handle this."

"Yes, Father." The young woman, head down in contrition, immediately made her way to the clinic without another word.

The priest turned to the four women. "I applaud your efforts, but I really don't think you understand what we do here at Avondale."

"We've been fed that, 'You don't understand what we do here at Avondale,' line all morning long. You know the old saying, Father, 'If it looks like a duck and quacks like a duck, it is a duck,' no matter how you sugarcoat it. Well, this is a pretty impressive building, but it looks like an abortion clinic and abortions are conducted here. So, I'd have to say it's an abortion clinic; a baby-killing factory. So, enlighten us, Father, when is an abortion clinic *not* an abortion clinic?"

The priest's face clouded. "You're free to exhibit your First Amendment rights," he said stiffly. "I just hope you'll be civil. The woman who come to see us are terribly fragile and they *do* need our help." Without waiting for a response, he returned to the clinic.

At 5:00 much of the staff—all women—left, stoically braving the catcalls the four women flung at them. Catherine, her head down, was among them. At the corner the women went separate ways, some in groups of two or three, most, like Catherine, alone.

"I have an idea," Lara said. "Toni and Christy, you two stay here. Yvette and I will try to find out where some of these ladies live. Maybe if we picket their homes we can get them to crack. I'll follow Catherine. She's most definitely a weak link. Yvette, why don't you follow the black girl just behind her. She looks almost as uncomfortable as Catherine. You'll be less conspicuous than the rest of us."

Lara followed Catherine, keeping her distance. The young girl, lost in her thoughts, seemed totally oblivious. Lara could have walked alongside her and the girl wouldn't have noticed.

Three blocks later, Catherine approached a waiting bus marked "Out of Service", entered and within minutes *all* of the other women who'd been with Catherine converged upon the bus. Lara saw Yvette keeping a discreet distance behind the woman she'd followed. When the last of the women got into the bus, it pulled away, travelling four blocks, without stopping, before it turned left out of view.

"What the hell was that?" Yvette asked when Lara joined her.

"Seems they're going to a lot of trouble to make sure no one knows they take the same bus," Lara answered. "Curiouser and curiouser, isn't it?"

"What now?"

"Tomorrow we stay here with the car and follow the bus."

The following day, the protesters ended their vigil at 4:30. At 5:00, Lara and Toni were parked around the corner from the "Out of Service" bus and at 5:15, a dozen young women, including Catherine, made their way to the bus from different routes. They were seemingly oblivious to one another, none speaking; to all appearances strangers arriving at the same time to make their way home.

Lara and Toni followed the bus for perhaps ten minutes, during which time it made no stops to pick up or discharge passengers. It made its way to the gates of a small self-contained community before stopping; the Faith Hope Charity Ministry of God. The grounds were dominated by a massive modern Church, with several dozen small bungalows branching out like tentacles from the main building.

The women disembarked from the bus and a number of them made their way to the bungalows. Catherine and several of the others, as a group but still without communicating, went to the side door of the main building. They were inside for no more than a few moments, leaving with children, ostensibly their own. Catherine emerged with a red-headed toddler, in stark contrast to her blond hair; a boy who silently held his mother's hand as they made their way to one of the bungalows.

Most of the others, likewise, left with one or two children. One, however, who looked to be about 25 emerged with six; the oldest about ten years of age.

"She can't be their mother," Toni said, as much to herself as to Lara, whose eyes had followed Catherine. "Lara, look at the one coming out of the Church with all the kids. They can't *all* be hers. Two are black and one's Oriental and she's a blond. What the hell's going on?"

They watched as one of the children, a boy about two, tripped and fell to the ground and began to wail. While the mother looked on, unsure, the Oriental girl, perhaps eight, knelt down and comforted the younger child. Within moments the boy was laughing, hugged her sister, who helped him to his feet.

"I think Christy was right," Lara said. "They are hers, though I'd lay odds she's still a virgin."

"You're talking in riddles, girl. They're hers, but she's a virgin," Toni said bewildered.

"Don't you see? The clinic *doesn't* perform abortions. They transplant the unborn fetus from one womb to another. Those women carry the children to term, but they never become pregnant in the traditional sense."

"Have the baby and then are implanted with another," Toni continued, finally following Lara's train of thought. "Did you notice the kids show no sign of affection towards the mother? The children seem more dependent on one another."

"The mother gives birth and houses the kids at night, like a babysitter," Lara went on excitedly, "but it's the Church that raises them."

"Raises and brainwashes them from birth," Toni corrected. "Then the females become surrogate mothers themselves." She paused, emotion clouding her voice. "Lara, in another six or seven years it could be *our* children, like Catherine, breeding every nine months... never questioning, never knowing love...never living except for their Church."

"They're not *our* children, Toni. Not anymore. We have to concentrate on what they did to *us*; punished us by making it impossible to ever conceive again."

"And how to do we do that?" Toni asked bitterly.

"Expose them for what they are. Discredit them somehow. Put them out of business before they breed a whole race of Catherines."

"How?"

"I'm thinking, girl. Let's tell Yvette and Christy. We know what we're up against now. Together we can figure out how to use what we've learned."

***

PHILADELPHIA - A bomb planted by anti-abortion terrorists caused minor damage at the Avondale Clinic in Upper Darby. There were no injuries. This was the third blast to occur at one of Avondale's 200 clinics in the U.S. in the past six weeks. Dr. Lloyd Frazier, clinic spokesman said the clinic received a phone call at 5:00 p.m., warning a bomb had been

planted. The explosion occurred at 5:17, after patients and personnel had been evacuated. Damage
was confined to the first floor, where police say, a
bomb had been left in a restroom. This newspaper
received a phone call at 5:30 from the Anti-Abortion
Underground, claiming responsibility for the blast
and warning attacks would continue against Avondale
clinics nationwide until they cease performing abortions. The groups purports to have supporters inside
the clinics themselves, sympathetic to their cause.

***

"We're not going to be able to keep this up much longer," Yvette
said, after reading aloud the newspaper account for the others.
"They've really beefed up security. It was pure luck they didn't search
the laundry truck."

"We're playing a game of chicken with them," Lara answered,
"and we just have to hope they break before any of us are caught. The
fact remains, they've spent a fortune on security at 200 clinics and we
still got in. Christy's idea to plant seeds of doubt by inferring we may
have had inside help just might induce the paranoia we need. All we
can do now is it and wait for some kind of sign from them."

The sign they were hoping for came three days later at a press
conference of the Pro-Life Action Alliance, an umbrella group for
hundreds of disparate anti-abortion groups. While Lara and her friends
each watched from their own homes, the Reverend Ralph Clancy put
out the long-awaited carrot. While decrying the senseless violence, he
told the assembled press, he could understand what drove this splinter
group to such excesses.

"This is no different than the schisms that developed during the
Civil Rights Movement," he reminded his audience. "While Martin
Luther King was preaching peaceful civil disobedience, just as we do,
there were groups that felt violence was the only answer to the injustic-
es heaped upon blacks. I can fully understand the frustrations of the
Anti-Abortion Underground as our tactics have met with mixed results."

The Reverend now looked directly into the camera, no longer
addressing the press, "However, I implore the leaders of this faction

to open a dialogue with the Pro-Life Action Alliance, so we can coordinate our efforts without resorting to violence."

Fifteen minutes of questions followed, but the Reverend had made his plea. His answers to often hostile questions were terse, at times dripping with sarcasm, at others matching the hostility of his inquisitors.

The women did not communicate until they met, as planned, two days later. They had outwitted the authorities because they had no ties with the anti-abortion movement and led seemingly normal lives. They befuddled police because they were nothing like they seemed. They met once a week at a different out-of-the-way motel and never contacted one another in between.

Lara explained her plan when they met.

"There's a reporter I went to college with, Jasmine DuBois, who'd give her first-born for this story. She's a respected investigative reporter, but is not so well-known that Clancy will recognize her. We meet with the good Reverend and let him convince us to steer clear of Avondale. Jasmine exposes him and the shit hits the fan."

"What if it's a trap?" Christy voiced the concern of the others. "You know, he hands us over to the police and reaps favorable publicity for the Alliance."

"It's a chance we have to take, but remember he honestly believes we're on his side. He'll draw as much heat from his supporters as praise if he turns us in. No, I think he'll try to manipulate us to continue our work where *he* decides its best. If we get caught down the line he's already distanced himself from us."

***

Jasmine, as Lara guessed, jumped at the opportunity. The four women met with the reporter and spared no details. Lara, upon seeing Jasmine for the first time in four years, was somewhat worried Reverend Clancy might not accept her as being one of their group. She cut an imposing figure; a tall black woman with the complexion of chocolate mousse. Her hair was combed back straight, tied at the back. She looked neither like a housewife nor a yuppie 60s radical. There was a self-confident aura about her that Lara thought might intimidate Clancy, who might clam up in her presence. All the same, she was a good listener who asked insightful questions without interrupting the flow of the conversation.

When Lara mentioned her concern about her appearance, Jasmine brushed it off.

"Girl, I've infiltrated any number of groups to get my story. I can be ghetto black or a homely housewife. I'm as much an actress as a reporter."

True to her word, she returned the next night, her hair in plats, baggy jeans and a sweater several sizes too big. She averted Lara's eyes when she was spoken to, answering barely above a whisper. Lara couldn't help but smile at the transformation.

That morning, Lara had called Reverend Clancy from a pay phone and he'd quickly agreed to a meeting. He was told there'd be directions where to meet when he landed at Kennedy Airport. At Toni's suggestion, they picked an isolated motel near the Meadowlands, in New Jersey.

Yvette would follow the Reverend from the airport to make sure he was alone. She'd wait outside, during the meeting. At its conclusion, or at the slightest hint of trouble, they could be off and all but impossible to track with Toni's knowledge of the area.

They needn't have worried. Reverend Clancy arrived alone, as instructed, picked up a message Yvette had left with the name of the hotel and caught a cab without making contact with anyone.

Fifteen minutes from the motel, at a rest stop on the Jersey Turnpike, Yvette called and let the others know Clancy would soon arrive. Christy met him outside the front entrance and conducted him through a side door so the front desk would not be alerted to his arrival.

The Reverend, congeniality exuding from every pore, immediately took control and got down to business. There were no introductions.

"You girls have stirred up quite a hornet's nest, by God. I applaud your devotion to the cause, but I must question your methods."

"Reverend, if you've come here to dissuade us from further attacks on Avondale clinics, you've wasted your time," Lara interjected. "With the first bomb we set, we committed ourselves and there's no turning back. We're sick and tired of marching, picketing and being hauled off to jail with negligible results. With three bombs and no injuries, we've hit the abortionists where it hurts most—in their pocketbook. Imagine the cost of added security? And, women are thinking twice about availing themselves of Avondale's facilities. We've got them on the run."

"But why Avondale?" the Reverend asked.

"Simple." Toni responded. "They're the McDonald's of abortion clinics, with franchises all over the country. Strike at one and *all* must respond."

Reverend Clancy shook his head in resignation. He was a commanding figure; 57-years old, with thick white hair. He was a big-boned, stocky impeccably-dressed man who had not let himself go to flab. He had a rosy Irish face and eyes that radiated a range of emotions. He'd tried speaking to them as a parent towards wayward children. Now his eyes blazed with the fury of a zealot as he told them the secret of Avondale.

"Avondale's a front. It's an abortion clinic run by a powerful segment of the Alliance. There are *no* abortions carried out at Avondale." He told them much of what they already knew. Told them as Jasmine taped the conversation. "I was, of course, skeptical when the Ministry first broached the notion, but they made it work. First one clinic, with their most fervent followers. Over the next several years more clinics opened and the Alliance provided funding. Women are counselled against abortions, but those who fail to heed our message get what they want; they lose their child, but not through an abortion. It's the best of both worlds. We spread our message to those willing to listen. We save the babies from those who want the convenience of sex without responsibility."

"But aren't you encouraging promiscuity?" Jasmine probed gently. "Anytime they get pregnant, it's Avondale to the rescue."

"They don't get pregnant a second time," Clancy said, his eyes now hard, devoid of sympathy.

"Sorry, Reverend, but birth control isn't foolproof," Jasmine countered with a bit more animation.

"At Avondale it is. Having an abortion is a sin, even if we don't really abort the pregnancy. And, sin is punished. During the procedure we make it impossible for the woman to conceive again. We can't stop sluts from sleeping around, but we can insure they will *never* have need for another abortion."

The Reverend sat back and let the women digest what he said for a few moments. Then, almost apologetic, he concluded. "Can you see now why you must abandon your attacks on Avondale?"

"You just want us to fade away, then?" Lara asked.

"I didn't say that." Hands on his knees, eyes locked on Lara's he made a proposal of his own. "I'm not one to advocate violence, mind you, but you've hit a nerve," he chuckled. "Pardon my French, but you women have balls. You act, not just react. Imagine if we had hundreds, *thousands* like you?" He paused for a second, deep in thought, then sighed. "But I'm straying. To answer your question, I would *never* suggest you abandon a method that can help the cause. There are many other abortion clinics aside from Avondale. Too many for my taste. Personally, and I speak for the Alliance as well, we wouldn't be adverse to seeing some of our competition run out of business. I look forward to the day when Avondale will have a monopoly and for all intents and purposes abortions will be a thing of the past. If you can bring that day closer, more power to you. Do we understand one another?" he concluded, radiating confidence.

"Perfectly," Lara answered. She stood up, signalling the end of the meeting. "I want to thank you for being so frank with us. Now that we know where the Alliance stands and how Avondale fits in we'll act accordingly."

"I'm sure you will. Ladies, it's been a pleasure," Clancy said, shaking their hands, a wide smile on his face. "I look forward to the fruits of our meeting, if you get my drift."

"You can expect something explosive quite soon," Lara said, and they all laughed.

***

Jasmine's expose was front page news the next day. Her tape was played, replayed and played again, much like the videotape of Rodney King's beating by Los Angeles police officers in 1991, as events unfolded over the next two weeks.

Reporters beaten out on the story of the year descended upon Avondale and the Faith Hope Charity Ministry of God with a bloodlust, groping for a new angle, a fresh perspective.

Avondale itself was overrun by irate women all over the country who could no longer bear children. Class action lawsuits in the billions were filed. Even with the clinics closed, until the furor passed, women stormed past bewildered security and seized records to search for their children. One clinic, which had shredded its records, was burned to the ground. The Ministry, in disarray, with the Alliance unsuccessfully trying to distance itself as much as possible, was slow to respond to the groundswell of outrage and hostility. It seemed one step behind each maneuver, legal or otherwise, the onslaught of the disclosure had wrought.

With its credibility destroyed the Alliance split and the anti-abortion movement was in disarray and fragmented. The more conservative groups attempted to fight in court and the political arena, with little success. Opponents thrust the Avondale horror in their faces at every turn, and they were constantly on the defensive.

More radical groups took their fight to the streets, forcibly blocking entrance into abortion clinics. Unlike the early nineties, however, demonstrators were arrested and given stiff fines and prison terms. District attorneys, bending to the prevailing political climate were not intent on being lenient and judges heeded their recommendations for severe sentences.

A small, but rabid fringe group, headed by Terrence McCauley, founder of the Faith Hope Charity Ministry of God went underground. McCauley, his dreams of an abortion-free United States in ruins, nevertheless decided to continue the work he'd started at Avondale.

Within a year, the Avondale backlash led to liberalized abortion laws with greater scrutiny and accountability of clinics to assure nothing of the sort could occur again.

Try as they might, no reporters were able to unearth the Anti-Abortion Underground, which vanished as abruptly as it had appeared.

Swept up in the storm that followed Jasmine's disclosures, all but Lara joined in the civil lawsuits, and all four attempted to locate their children. They did so separately, deciding to keep their distance from one another until at least their next high school reunion.

***

Lara sat in the back of the 6th grade graduation at St. Charles. Among the seventy boys on stage, third from the left in the first row was her son. He'd been enrolled at St. Charles soon after the Ministry school he'd attended since Day Care had closed four months before.

His eyes were flat and vacant as he voiced songs learned by rote. Four of his brothers and sisters had been taken from his "mother" after successful lawsuits by their natural mothers.

Looking at the child, Lara knew she would not do the same. The child was too old to reclaim. Psychologically scarred for life. She remembered the words from so long ago: "a lifelong decision." He was no longer hers; hadn't been since she'd first walked into Avondale.

Walking out in the midst of the ceremony, she thought the time right to bring up the subject of adoption with Benjamin. He'd broached it many times over the years, but she'd harbored guilt that her inability to conceive had been God's punishment for her abortion. She'd thought that any child she might adopt would, likewise, face God's wrath and meet some dreadful end. She knew now she was wrong. A *human* hand, not God's, had choreographed decisions she'd made since her visit to Avondale. It was now time to reclaim her life.

She'd made one lifelong decision as a teenager; a decision she'd finally come to terms with. She'd made another that day and damn if it didn't feel good.

She held the door open and allowed a young woman with blond hair to enter, her head down, possibly in prayer.

***

Catherine made her way down to the basement of St. Charles. Father McCauley was speaking to several dozen people, the great majority of them women.

"One woman at a time, my friends," he exhorted these most fervent of his followers who'd refused to abandon the cause. "Human greed is our ally. A spiritual vacuum has enveloped the Nation. Do you know what that means?"

"Tell us, Father," his followers chanted in unison.

"Young women, little more than children, will become pregnant and seek the easy way out—through abortion. But abortions aren't free anymore, for the most part. We mustn't allow the unborn to die. We can offer a better alternative and punish them for their sins at the same time."

"Tell us Father."

And he did.

***

Catherine watched a girl, no more than fourteen, leave the Farris Clinic, tears streaming down her face. Catherine approached, as the girl turned the corner.

"What's the problem, my child?" she said, scarcely above a whisper. "Maybe I can be of some help."

"Leave me alone," the girl shot back.

"You're pregnant," Catherine said, ignoring the girl's hostility.

The girl stopped. "What's it to you?" Snappish, but with less rancor and a tinge of curiosity.

"You're contemplating an abortion, aren't you?"

"Not contemplating, lady. I've made up my mind. Just have to raise the money." More tears welled in her eyes. "Somehow have to raise the money..."

"Nonsense." Catherine opened her purse and removed five one hundred dollar bills. "This is yours, no strings attached, in exchange for the fetus."

"Five hundred dollars for a baby I don't want. What's the catch?"

"$500 for the fetus. You'll be rid of it and the baby'll live a happy life. You can have a child of your own when you're ready."

The girl greedily grabbed the money and followed Catherine across the street.

Barry Hoffman is the editor of Gauntlet, *an annual publication that examines the subject of censorship. Most recently, Barry has had fiction published in* Fear, Cemetery Dance, Cold Blood, Twisted, *and* The Sterling Web. *He also has a story in the upcoming anthology,* The Day the Earth Struck Back.

Khellie

Mike Hurley

Hammurabi Renfield clawed his fingernails into his temples as Dr. Amoralis approached. The news was disastrous; Ham knew by the doctor's grimness.

"We did everything we could."

Ham knew what that meant but he asked anyway. "My wife?"

The doctor shook his head. "There's no hope; there never really was."

"Is...is she—" He sobbed and buried his face in his hands. He couldn't force out the word.

Dr. Amoralis sat down beside Hammurabi Renfield and placed a compassionate hand on his shoulder. "Brain stem. The machines, however..." His fingers traced circles in the air while his voice trailed off; he was having difficulty with the right words himself. "We have to talk."

Ham Renfield swallowed a great welling of spit. His throat constricted and tired to refuse the burden. At last he forced it down. "She's being kept alive on a machine. Is that it? You want to unhook her?"

"We need to talk about it."

Renfield nodded. Tears flooded his eyes. He blinked them away and swallowed again, painfully. "Khellie!" he called.

The doctor patted Renfield's shoulder. "She's gone," he said softly, "but we need to talk about something else"

* * *

Yes, they had talked about such things before—many times—but never (that he could recall) before their marriage...unless it was silly chitchat that neither of them took seriously. But on their wedding night, the very night—

They had made love repeatedly and were lying in each other's arms, languid, gathering strength for the third encore. Suddenly she pushed him away and sat up in the bed.

"I don't want any children," she said, "not right away."

He looked at her with a puzzled expression. "It's a little late to be concerned," he said.

She looked down at his nakedness and grinned. "Oh, that's got nothing to do with it."

Hammurabi Renfield reached up and traced his fingers around her breasts. "My dearest darling wife," he said, "I was taught it had everything to do with it."

"I'm on the pill."

He shrugged. "So much for biology." He kissed her and tried to pull her down again.

"No," she protested. "We've got to talk about this."

"You don't want kids and you're on the pill. So what's to talk?"

"Oh, Ham, it's not that simple. You're part of me now. I need to know where you stand. You probably want children—most men do—but I'm not ready for it. Someday, maybe, I'll want kids, but not now, and I don't want to lose you because of it. I need your support...your understanding."

He had given it or at least he had tried to but as their marriage entered its seventh year, he began to yearn for a child.

"No," she declared. "Not yet."

"Why not?" he asked. "When we were first married it was different. You wanted a job, college, a career. A baby then would have been difficult. But you haven't done any of those things. You stay home or go out and amuse yourself. Why not start a family?"

"No."

"Your mother would like a granddaughter," he argued. "And I would like a son."

She pressed her hands against the sides of his face and played a thumb over his lips. "I know," she said, "but it's my body."

"It's my body, too. It's my body that gets up every morning and goes to work, at a job I don't really enjoy, just to support us. If I was single, I could take a job I liked, any job, without having to ask what it pays."

"What are you trying to say, Ham? Do you want me to get a job?"

"No. I'm trying to say that marriage has its responsibilities—mine is to protect and support."

"And it's my responsibility to have babies? Is that it? My God! that's Neanderthal!"

"So what? Evolution hasn't changed anything. You can take over my job but anatomy won't let me do yours. All your liberation and equality and role-reversal jazz is artificial, and always will be until men can have babies. Or maybe someday we can grab a Sears catalog and order a Baby Hatch. Won't that be great? Comes like a blow-up doll, with a sex organ for you and another for me. We take turns taking it to bed and then stick it in the closet to gestate."

"Now you're talking stupid."

"Oh am I? Well maybe it's the sort of stupid we need. Maybe men need to get together in a Male Restoration Society to re-establish masculinity or create a world where we don't need women."

She laughed and moved closer to wrap her arms around him.

"What's so damn funny?" he demanded.

"You," she said. She kissed him on the cheek and nuzzled against his shoulder. "Do you realize what you're promoting?"

"Male liberation!"

"Restoration was the word you used. The Male Restoration Society...commonly known by its initials: Mrs."

He pulled her around to look into her eyes. They sparkled with good humor. He grinned. "See!" he said in a put-on voice, "women getting their hands on everything. Nothing is sacred anymore. Gone are the last bastions of male superiority!"

"As it should be," she said demurely, her lips pouted.

He sucked in a breath and assumed a soap-box position: "If we still had caves and saber-tooth tigers, things would be different. You wouldn't be so eager to be independent then."

She backed off a step and curtsied. "We thank you for the past, kind sir. And now that society no longer needs muscle, we want equality."

"And tomorrow?" he asked, folding his arms and standing god-like before her. "Then what will you want? Superiority?"

"Oh, I don't know," she said as she put out a hand and began to rub an area below his belt buckle. "But whatever happens, we'll keep a few of you around for sex."

He lifted her in his arms and carried her off to the bedroom. Two months later, she shrieked at him:

"*You bastard!*"

Hammurabi Renfield flinched, expecting something to come flying at him. "What did I do?" he yelled.

"I'm pregnant, you son-of-a-bitch."

"Are you sure? That's great! I mean, I'm sorry. Why are you blaming me?"

"Who the hell else should I blame?"

"I don't mean that—I mean the pill—for Chrissakes, you're on the pill."

"Hell of a lot of good it did."

"Hey, I'm sorry," he said, reaching out to take her hand, "but I didn't make the pills, you know."

"Oh! oh! shit!" She came close to him and cried against his chest. "I know it's not your fault, Ham. I've got to blame someone and who else have I got?"

"So what are you going to do?"

"Do?"

"About the baby?"

"I'm not ready for it, Ham."

"I know, but that's always been theory. Now it's real. What are you going to do?"

She pulled back and stood apart from him. "What choice do I have?"

"Have the baby. Start a family before you get too old. Let your mother spoil her grandchild. Give me someone to continue the family name."

"I'm not ready."

"When will you be ready, Khellie? When you're old enough for child-bearing to be risky? When you're too old to conceive at all? When you're dead?"

"I don't know—not now."

"So you're going to abort?"

"A week from Monday."

"Just like that? No asking me how I feel about it?"

"I already know how you feel."

"And?"

"My decision's made."

"Did my feelings count for anything?"

She looked at the floor. "I'm sorry, Ham. This is between me and this thing inside my belly."

"It's my thing, too."

"It's not your body, dammit—it's mine—and I'm not going to let it become a mindless incubator. Here, Khellie, here's a little present for you! Get pregnant. Have a baby. Drop out of the world for a year—Get tied down for three or four—deal with the consequences for twenty—take on extra responsibilities for life! Here, Khellie, nice Khellie, good Khellie, have another...and another—My God! I'm not a breeding machine that you can switch on or off!"

"You're upset. We'll talk about it later."

"There's nothing to talk about. You or nature or the goddamn pill makers flipped the 'on' switch. Well, I'm pulling the plug. That's all there is to it. And it's none of your business. End of discussion."

* * *

"We have to talk about the baby," Dr. Amoralis said.

Hammurabi Renfield sat, head low, hands on his lap. His fingers traced aimless whorls upon each other. At last he nodded his head. "I know," he said.

"I understand she was on her way to an abortion clinic when the accident occurred," the doctor said, "so I assume she didn't want the baby."

"Yes..."

"But if she knew there'd never be another, what would she have wanted then? What do you want?"

"What are you asking, doctor?"

"Do you want the baby, Mr. Renfield? Do you want to save the last opportunity you and Khellie will ever have at giving life to an expression of your love?"

"Khellie's dead."

"The baby's alive and perfectly well for the moment."

"I don't understand."

"It's quite simple—we've done it before. Your wife is dead, Mr. Renfield—brain dead—but her body is otherwise in good condition. We keep things hooked up and we keep the baby alive and growing. When it's strong enough, we'll remove it."

"How long?"

"At a minimum, three months. Probably longer; full term if we can keep it."

"My God! she'd be a machine herself, lying there all that time —another paper for the medical journals—nothing more than an incubating piece of meat—"

"She's beyond caring. You've got to think of yourself and what you want."

"But it's her body."

"Yes, I know that line but it's not true anymore. She's dead and the disposition of her body belongs to you. Think about it and let me know your decision tomorrow. It's your body now."

———————————

Mike Hurley has fiction publications in the United States and abroad, in such varied places as Belgium, Chile, the former U.S.S.R., Hungary and Argentina. His domestic credits include Haunts, Space & Time, New Dimensions, Detective Story, Other Worlds, Midnight Zoo, *and many others. He hails from the English Department of Bridgewater State College in Massachusetts.*

The Days of Babies

Joyce Hunt

My mother smiles across the dinner table and asks me if the chili is too hot. I try to smile back. "A little," I say. "But it's good."

Let her think the reason I can't smile is too-hot chili. She will never guess the real reason. She will never guess it's because Leanna, my best friend, is pregnant.

I look at my family as they sit with me eating our dinner as usual. It would never occur to any of them, my lawyer dad, my jock brother, Petey, or Cindy, at seven the "caboose" of the family, that such a thing could happen. Until just after school today it wouldn't have occurred to me either. And the truth of how I feel is this: I wish I didn't know.

If that sounds like an awful best friend, then I guess that's what I am. Because a little corner of me is mad that Leanna told me—just me, no one else, not even Jeremy Phillips, the guy who made her pregnant. A little corner of me doesn't want to carry this secret. And then I think of Leanna, and what a secret she's carrying and I'm totally ashamed of myself.

"I don't *know* what I'm going to do!" Leanna told me this afternoon. We were sitting on her bed with its pile of bright pink flowered pillows, covered in the same rich chintz material as the curtains and the ruffle around her dressing table.

Mrs. Rice, Leanna's mother, calls herself an interior consultant. She decorates for people whose names everyone in town recognizes and she doesn't believe in posters or stuffed animals or anything that could be called trendy or cute. She likes things that are classic and timeless and she had told Leanna that's just what her bedroom is. "You'll never outgrow this room," she told her, when Leanna objected to the chintz saying it reminded her of an old lady's sitting room. "You'll love it when you come home from college, you'll love it when you come home from your first job and you'll still love it when you come home to get married."

This afternoon, Leanna was crying. "I can't tell them," she said. "You've got to," I told her.

We are both high school juniors this year. We have been hearing about pregnancy in school for ages and the advice has always included confiding in your parents or some sympathetic adult as soon as possible. "They can help you," I say weakly. Then I hate myself because I know I'm only saying that because I think it's the right thing for a person in my situation to say. I don't really believe her parents will help her. In fact, I know Leanna's parents will scream and carry on and be disgraced and make her do what *they* think is right, not what she wants to do and it will only make things worse. And I hate being here with my best friend saying things I don't believe. Up until now Leanna and I have never done that. But up until now Leanna was never pregnant either.

"They'll make me have an abortion," Leanna said softly. "I don't know if I can do that."

"So, you can have the baby. And then give it to someone to adopt."

"I don't know if I can do that either." Leanna's face, always so pretty, now so serious, pleads with me to understand. And I do. I think I understand that all she can do right now is not know what to do.

"You don't have to do anything today," I say. "You've got time. Are you sure your period's just not late?"

"I did the test. Twice. Both times it was positive. And I can feel it." Leanna runs her hands over her breasts and down to her belly. "I feel different inside," she says. "I just know."

"I think you should tell Jeremy," I finally say. I am not sure if I want Jeremy to know because he must take some responsibility as the father, or if I hope that his knowing will ease some of my burden.

Leanna only shakes her head. "If it comes to that, I will," she says. "Only if it comes to that."

"Comes to what?" I ask.

"If I keep the baby I'll tell him," she says. "If I don't, I don't want anyone to know. Just you. That way I know it won't get around."

"It won't get around," I say getting up to leave. I give her an awkward little hug and then go home to have chili.

On the way home I think about Jeremy. He lives with his dad and two brothers in a tiny house with a cracked crooked fence and weeds growing all around it. When we were in junior high his mom took off—went to New York City to be an actress, some people said, went to Los Angeles with a salesman she used to work with at the discount store other people said. Jeremy is handsome, we all agree on that. But sometimes he looks like someone whose mother ran away and left him in a rundown house. He does not look dirty, I decide, as I approach my own driveway, which is swept clean and has four matching trash cans lined up for the early morning pick-up tomorrow. He just looks disorganized.

***

I have not been a good friend to Leanna, I think as I pick at the corn bread my mother has bought to go with the chili. I remember the times I've been jealous when guys we both knew have asked Leanna to go to movies or parties. I think of the time I agreed with Charlotte McGrew when she said Leanna was just as snobby as her mother and how I was secretly glad a couple of months ago when Jeremy started paying attention to Katie Sigmund. I was sort of going with Billy Kendall at the time and Billy said, even though he thought Leanna was one of the best-looking girls in the high school, he wasn't sure if you could trust her. I didn't disagree with him.

"I'll eat your corn bread if you're not going to eat it." My brother, Petey, reaches over to my plate and I slap his hand away as if I'm swatting a fly.

"That is rude and uncouth," I say. "I'm not done eating."

"You're just making a pile of crumbs," Petey says. "That is rude and uncouth too."

"Cut it out, Petey," my father grumbles. "You've had three pieces of bread already. Now hurry up and finish or I'm not taking you to the mall to get those new sneakers."

He and Petey push their chairs from the table. "Does anybody need anything from the mall?" my father calls as they head out the door.

"A diamond bracelet," my mother says as the door slams behind them.

I am helping my mother load the dishwasher and we are both listening to Cindy spell her second grade spelling words when Leanna calls. "I'm going to tell Jeremy," she says. "I think you're right. He ought to know. After all, I didn't do this all by myself." She sounds bright and cheery, and I picture her sitting in that flowered room, her face as shiny as the chintz fabric, her skin as pink.

"You're doing the right thing," I say. I have lowered my voice and my mother and Cindy look suspiciously at me. "Gotta go," I tell Leanna. I hang up and give them both a fake happy smile. It's not totally insincere, though. Leanna's telling Jeremy brings me a feeling of relief. I like what her decision means. I think it means Leanna will keep the baby.

***

Later that same night my Aunt Molly and her husband, Jeff, come over. Aunt Molly is my mother's younger sister, 'the afterthought', my mother jokes, 'the accident', I've heard my father call her. I think of Leanna's baby. I don't think anyone will joke and call that baby an accident. My aunt is called that because my grandmother was forty-five when Aunt Molly was born. My mother was fifteen. Aunt Molly was more like a daughter to my mother than a sister, "like a little living toy for me," my mother has told me.

Tonight Aunt Molly and Uncle Jeff are holding hands. They've been married for eight years and they don't have any children.

"They don't know whose fault it is," my mother told me a little sharply once, when I'd overheard Aunt Molly saying that Uncle Jeff refused to go and have tests done. "They don't know so they'll keep on trying until something happens."

My mother talks about sex a lot that way. She doesn't come right out and say anything, she just uses expressions like 'keep on trying' and 'until something happens' and she thinks I know just what she means. I suppose I do, but I also think that until you actually do it, you'll never quite know what any of it means.

Aunt Molly and Uncle Jeff are holding hands because they say they have an announcement to make. A knowing look passes over my mother's face. Her eyes sparkle and she winks at me. I know what they're going to say too. I can not believe twice in one day I'm going to hear that someone is going to have a baby.

Uncle Jeff clears his throat and looks to Aunt Molly to make the announcement. A little shiver of pleasure quivers in her shoulders before she says anything. Then she tells us.

"We didn't want to say anything, but last year we put our names in to adopt a Korean baby," Aunt Molly begins. "And tonight we got the call. Our baby has been born. They're sending us a picture tomorrow and he should be here within a couple of months. But think of it. Yesterday was his birthday!"

There is silence for a second as all the features on my mother's face shift into her look of severe disappointment. I've seen this look before. I saw it a lot a couple of months ago when my father changed his mind about joining a bigger law firm because he didn't want to commute for over an hour each way. And I saw it briefly when I showed her this gorgeous dress I picked out myself to wear for Thanksgiving dinner in a restaurant.

"A Korean?" my mother asks. "Why a Korean? Do you know how difficult that will be? Culturally it's so vastly different from how we live. Do you really think it's fair to those children?"

"We've given it a lot of thought," Aunt Molly says. She is clutching Uncle Jeff's hand more tightly and I realize she was expecting an argument. "The children aren't wanted in Korea if they're illegitimate. They live the lives of outcasts. At least here they have love and acceptance."

"It's your decision, of course," my mother says mildly.

"I think it's nice," I say. I try to picture my new Korean cousin, and I see him as plump with dark spiky hair and happy slanted eyes. There are some Vietnamese and Japanese students in my school. But no Koreans. "What do you think you'll name him?"

"He has a Korean name," Aunt Molly explains. "But since he's going to be an American, we'll give him an American name." My mother's eyebrows raise slightly, but she doesn't say anything.

"Why didn't you just get a regular baby?" Cindy asks.

Aunt Molly smiles patiently, but Uncle Jeff looks away, uncomfortable and flushed. "This will be a regular baby," Aunt Molly says. "He'll eat, and cry and dirty his diapers." Cindy smiles.

To my mother Aunt Molly says, "To get a healthy American baby we'd have to wait years maybe. The Koreans come much quicker, although so many people want them it's getting harder all the time. We think we've been very lucky."

"I mean why don't you have the baby yourself?" Cindy persists.

Aunt Molly gives my mother a look and I say, "Cindy, that's an impolite question."

"This could very well be the thing that makes it happen," my mother said quickly. "You know how they say as soon as people adopt they have their own. Now, how about a cup of tea to celebrate?"

"I like Timothy, but Jeff likes Joseph," Aunt Molly is saying a few minutes later in the kitchen. She and my mother are sipping mint tea and talking about baby names and planning a shower. But there is a faint tension still in the air. My mother is not completely pleased with her new nephew and his parents know it. "Joseph Timothy or Timothy Joseph. Which sounds best to you?" Aunt Molly asks me.

"They both sound find," I say. Then I excuse myself. Suddenly I don't want to hear another word about babies. The whole thing is scaring me. It's not what I always thought it was, just a simple thing that everyone was excited about. I touch my stomach. I have been getting my period for a couple of years. Like Leanna I could have a baby. Or would I be like Aunt Molly and not be able to have one? And what would it feel like if either of those things happened to me?

***

I must go to sleep thinking about this because I awaken suddenly in the middle of the night. I had a dream that had a baby in it, and when the baby started to cry I woke up. For a while I just lie in the darkness watching the dots on the digital clock change. Then an idea starts to come to me. What if Aunt Molly adopted Leanna's baby? Then the baby would have a good home, Leanna could see it whenever she wanted, and Aunt Molly and Uncle Jeff would have an American child. In the middle of the night, the more I think about it, the more wonderful it seems. I want to wake up everyone and tell them my plan. But I decide to wait. Instead, I roll over feeling very contented as I fall asleep again.

But in the morning my idea seems stupid. Besides, when I get to school Leanna is at my locker to tell me that Jeremy is going to talk to his older brother about getting money for an abortion. "Jeremy said he'd go with me," she says. "But I'd want you to go too. And he said he'd pay for it and never tell a soul."

"So that sounds good," I say.

"I don't know if I can do it," Leanna says. "I heard about a girl who almost died having an abortion."

"You won't die," I say. "And if Jeremy is going to help you, I think you should do it."

Standing by our lockers I can't bear to think of Leanna's stomach growing huge. I can't stand the thought of her screaming in pain for hours while she's in labor and of having a baby she'll have to give up to some stranger. Everything I thought yesterday about her having the baby, or about her giving it to Aunt Molly has changed. Now I think she should have an abortion and get it over with.

When I meet her for lunch that noon Leanna is pale and shaky. "I just threw up," she whispers, her eyes watery in front of mine as they avoid her lunch tray.

"Are you all right now?" I ask.

"I think so," she says. "I just don't know what to do."

We sit in silence at lunch because there is nothing I can tell her. I have seen the same news shows that she has, shows with demonstrators in Washington, some of them talking about killing babies, some of them talking about women's rights to decide. I have seen TV shows about teenage mothers and movies where having a baby looks like the most joyous thing you can do. But they all mean nothing. Because none of them are about my best friend, Leanna Rice.

Later that afternoon toward the end of the day, in Mr. Schreider's class when we're talking about India and how hard Indira Ghandi worked for her country, I decide Leanna should have her baby after all. I think of the beautiful house she lives in and how much money her parents have and how wonderful babies are and it seems as if it wouldn't be such a bad thing after all. Mrs. Rice isn't so terrible really. She would probably love her grandchild on first sight and want to take care of it while Leanna was in school.

I have just decided this when Mr. Schreider shuts off the lights and puts on a video about India. The camera follows a young man through New Delhi and pans over tired-looking dark faces. Then it pauses to tell about starvation and two tiny boys, their bellies bloated like balloons, their eyes wide, hungry and sad, stare into the camera and seem to be looking right at me. I can't look away, but I am glad the lights are off because suddenly my eyes are filled with tears. I think of my tiny Korean cousin who will never know his Korean mother and I am suddenly crying out of the sadness and frustration of my confusion. Who should be born and who shouldn't be born? I don't know and I don't want to think about it. But I have to think about it, because Leanna is my friend, and Aunt Molly is my aunt and just like them I am a woman and I will have to make these kinds of decisions too.

I wipe my eyes quickly before Mr. Schreider can turn the lights back on and I get up and take the bathroom pass. I slip out of the room and head down the hall and go into the bathroom which is deserted and silent except for the squeaky trickle of a faucet that won't shut off. I stare at my blotchy eyes in the mirror then splash cold water over my face and when I look up again I find I can smile.

Suddenly I am filled with gratitude. I am grateful for something that I have never thought to be grateful for before, and that is that none of these decisions are mine. Leanna will decide what she wants to do, the same way Aunt Molly has, and whatever she chooses it will be right for her. I will help her with any decisions. I will babysit for her. I will go with her if she decides to have an abortion. But I will never tell her that I am rejoicing right now. I will never tell her that standing before this bathroom mirror I am filled with a new and sudden happiness.

I want to hug myself and shout thanks because I know I am too young—and for a long time I will stay too young. And I am almost giggling because I am so relieved that today these are not decisions I have to make.

Joyce Hunt is a children's writer who has had numerous pieces of fiction and nonfiction published in magazines such as Child Life, Highlights for Children, and Cobblestone. She is also the author of two novels, Eat Your Heart Out, Victoria Chubb (Scholastic 1990) and The Four of Us and Victoria Chubb (Scholastic 1991). She is presently working on a novel for young adult readers. Ms. Hunt lives in Albany, New York, and is an elementary school teacher.

Rock-A-Bye

Edward Lodi

Darryl Spencer gnawed at his knuckles, a habit he had when nervous. As a rule he caught himself before inflicting any great damage, but this time he chewed through skin and flesh before the salt, metallic taste of his own blood penetrated his consciousness. He drew his hand away from his mouth and examined the ravaged knuckles with the dazed abstraction of an accident victim contemplating a severed limb.

On the sofa beside him the agent of Darryl's distress rested comfortably with outstretched forepaws. Alternately exposing and retracting his claws in a gentle kneading motion, Whiskers purred in smug contentment preparatory to dozing off.

How Darryl envied his pet's feline unconcern!

That Whiskers was the immediate cause of the morning's horror wasn't, of course, the cat's fault. Darryl had trained him to be a mouser. Train wasn't exactly the right word—*encouraged* the cat's natural proclivity to hunt was more like it. They'd had Whiskers how many years now? Seven or eight at least. Yes, it must be eight. He and Deborah had rescued the kitten from the Animal Shelter when they were overrun with rodents because of a neighbor's horses and carelessly swept barn. The kitten had earned his keep, bringing home mice on an almost daily basis before he was fully grown. And Darryl had rewarded him for each tiny body with a nugget of Kitty Treat. No reward for birds, naturally, but birds were harder to catch than mice and were seldom laid at the Spencer doorstep.

Even so, the variety of kills was astounding. In addition to the desired rats and mice they included chipmunks, squirrels, frogs, small turtles and some not so small snakes. The absurd image of Whiskers leaping over a picket fence dangling a three-foot-long snake in his jaws usually brought a smile of recollection to Darryl's face, but not today.

Today there was nothing to smile about. Darryl glanced toward the kitchen. Deborah would be home soon. He couldn't let her see *that*.

With an effort of will he got off the sofa and made his way slowly back into the kitchen. Maybe it would be gone, would prove to have been a figment of his imagination—a sign that he was going insane, no doubt—but wasn't madness preferable to a reality that could hold such an abomination?

But no, it was still there, inside the screen door where Whiskers had proudly dropped it and where Darryl, unsuspecting, had stooped down to examine it. And immediately staggered into the bathroom to be sick.

After heaving his breakfast he had gone back to examine it again. And again been sick. This time, he told himself, he would look at it closely, *not* be sick, then think of some way to get rid of it. Before Deborah returned.

After all, he still loved her. Despite all that had happened between them. The arguments. The recriminations. It wouldn't do for her to see it.

Or would it? The thing about it was, it had Deborah's hair. Those blond, taut, kinky little pubic wires that he liked to tug at playfully when they made love. All over its head. It had blond pubic hair, just like Deborah's, only in the wrong place. All over its head. He kept repeating this to himself, a litany of disbelief: blond pubic hairs, all over its head. Its tiny fuzzball head.

He prodded it gently with the tip of his shoe. Then flipped it over, shifting it from belly to back. It was a wee bit of a thing, scarcely eight inches long. A perfect little manikin. With perfect little eyes. And perfect little ears. And tiny pink fingers. And tiny pink toes.

And a teeny weeny pink peenie.

The penis. The thing about the penis—well, first of all it was erect. The creature was dead—very much so, riddled with wounds where the cat had mauled it—yet the penis remained erect. But the worst thing about the penis—it was pronged. Just like a tuning fork. With—and now Darryl knew he was cracking up—with a stinger—a pointed, venomous stinger, just like the tail end of a wasp—on each tine. Each tiny tine.

Hah, gotcha! Take that! And that!

Darryl knelt on the linoleum and wept. His mind was going, was all.

He had always thought their child would have been a boy. It was Deborah who wanted the abortion. Darryl had resisted. But not too much. No, he had not resisted much. They were not ready to have children. Not just yet. Later. They would have children later, when they could afford them.

He picked the creature up, cradled it in his arms, cooed to it softly. He nuzzled his nose against the tiny furred head. Discreetly tucked the stiff little penis between the spindly legs. Rocked the bruised body back and forth. Sang to it softly.

When Deborah returned home she opened the screen door to find her husband sitting on the kitchen floor swaying to and fro, blathering idiotically to an object cuddled in his arms. He glanced up at her and grinned.

"Hi, Deb. Look what the cat dragged in." He held it up for her to see. "Baby's home!"

Edward Lodi published his first story in **The Horror Show** *in 1985. Since then he's sold more than one-hundred stories, articles, reviews, verse, etc. in such publications as* **Ellery Queen's Mystery Magazine, 2AM, GAS, Grue, The Tome, Nuclear Fiction, The Armchair Detective,** *and others. He has a column in* **Writer's Nook News,** *and another on grammar tips in* **Calliope.**

We Are Flesh, We Are Flame

P. Willis Pitts

I am Starfire, he is Gold. We are Flesh, we are Flame. We know the secrets of the Stars; we know the atom's azure dance. We are the last of the Anusetti. We have returned from the Stars. We know many things. We dance, we love, we share Star-secrets, Flame-knowing. Many years have we travelled thus. I have seen the comets flare across the empty reaches of Space, heard the crackling moan of dying suns. Many races; many planets. We have reaped the knowledge of the universe, and we are Home, Home, Home.

Seen as in a dream, it lies below in all its blue-wreathed beauty. So many millennia it has been; we almost doubted it existed. Home.

Gold dances for joy, streaking through the stratosphere like a burning meteor.

"We are here! We are here!" he calls.

I cannot but respond—so many millennia we have been disincorporate; whispering along gaseous trails, riding the tides of hell-force on planets of crystal, planets of sand, gas giants that would consume this Earth in a single gulp. It is Bright; it is Blue; it is Beautiful. The planet of the Blue Seas. Far below us lies the crashing ocean, the ceaseless surf we have only imagined for so long.

We wonder: what, then, shall we find now? We descend.

Joy. Giant structures; glittering surfaces as hard as basalt; teeming, ebullient life. The air is conquered; the land, their domain. They fly, they build, they live, superior. Thousands upon thousand, the mammalian species has risen once again to take this lovely orb and call itself King. So many millennia it has been. And now we are Home, we have much to say, much to share. Our destiny is fulfilled. It is time.

We dart hither and thither, looking for a place, a moment to incorporate. It is a waving, weaving dance; only the briefest of opportunities will present itself; less than the space of an atom, faster than light; we must act quickly. Anticipation. Oh, delicious anticipation:

No Star-secret is so awesome as the miracle of the flesh: the heart's thudding lope; the scents; the sounds; the pheromonic cascades that ripple through the body. The sensual tang of ocean tides; the ride through blue-white foam; scent of sea spray; boom of surf. Touch, taste, sound, feel. All Life is therein. So long it has been that we are disincorporate.

The moment comes. The strange, sickly metamorphic tug that is like an electro-magnetic thrill to the disincorporate. A burgeoning, tiny consciousness beckons—in itself like starfire, embedded in receptive flesh. It knows us. It calls.

"Come, come, brother, sister, come!"

Like darting minnows in dappled streams, we flash downward. Thrust. Wriggle. The dying, choking sensation we have all but forgotten; prelude to Transition and Incorporation.

Delight. We are whole again.

Beyond description! Is it not the supreme joy, this fleshly state? Yes, to dally in the Stars and dive through the heart of a sun is awesome—a knowing state, but, at best, a distant knowing. But when the blood pounds through the veins, and rivers of lymph surge; when a stray thought sends a billion molecules tumbling towards a single synapse; when multi-hued clouds of protein cascade and metamorphose, each one a star guided by the inner pulse of Life, even for the tiniest twitch of a muscle. In this we know God as surely as we have seen the Supreme Intelligence work its magic in the Stars. We are here in the Temple; every cell, a miracle; every synapse flaring with its song of Mystery.

Yes, we, the Anusetti, know there is a God; we have sat at his throne. And this we know the Intelligence that charts and moves the planets on their cosmic paths is no less alive in the body. Though the stars are God's lanterns, the body is his blessing.

And we have returned. We are silent; observers only, awed before the miracle that informs the dead, inert chemicals of the body and renders them Divine.

We are twice blessed, for we lie together, Gold and I; two within a female-receptive. Nestling side-by-side, nurtured by the slow tug of her inner tides, the warm lap of placental fluid and the deep boom of her heart—like the crash of surf on the world that waits outside.

Luck. Fate. Destiny. Call it what you will. Gold is as ecstatic as I; two adjacent unborns ensconced within this mother's flesh; the lovely, crimson secret that is mammalian birth. Once before, I was mother, and now I know it for what it is—the breath of the Divine animating dust.

"We will see this world together, corporate," we whisper.

Snug and fed, we sleep, we sing, we chant the Anusetti litanies learned in the Stars:

"I am Starfire, he is Gold; we are flesh, we are flame. We have been to the Stars and we return Home to offer you our Star-secrets, to counsel with the wise, to love, to share our Flame-knowing. We are flesh again. We are the Anusetti. We are you."

Movement. It is ecstacy. The female receptive is moving. Gold flexes his newfound body. The mother registers this, stops and changes position. This single act of kinaesthesia is a drunken delirium for we who have been disincorporate for so many millennia. To move, to turn, to feel, floating within the warm ocean of the mother's belly. Eventually, we sleep, lulled by the beat of her heart and dream of being born once again into our Home world. Soon.

Gold screams. He has no breath, and yet he screams. It tears across my mind, ragged and raw, and, instantly, I am awake. Wrapped within our oceanic placental fold, we are as one. I am he, he is me, his pain is mine. For a moment, the agony obliterates all thought. And then, horror upon horror, I realize what is happening.

Through the vaginal fold, thrusts a thin, cruel weapon. Cold, metallic, it pierces the placenta. Fluid gushes as it violates the warm sanctity of our haven. Jabbing fiercely, it rips into the soft, growing tissues of Gold's unborn body.

Horror freezes me into inaction as the weapon tears through the pristine patterns of musculature, the delicate fronds of the nerves. Gold's anguished thoughts race through the capsule of flesh that is now our prison of pain:

"Starfire! Starfire!! I am dying!!"

He is lost. We have corporated. The price for this kingly state is fragility, mortality; pain lives with pleasure. And it is pain, not pleasure, that sears his synapses now. The steel rod rips and tears, desiccating soft tissue, nerve and sinew.

Like a dying sun, Gold's spirit winks feebly, and I know for the first time in millennia the horror that is the expiration of the Life flame. Then it is gone. Into the void. Gold is no more.

The corpse sags in the folds of flesh that once nurtured it. Blood seeps through the punctured tissues to join the steady drip of leaking placental fluid.

I am aghast. Never had I thought that this sacrosanct space could be so violated. But my horror is rendered mute by the most horrendous fact of all: It is the mother that has murdered her unborn child.

I am unable to move, unable to think, held in a kind of thrall by the unthinkable. This delicate balance of blossoming blood and bone, the miracle of a billion knitting cells and nerves, violated by the very creature that gives it life!

Then I act. The body I inhabit is weak and not yet ready for birth for two more passages of Earth's moon. Still I act. I rip and scrabble at the placental sac with a fury that is as insane as the act that precipitated it.

The mother registers pain, horror, fear. But I care not. Murderer she is; and a murder will out: an eye for an eye, a tooth for a tooth.

My brother's inert body begins to heave and pitch with the peristalsis of agony I enforce upon the treacherous creature that bears us. The placental folds engulf me, squeeze, pummel my own body. But I will not die. I will be avenged. It is the way. It is sung in the litanies of the Anusetti—a sacred trust cannot be usurped.

"Kill, kill," I sing.

I tear though the suffocating layers of flesh. Blood gouts, tissues rend, and still I tear, rabid, remorseless. I rip aside the shroud of flesh that was once my sanctuary and burst through into light.

And with my first breath, I scream my victory, my defiance for the murderer who has betrayed innocence. Oh, yes, but now a savage innocent. As my lungs inflate and I am a creature of the air and light, I hear the murderer's dying wail. I am triumphant. Revenge.

Then I comatose. Blackness.

Comatose I remain. I assess my damage. I trickle down the synapses, muscles, blood and nerves; see the ravages my bloody fight has wreaked upon my premature body. I will live. I have revenged the crime against nature and I shall overcome. My brother is gone. Loss clutches at my heart, but I try to put it aside. Many millennia we have travelled to fulfill our purpose—and fulfill it, I will. He is me and I am he. I comfort myself that he lives in my blood. I am Starfire. He is Gold. I am the last of the Anusetti.

I repair my body. Slowly, I renew my senses—sight, sound, smell—and soon I am whole enough to realize I am in the hands of wise humans.

They surround me with lights, with the science of corporation—the extensions of the body that the Anusetti once eschewed, choosing instead the extension of our spirit into disincorporation. These, then, are the sages of the Earth.

I am comatose but aware. I essay a reaching-out.

There are beings of wisdom. In white garments, they move about their tasks gravely. I sense them and know they share my revulsion at this creature who was our mother. Wise they are. They, too, condemn their fellow who would murder the innocent life within. They view her yawing body and gaping eyes without compassion, knowing, as I do, she broke the sacred trust.

I do not see the pitiful remains of that which once was Gold, but I remain resolute in my purpose. To give me strength, I sing the Song that the Anusetti sang through the galaxies, through the empty tracts of Space where comets span and suns eclipsed, deep in the moribund hell of a neutron star, riding on the pulsar's waves. The Song is our Destiny, our Reason to live:

"We are the Anusetti. We have come Home. We have travelled to the stars. We bring our wisdom Home to you, O people of wisdom."

I realize I am lying on a cold surface. It is pleasant. The lights are hot, glowing. I remain comatose to conserve my strength as I knit and repair my ravaged body. I am weak, I am premature. But I am with good people; people of wisdom, people of science. They do not hear my Song. But they will. They will.

I realize they have cleaned me meticulously, that they have affixed me to the cold surface. I marvel at the ingenuity of that which restrains without damaging. I have broken a fin in my savage bid for revenge. The humans have spread it out with a reverent care for the miracle of flesh that is the sign of their wisdom. I knit the broken appendage and await Release and Contact. We shall find a way. I am Anusetti; they are wise.

One of them approaches. Aaah. I sense his curiosity, his sagacity. He examines the changes I have made in my body. He knows. He is impressed. He sees I am not alien. I have simply returned the foetus to a form which has been built into its structure from ancient days. I am his ancestor. I am Anusetti.

He becomes excited. I greet this with quiet joy. He knows I am he and he is me. Soon I will return to the sea from whence we both came so many millennia before, he and I. And now these our sons and daughters walk the Earth as creatures of science. I am proud. I am impatient. But I must wait. Beneath the burning lights, I sing my silent Song.

The moment has come.

I am Starfire. We are flesh, we are flame, we are the Anusetti, oh brothers, oh children of the land. Many years have we travelled thus, now we return. We are Home. I bring you the secrets of the Stars. I will teach you the comet's azure dance, the inner flame of the atom, the miracle of the flesh and of disincorporation. Once again, we are one.

The humans gather around. I grow excited. It is a ceremony. They bear a platter of glittering metal with a quiet reverence. The instruments of joy and science. They will slice me from my bonds and I will grow slowly. We will grow together. I wriggle impatiently. I sense, too, his feeling of impatience. I register his sounds, for I have ears, I can hear; I have eyes, I can see. I am flesh again. Come, come, come, brother.

He leans over me and he speaks. Airborne sound.

The sound is lovely. Subtle cadences, dissonances and assonances, much more complex than the simple pipings of our kind. What a creature we have evolved into—our son, our brother, our destiny. I store the sound for its poetry, for its subtle clash and cadence without knowing its meaning—yet. Soon I may sing their Songs. These are people of science. We are the Anusetti. We will share. I have recorded it faithfully.

"CutthegoddamnfishforCristssake!" is the Song he sings.

Lovely, lovely sounds.

The knife descends.

I know the secrets of the Stars.

P. Willis Pitts has written and produced hundreds of programs as an executive staff producer for the BBC World Service, including programs translated into over thirty languages, and an audience averaging thirty million. He's been a professor of English in England and South

America. He's won awards through the Writers of the Future contest and the National Writer's Club, among others. He's written novels, plays, radio dramas, short stories and articles for national and local publication. The Sacramento resident is finishing the final draft of a science fiction trilogy which is under consideration by a publisher. All-in-all, a very busy writer. He's also written one of the best accounts of the 1989 Loma Prieta earthquake I've read.

Factors

Gregory Nyman

Little children laugh and sing, even though they may never amount to anything. Such a morbid thought, I agree, but for some of them, their lives will barely rise above the grime and the shit. That is, if their parents let them. If only their parents...

The ONLY IF factor.
Conventional wisdom wrapped in a bow and handed to children on a platter filled with holes.
A legacy dished out at birth to a suckling child who knows only the warmth of its mother's breast.
Should previews of coming attractions be featured on the walls of the womb, I daresay half the children of the world would welcome death. I know I would have.

We have inevitably entered a time where the abortioner is criminal and the afforded liberal protections are mere antiques soon to be relegated to the incinerator. A woman's right to choose has found its place next to the ashes tossed in the wind and dissipated to the four corners of Hell.
"Protect the unborn," the chant reverberates. "It's their choice to live, too."
Shit, I'm for that. God knows I never had a choice until later, and now that I'm...Christ, it's a bloody crime I was ever born at all.

I'd surmise I'm anti-social. Maybe even a danger to the community, but I'd be willing to bet there's more support for my methods than they're willing to admit. If my theories were adopted, then they'd see the real misfits.
You see, the answer to all this abortion shit has been so simple, I'm surprised no one has ever thought of it before.

It's all very basic, you see. Maybe even archaic, but proven very effective. The VERY FACTOR, I like to call it.

You simply abort the conceivers of a child, either before it's born or after. Preferably before, that way you're not punishing the child twice. Once for coming into the world without a choice, and second for having to live an abused childhood. I know the hell of parents who are subhuman and parasitic.

Forget about sterilization. Impose elimination.

Children have a right to healthy lives. Most everyone agrees with that, but why society allows the same children to live under the same roof with parents and guardians who misuse or even refuse to treat them right is criminal, warranting extinction.

This isn't a diatribe but a call to action. I do more than talk.

When I'd discovered the legacy *my* conceivers left me, I killed them. It took me fifteen long years, but I did it, and when I found my mother's diary, its entries only supported my actions. My cause was just. It still is.

I love the children of the city. I love to hear them sing and play in the parks.

Most parents tend to protect their children from perceived dangers. That's pretty standard stuff, even for an unfit parent, but when they perceive the danger to be me, it hurts, especially to my little friends. They know whose wings keep them from harm.

Like Tommy.

When his Daddy beat him to a pulp in the alley, I was waiting in the shadows. It wasn't the kid's fault he happened to be around when his old man wasted the grocery money on the white powder, but the Daddy never had to worry about accidental overdose. My Bowie knife made sure his throat was cut before the straw went into his nose.

Like Sandy.

When her Mommy gave her to the landlord to pay for the rent, my eyes were wide open, and before the co-conspirators could benefit from the transaction, the pick I called ICE sliced and spliced their eyes together with their brains. Adulthood hadn't taught them anything.

Then there were the twins.

They were barely two when Grammie took custody of them. It'd been a bitter court battle, but when it was over, the issue was far from being resolved. Grammie said the parents were unfit, but had she studied her biology instead of the *TV Guide*, she would've realized fitness lived in the blood and genes.

When the old hag got loaded and locked the kids in the closet, my ears heard their cries, and it wasn't long before the old bitch was pitched twenty stories below on her drunk ass. Twenty stories to read about. EXTRA, EXTRA, EXTRA. The morning edition sold out.

Tonight I'll be watching from my tenement window. Spying, crying, and lying in wait with my semi-automatic. I keep the safety off and the silencer in, and my telescope tells me who to do in.

It's for the children, you know.

My mother made the fatal mistake of letting me live. Twice she made the mistake. Once while I was in the womb (God, I hated being stuck with the hanger) and once when she found out what I was.

Like I said before, it took fifteen years for me to realize how much of a freak monster I'd become. Erroneous conceptions, for sure.

I'll never be found out. This I know.

Those who see me usually turn their eyes away. Something about misshapen heads and distorted features tend to do that.

Someone like me would never be credited with most of the random murders in the city. The police are looking for someone else, or so I've read.

My young ones still sing and my heart rises with them.

That some of them now have the State for a parent doesn't phase me in the least. If the bureaucratic agencies start abusing kids, I'll have a new nemesis to deal with, and I will. VERY EFFECTIVELY.

Dead people can't conceive, and this is what it's all about. It's the real beauty.

Abort the ones who take no responsibility or care for their children. Forget sterilization. Adopt massive elimination.

As you read this, there are children who are being beaten to death, sexually abused, tortured both physically and/or psychologically, or either being born into addiction or sold into it. Kids have always been slaves. Just read the Bible or a Dickens novel. Do you give a shit?

My mother mated with a demon, but she gave birth to something far worse than a son-of-a-bitch. More like a conscience with an itch, and it's this itch I need to scratch. Across sex, race, and economic levels. Monsters exist at the highest levels, and the rich eat their kids, or haven't you heard? Maybe you eat your own, and maybe I'll come looking for you.

The songs of rhymes echo through my mind, and I remember a time when my mother was my only world.

Now the children fill my life, and I peep and snoop, and bloodlet their enemies, whether they're black, white, decadent, or blight.

Abortion is not so much about the unborn, dear friend, but about the born who treat their children like the expendable unimportant. Eliminate them and you save the world. We must do it VERY QUICKLY.

Gregory Nyman assures me he hasn't killed anyone. After reading his story, it was a question I felt I had to ask. Mr. Nyman has spent the past 10 years in the criminal justice system, most recently with the State of Massachusetts Parole Board. As a writer, he's been published in After Hours, Haunts, Godsend Magazine, Virgin Meat *and* The Nightside. *A collection of his stories will soon be published by* The Nightside.

Dr. Pak's Preschool

David Brin

Hands, those strong hands holding her down upon the table-top...in her pain and confusion, they reminded her of those tentacled sea creatures of fabled days which ola-chan had described when she was little, whose habit it was to drag unfortunate mariners down to a watery doom.

Those hands, clasping, restraining—she cried out for mercy, knowing all the while that those hands would ignore her protests, along with any pretense at modesty.

Needles pricked her skin, hot localized distractions from her futile struggle. Soon the drugs took effect. A soporific coolness spread along her limbs, and she lost the will to resist any longer. The hands loosened their grip, and turned to perform yet other violations.

Stormy images battered her wavering sense of self. Moiré patterns and Moebius chains—somehow she knew these things and their names without ever having learned them. And there was something else—something that hurt even to contemplate—a container with two openings, and none at all...a bottle whose interior was on the outside...

It was a problem to be solved. A desperate quandary. A life or death puzzle in higher level geometry.

The words and images whirled, hands groped about her, but at the moment all she could do was moan.

"Wakarimasen!" She cried aloud. "Wakarimasen!"

1.

Reiko should have been more suspicious the night her husband came home earlier than usual, and announced that she would accompany him on his next business trip to Seoul. That evening, however, when Tetsuo showed her the white paper folder containing two red and green airline boarding passes, Reiko could think only in the heady language of joy.

He remembers.

Her elation did not show, of course. She bowed to her husband and spoke words of submissive acceptance, maintaining decorous reticence. Tetsuo, in his turn, was admirably restrained. He grunted and turned his attention back to his supper, as if the matter had really been of little consequence after all.

Nevertheless, Reiko was certain his gruffness overlaid a well of true feeling.

Why else, she thought, would he do such an unheard of thing? And so near the anniversary of their marriage? That second ticket in the envelope surely meant there was still a bit of the rebel under Tetsuo's now so-conventional exterior—still a remnant of the free spirit she had given her heart to, years ago.

He remembers, she thought jubilantly.

And it was not yet nine in the evening. For Tetsuo to return so early for supper at home, instead of having it with business colleagues at some city bar, was exceptional in itself. Reiko bowed again and suggested awakening their daughter. Yukiko so seldom got to spend time with her father.

"Iye," Tetsuo said curtly, vetoing the idea. "Let the child sleep. I wish to retire early tonight, anyway."

Reiko's heart seemed to flutter within her ribcage at his implication. After clearing away dinner she made the required preparations, just in case.

And indeed, later that night he joined with her in their bed—for the first time in months without beer or tobacco or the scent of other women commingling in his breath. Tetsuo made love to her with an intensity she recalled, but which, of late, she had begun to think she had imagined all along.

Almost exactly six years ago they had been newlyweds, trapped joyously in each others' eyes as they honeymooned in Fiji, hardly noticing the mountains or the reefs or the exotic native dancers for the resonant happiness, the amplified autarchia of their union. and for the following year, also, it had remained that way for the two of them, as if they were characters from a happy romantic tale, brought into the real world. In those days even the intense pressure of Tetsuo's career had seemed to take second place to their love.

It had lasted, in fact, up to the time when Reiko became pregnant. Until then she hadn't believed they would ever stop being lovers, and begin the long tedium of life as a married couple. But they did.

Tetsuo closed his eyes tightly and shuddered, then collapsed in a lassitude of spent coitus. His breath was sweet, his weight a pleasure for her to bear, and with her fingertips Reiko lightly traced the familiar patterns of his back. The boy she had known was filling out, gaining the looser fleshiness of a grown man. Tonight however she felt a slight relaxing of the tension that had slowly mounted along his spine over the grinding months and years.

Tetsuo seldom spoke of his work, although she knew it was stressful and hard. His supervisors seemed still to hold him under suspicion over an incident a few years ago, when he had tried unsuccessfully to introduce un-Japanese business practices into the firm. This, she imagined, was one reason why he had grown so distant, allowing the flame of their passion to bank back in favor of more important matters. That was, of course, as it would have to be.

But now all seemed restored. Tetsuo had remembered; all was well in the world.

When, instead of simply rolling over and going to sleep, Tetsuo stroked her hair briefly and spoke to her softly in unintelligible mumblings of fondness, Reiko felt a glow like the sun rise within her.

2.

It was her first trip to the airport since the honeymoon, so long ago. Reiko could not help feeling disappointed, for the experience was not all the same this time.

How could it be? She chided herself for making comparisons. After all, different destinations attracted different classes of people. The occupants of this departure lounge could hardly be expected to be like those down the hall a ways, bound from Tokyo to Fiji, or Hawaii, or Saipan—young couples close-orbiting on trajectories of bliss.

Sometimes on such honeymoon flights groups of newlyweds would have singing contests to help pass the time, clapping with courteous enthusiasm however terrible the voice. After all, there were harmonies that went beyond music, and much holding of hands.

Travelers not bound for the resorts dressed differently, spoke and behaved differently. It was as if the departure terminal were a series of slices of modern life each distinct, representing a separate phase or molting.

Jets destined for Europe or America generally carried tour groups of prosperous older couples, or gaggles of students, all dressed alike and hanging together as if their periphery was patrolled by dangerous animals, ready at any moment to snap up the unwary straggler.

And, of course, there were the intense businessmen, who spent their transit time earnestly studying their presentation materials... modern samurai...warriors for Japan on the new battlefields of commerce.

Finally, there were the gates nearest Reiko, from which departed flights for Bangkok, Manilla, Seoul. These, too, carried businessmen, but bound instead for the rewards of success. Women told each other rumors about what went on during these...Kairaiku expeditions. Reiko had never really been sure what to believe, but she sensed the anticipation of the ticket holders in their particular lounge. Most of the passengers wore suits, but their mood did not strike her as businesslike. They carried briefcases, but nobody seemed much interested in working.

Reiko had few illusions about the "commerce" that went on during such trips. Still, the Koreans were industrializing rapidly. Certainly there were many bona fide dealings, as well as junkets. Tetsuo's company had to be sending him for real business reasons, or why would he have invited her along? Reiko wondered if all those stories had been exaggerated after all.

A contingent of foreigners awaited the opening of the gate with typical gaijin impatience, speaking loudly, staring impertinently. An orderly queue of Japanese formed behind the jostling Europeans and Americans.

Reiko's sister, Yumi, held Yukiko up to wave goodbye to her parents. The little girl seemed confused and unhappy, but determined to behave well. Already Yukiko exhibited a sense of public propriety, and she did not shame them by crying. As Tetsuo led her down the crowded ramp Reiko felt a pang of separation, but she knew Yukiko would be all right for a few days with her aunt. At worst their daughter would be spoiled by too much attention.

On board, Reiko saw there were a few other married couples besides themselves, all seated toward the rear of the airplane. The women seemed less at ease than their husbands, and listened attentively as the stewardesses went over emergency procedures. Finally, the great machine hurtled down the runway and propelled itself into the sky.

When the safety lights turned off, the cabin began to fill with a haze of cigarette smoke. Men got up and drifted forward toward the lounge. Soon there was heard, beyond the partition, the clinking of glasses and harsh jesting.

Reiko discreetly observed the other women, sitting quietly with empty seats between them. Some gazed out upon the green mountains of Honshu as the plane gradually gained altitude. Others conversed together in low tones. A few just looked down at their hands.

Reiko pondered. So many husbands could not be bringing their wives if their business in Seoul were only concupiscent pleasure. Could they?

She realized she was staring and quickly lowered her eyes. Still, Reiko had noticed something; all the other wives aboard were young, like herself. She turned, intending to whisper this interesting observation to her husband, and blinked quickly when she found herself facing an empty seat.

While she had been looking around, Tetsuo had quietly slipped away. Soon Reiko heard his familiar laughter coming from just beyond the partition.

She looked down then, and found fascinating the texture and fine lines that traced the backs of her own hands.

3.

That evening, in their hotel room, Tetsuo told her why he had brought her along with him to Seoul. "It is time for us to have a son," he said, matter of factly.

Reiko nodded dutifully. "A son is to be hoped for."

Tetsuo loved his daughter, of course, but he clearly wanted to have a boy in the family, and Reiko could hope for nothing better than to please him. And yet, had he not been the one insisting she buy birth control devices weekly from the neighborhood Skin Lady, and use them so carefully?

"We can afford to have only one more child," he went on, telling her what she already knew. "So we shall want to make certain the second is a boy."

Only half seriously, she suggested, "Shujin, I shall go to Mizuko Jizo Temple daily, and burn incense."

If she had hoped to draw a smile from him, Reiko was disappointed. Once upon a time, he had been witty in his mockery of the ancient superstitions, and they had shared this delicious cynicism between them—she the daughter of a scientist and he the bright young businessman who had been to university in America. Now, though, Tetsuo nodded and seemed to accept her promise at face value.

"Good. However we shall supplement prayer with technology." From his jacket pocket he withdrew a slim brochure which he handed to her. He left Reiko then to read the pamphlet in their small room while he went down to the bar to drink with friends.

Reiko stared down at the bold type, glittering in stark romanji script.

Pak Jung Clinic
Gender Selection Service
Seoul, Hong Kong, Singapore, Bangkok,
Taipei, Mexico City, Cairo, Bombay
Satisfaction is Guaranteed

A little while later she got undressed and went to bed. But lying there alone in the darkness, she found she could not sleep.

4.

They were actually quite kind at the clinic. Nicer, at least, than Reiko had anticipated. In her mind she had pictured a stark, sterile-white hospital setting. It was reassuring, then, to sit in the pastel waiting room, with cranes and other symbols of good fortune traced out delicately upon the wall reliefs. Tetsuo remained behind when her name was called, but he did smile and offer her a nod of encouragement as the nurse bowed and ushered her into the examination room.

The doctors were distant and professional, for which Reiko was grateful. They tapped and thumped and measured her temperature. When it came time to take various samples there was only a little pain, and her modesty was protected by a screen across the middle of her body.

Then she was returned to the waiting room. One of the doctors accompanying her bowed and told Tetsuo that she would be ready to conceive in three days time. Tetsuo replied with a polite hiss of satisfaction, and exchanged further bows with the doctor before they turned to leave together.

During the next few days Reiko saw little of Tetsuo. He really did, it seemed, have business to do in Seoul—meetings and sales analyses. The clinic provided a guide to show Reiko and a few other prospective mothers the sights, such as they were. The women saw the

Olympic Village, the war memorials, the great public museums. Only occasionally did some passerby glance sourly at them on hearing spoken Japanese. All in all, Reiko found the Koreans much nicer than she had been led to expect from the stories she had heard since childhood. But then, perhaps the Koreans she met felt the same way about her. It was all very interesting.

Still, this was no second honeymoon. Not the resumption of bliss she had hoped for. When Tetsuo returned late to their hotel room the following two nights, she could tell that he had spent part of his day in close proximity to other women.

Even the explanation offered by one of the other wives did not much ease Reiko's disappointment. "The clinic prefers to have some fresh semen to supplement the frozen samples they stored during our husbands' past visits," Mrs. Nakamura confided while they waited together on the third day. Reiko's head spun in confusion.

"You—you mean he has been...donating for some time?"

Mrs. Nakamura nodded, confirming that Tetsuo had had this in mind for months, at least. On his last two trips to Seoul, he must have visited the clinic to collect his seed for freezing. Or, more likely, he had used the *kairaku* house next door, which Reiko was now certain maintained a business relationship with the Pak Jong doctors.

"I am sure the place is licensed and regularly inspected," Mrs. Nakamura added. And Reiko knew which establishment she meant. Reiko nearly bristled at the presumption, that Tetsuo would ever *think* of patronizing an unlicensed house, and so risk his family's health with some filthy *gaijin* disease.

She restrained herself, knowing that part of her passion arose out of a sense of bitter disappointment. Somehow, Reiko managed to see a bright side to it all. The donated material probably had to be prepared quickly. That is why he continued to use the pleasure house, even when I was *here*.

She was well aware that she was rationalizing. But right at the moment rationalization was all that stood between Reiko and despair. When, a little while later, she had to endure intromission by cold glass and plastic, Reiko lay back and clasped her arms tightly across her breasts, dreaming of her first conception, which had come the natural way, with her hands and legs wrapped around a living, breathing, sighing man, her loving husband.

5.

Three weeks after they returned to Tokyo it became apparent they had succeeded—at least so far as impregnation was concerned. Queasiness and vomiting confirmed the joyous news as surely as the stained blotter of the little home-test kit. As for whether the child-to-be was male, several more weeks would pass before anyone could tell. But Tetsuo was full of confidence and that made Reiko happy.

Little Yukiko had reached the age where she attended preschool half of every day. Reiko would deliver her daughter to the playground entrance and watch all the children line up in their little uniforms, attentive to every phase of the carefully choreographed exercise activity. They seemed to be enjoying school, clapping together in time as the instructors led them through teaching rhymes. But who could actually tell what was best for a child?

Reiko often wondered if they were doing the right thing, starting Yukiko's education so early, a full two years before the law required.

"Doozo ohairi, kudasai!" the headmaster called to her little charges. The neat rows of four-year-olds filed indoors under an arched doorway decorated with origami flowers. It all felt so alien and remote from Reiko's own childhood.

Modern times are very hard, she knew. And Tetsuo was determined to provide their children with the very best advantages to face such a competitive world. Yukiko was one of only ten little girls in her *juku* preschool class, all the rest being boys. It was commonly said to be a waste to bother much on a female's education. But Tetsuo believed their daughter should also have a head start, at least compared with other girls.

Piping sounds of earnest recitation...Reiko remembered that examinations in only four more weeks would determine what kindergarten would accept little Yukiko for admission. And for boys the cycle of *juku*, of compressed learning and scrutiny, began even earlier, with some parents spending small fortunes on special "baby universities."

A month ago there had been a news story about a six-year-old who took his own life in shame when he did not do well in an exam...Reiko shuddered and turned away. She straightened her obi and looked downward as she hurried to the nearby station to catch the next train.

It seemed there was no escaping rush hour anymore. Staggered work schedules only spread the chaos over the entire day. Reiko endured being packed into the car by white-gloved station proctors. Automatically, she raised invisible curtains of privacy around her body and self, ignoring the close pressure of strangers—women with shopping bags at their feet, many of the men hiding their eyes within lurid, animated magazines—until the train at last reached her stop and spilled her out onto a platform near Kaygo University.

Smog and soot and noisy traffic had erased the semi-rural ambience she recalled from long ago. Reiko's earliest memories—from when she had been Yukiko's age—were of this ancient campus where she had grown up as a professor's daughter, playing quietly on the floor of a dusty study stacked high with aromatic books, the walls lined with fine works of makimono calligraphy. Unknown to her father, she used to concentrate and try to listen to his conversations with students and faculty and even gaijin visitors from foreign lands, certain in her childish belief that, over time, she would absorb it all and one day come into that world of his, to share his work, his pride, his accomplishments.

When did I change my dreams? Reiko wondered.

Usually, memories of such childish fantasies made her smile. But today, for some reason, the recollection only made her feel sad.

I changed very early, she knew. And how can I be regretful, when I have everything?

Still, it was ironic that her sister Yumi, so reticent as a child, had grown to become assertive and adept, while she, Reiko, could imagine no higher role, no greater honor, than to do her duty as a wife and mother.

It would have been nice to stop to visit her father. But today there would not be time. Anyway Yumi should be the first one told the news. Reiko hurried across the street to the great row of commercial establishments facing the university—the phalanx of industrial giants whose benign partnership had helped Kaygo to thrive. The guard at the side gate of Fugisuku Enterprises recognized her as a former employee and frequent visitor. He smiled and bowed, asking her merely to impress her chop upon a clipboard before she passed through.

Reiko took the quickest route toward the Company Garden of Contemplation, a path taking her along a great glass wall. Beyond that barrier she could view one of the laboratories where Fugisuku manufactured the bio-engineered products it was famous for worldwide.

Thousands of white cages lined the walls of the vast chamber, each containing three or four tiny, pale hamsters, all cloned to be exactly alike. Automatic machines picked up cages and delivered them at precise intervals to long benches, where masked technicians in white coats worked with needles and flashing scalpels, all to an unheard but insistent tempo.

Even through the glass, Reiko caught the familiar, musty rodent aroma. She had worked here for some years, up until the time of her first pregnancy. Gaijin "liberalism" had penetrated that far, at least. Women no longer had to retire upon getting married. Frankly, though, Reiko did not miss the job all that much.

The rear doors opened upon a walled setting of peace and serenity in the middle of sprawling Tokyo. Out in the garden, beside the carefully tended dwarf trees and neatly raked beds of sand, a ceremony was nearing completion under a delicately carved Tori spirit gate. Reiko folded her hands and waited politely as the priest chanted and many of the women of Fugisuku bowed to an altar swathed in incense. Unconsciously, she joined in the prayer.

Oh Kami of little mammals, forgive us. Do not take revenge upon our children for what we do to you.

The monthly ritual was intended to appease the spirits of the slaughtered hamsters, who gave their lives in such numbers for the good of the company and their common prosperity. Once upon a time the prayer gatherings had amused Reiko, but now she did not feel so sure. Did not all life strike a balance? The gaijin argued endlessly about the morality of mankind's exploitation of animals. "Save the whales!" they cried. "Save the krill!" But why would the westerners be so obsessed with preserving inferior animals unless they, too, feared the implacable retribution of karma?

If animals did indeed possess kami, Fugisuku would certainly be haunted without the right protections. Barely after their eyes opened, the young hamsters were injected with viruses to stimulate production of antibodies and interferons. They were sacrificed by their thousands in order to produce just a few milligrams of precious refined molecules.

With new life now taking form within her, Reiko was not of a mind to ignore any possible danger. She fervently added her own voice to the chant of propitiation.

Oh angry spirits, stay away from my child.

Later, Reiko sat with Yumi in the garden, sharing lunch from the lacquered box she had brought along. Yumi reacted to her news with enthusiasm, speaking excitedly of all the preparations that must be made in order to welcome a new child into a home. At the same time, though, Reiko thought she felt an undercurrent of misgiving from her sister.

Of course Yumi had suspected early on the true reason for the journey to Seoul. In many ways Reiko's younger sister was much more worldly. Still, Yumi would never rebuke her, or ever say anything to bring down her hopes. About Tetsuo she had only this to say:

"When our family first met him, Father and the rest of us thought you might face problems from Tetsuo's unconventionality, his western, liberal ideas. He has certainly been a surprise, then. Who ever would have expected, so few years later, that your husband would try so very hard to be perfectly Japanese?"

Reiko blinked. Is that what Tetsuo is trying to do? She wondered. But no encouragement would force Yumi to say anything more.

7.

The next trip to Seoul was even briefer than the first, and taken on even shorter notice. Reiko barely had time to pack a satchel for Yukiko and deliver her to Yumi before they had to rush to the airport to catch the flight Tetsuo had arranged.

Again, the Pak Clinic doctors took samples just beyond the curtain of modesty. Reiko was well enough educated to understand much of what she overheard them saying.

They spoke of tests...tests for potential genetic defects, for recessive color blindness, for the insidious trait of nearsightedness, for the correct sex chromosomes. When the implications of their discussions sank in, Reiko's knees shook.

They were holding court on whether the fetus—still so small that Reiko wasn't even showing yet—was to live or die.

She'd heard that in parts of rural China they were drowning girl babies. Here though, they were tested, discovered, and taken from the *womb*, before their first cry. Before their spirits could even form.

Reiko was terrified they were about to tell her the fetus carried some unpalatable defect, such as femininity. So when they returned and bowed, smiling, with the good news, Reiko nearly fainted with relief. The very real attentiveness Tetsuo showed her afterwards caused her to feel as if she had achieved some fine accomplishment, and had made him very proud of her.

They held hands during the flight home. And for the following four wonderful months Reiko thought her trials were at an end.

Now Tetsuo came home early often, spurning all but the most important business-and-dinner parties with colleagues. He played with Yukiko and laughed with his family. He and Reiko spoke together of plans for their son, how he would get the finest of everything, the best attention, the best schooling, everything required to arm him for success in a competitive, judgmental world.

His son's fate, Tetsuo swore, would not be to face an endless subservience to subtle hierarchies and status. He would not be one of those who were bullied in school, in cruel rituals of kumi group solidarity, by children and teachers alike. His son would *head* hierarchies. When his son toasted kampai, it would be *his* glass that would be highest.

Touching her swelling belly, Tetsuo's eyes seemed to shine, making Reiko feel it all had been worthwhile, after all.

Then, in her fourth month, Tetsuo came home with yet another slim white folder containing two pink and green airline boarding passes.

8.

She gasped in surprise when she saw the image on the screen. The Pak clinic doctors focused beams of ultrasound into her womb and computers sorted the muddled reflections into a stunning image of the life growing within her.

"It looks like a monkey!" she cried in dismay. Her thoughts whirled, for surely this was something the doctors would never allow!

One of the men laughed harshly. The other doctor was kinder. He explained. "At this early stage of development, the fetus has many of the attributes of our distant ancestors, who lived in the sea long ago. Only recently, for instance, it had gills and a tail. But these were reabsorbed. And in time he will look like later forefathers, until he at last appears quite human."

Reiko sighed in relief. Someone mentioned the gaijin-sounding term, "recapitulation", and suddenly she did remember having heard or read about it. She blushed, shamefaced, certain her outburst had made them think her a hysterical woman.

"The important thing we have determined," the doctor went on, "is that the acoustic nerves are already in place, and soon the eyes will be functional."

"So all is well now?" she asked. "My baby is healthy?"

"A fine, strong little boy, your Minoru will be."

"Then I can go home now?"

The second doctor shook his head. "First we will be fulfilling the next phase of our contract. We must install a very special device. Do not be alarmed. We are very skilled at this. It will not cause much discomfort. You will only have to stay for two nights."

Dazed, Reiko did not even think of complaining as they gave her an injection. With sudden drowsiness swarming over her she watched the world swim as they wheeled her into an operating room. There was hushed, professional talk. Nobody spoke to her.

"S'karaimas. Gomen nasai," she said as the anesthetist's mask came down and a sweet, cloying odor filled her mouth and throat. "Forgive me, I am very tired."

Reiko's shattered thoughts orbited a burning core of shame. She seemed to have forgotten the reason she was apologizing, but whatever she had done, Reiko knew it had to have been terrible.

9.

Dreams began disturbing her sleep soon after her third homecoming. They started out as muddy, uncertain feelings of depression and fear, which did not rouse her but left her tired in the morning when it came time to prepare Tetsuo for work and Yukiko for preschool. Often she would collapse back upon the tatami after they were gone. She had no energy. This pregnancy seemed to be taking much more out of her than the first one.

Then there was the music. There was no escaping the music.

At first it had been rather pleasant. The tiny machine that had been implanted into her womb could barely be traced with her fingertips. Nothing extruded. It drew power from small batteries that would easily last another five months.

And at this stage in the fetus's development, all the device ever did was play music. Endlessly, over and over again, music.

"Minoru wa, gakusei desu," Tetsuo said. "Little Minoru is now a student. Of course his brain is not yet advanced enough to accept more complex lessons, but he can learn music even this early. He will emerge with perfect pitch, knowing his scales already, as if by instinct."

Tetsuo smiled. "Minoru kun wa on'gaku ga suki deshoo."

So the harmonies repeated, over and over again, throbbing like sonar within the confined sea of her insides, diffracting around and through her organs, resonating at last with the beating of her heart.

Yumi no longer visited when she thought Tetsuo might be at home. Their father had voiced his disgusted disapproval of Tetsuo and this invasion against the ways of nature. Reiko had been forced to answer loyally in Tetsuo's defense.

"You are too westernized," she told them, borrowing her husband's own words. "You too-blindly accept the gaijin and their alien concepts about nature and guilt. There is no shame in this thing we are doing."

"A dubious distinction," her father had replied, irritably. Yumi then interjected, "*Guilt* consists in doing the right thing, even when nobody is watching, Reiko. *Shame* is making sure you don't get caught doing what others disapprove."

"Well?" Reiko had answered. "You two are the only ones expressing disapproval. All of Tetsuo's associates and friends admire him for this! My neighbors come by to listen to the music!"

Her sister and father had looked at each other at that moment, as if she had just proven their point. But Reiko did not understand. All she knew for certain was that she must side with her husband. No other choice was even conceivable. Yumi might be able to have a more "modern" marriage, but to Reiko, such ways seemed to promise only chaos.

"We plan to give our son the best advantages," she concluded in the end. And to that, of course, there was very little the others could reply.

"We shall see," her father had concluded. Then he changed the subject to the color of the autumn leaves.

10.

At the end of Reiko's sixth month the thing in her womb spoke its first words.

She sat up quickly in the dark, clutching the covers. In a brief moment of terror Reiko thought that it had been a ghost, or the baby himself, mumbling dire premonitions from deep inside her. The words were indistinct, but she could feel them vibrating under her trembling fingertips.

It took a few moments to realize that it was the machine once again, now moving into a new phase of fetal education. Reiko sank back against the pillows with a sigh. Next to her Tetsuo snored quietly, contentedly, unaware of this milestone.

Reiko lay listening. She couldn't make out what the machine was enunciating slowly, repetitiously. But the baby *responded* with faint movements. She wondered if he were reaching out toward the tiny speaker. Or perhaps, instead, he was trying to get away. If so, then he was trapped, trapped in the closest, most secure prison of all.

The doctors were certain it was safe, Reiko reminded herself. Surely those wise men would not do anything to hurt her child. Anyway, though it was a pioneering method, she and Tetsuo were not the very first. There had been a few before them, to prove it was all right.

Consoled, but convinced that sleep would not return, she rose to begin yet another day before the sun turned the eastern sky a dull and smoggy gray. Reiko bent her attention to daily life, to chores and preparation, to doing what she could to make life pleasant for her family.

One evening soon thereafter they sat together, watching a television program about genetic engineering. The reporters spoke glowingly of how, in future years, scientists would be able to cut and splice and redesign the very code of life itself. Human beings would specify everything about their plants, their animals, even their offspring, making them stronger, brighter, better than ever.

She heard Tetsuo sigh in envy, so Reiko said nothing. She only laid her head on his shoulder and concealed her own relieved thoughts.

By that time, I will have finished my own childbearing years. Those wonders will be for other women to deal with.

Reiko knew what was coming next. She tried and tried to prepare herself, but still it came as a shock when, a week or so later, her belly began to glow. At night, with the houselights extinguished, faint shimmerings of color could be seen emerging through her flesh from one corner of her burgeoning belly. It flickered like a tiny flame, but there was no added warmth. Rather, it was a cold light.

Soon the neighbor women were back, curious and insistent on seeing for themselves. They murmured admiringly at the luminance given her skin by the tiny crystal display, and treated Reiko with such respect that she dared not chase them away, as she might have preferred.

A few of Tetsuo's envious comrades even persuaded him to bring them home to see, as well. One day Reiko had to rush about preparing a very special meal for Tetsuo's supervisor's supervisor. The great man complimented her cooking and spoke highly of Tetsuo's drive and forward thinking.

Reiko did not much mind showing a small patch of skin in a dim room, nor the cold touch of the stethoscope as others listened in on Minoru's lessons. Modesty was nothing against the pride she felt in helping Tetsuo.

Still, she did wonder about the baby. What was the machine showing him, deep inside her? Was he already learning about faraway lands Reiko herself had never seen? Was it describing the biological facts of life to him? Where he was and what was happening to him?

Or was it imprinting upon him the cool, graceful forms of mathematics, fashioning genius while the brain was still as malleable as new bread dough?

Her father explained some of it to her during Reiko's next to final visit to her parents' home. While Yumi and their mother cleared the dinner bowls, Professor Sato looked over some of the titles of the programs listed on the Pak Clinic brochure.

"Abstract Geometry and Topology, Musical Tone Recognition, Basic Linguistic Grammar...Hon ga nan'satsu arimas'ka? Hmmm." Her father put aside the brochure and tried to explain to her.

"Of course the fetus cannot learn things that an infant could not. It cannot really understand speech, for instance. It doesn't know yet about people or the world. The technicians apparently know better than to try to cram facts into the poor little thing.

"No, what they appear after is the laying down of tracks, pathways, *essences*...to set up the foundations for talents the child will later fill with knowledge during his schooling." Reluctantly, her father admitted that the doctors seemed to have thought these things out. "They are very clever," he said.

With a sigh he added: "That does not necessarily mean, of course, that they really know what they are doing. They may be too clever by half."

A warning glare from Yumi shut him up, then. But not before Reiko shivered at the tone in his voice.

Soon she started avoiding her father, and even Yumi. The days dragged on as the weight she carried grew ever heavier. The fetus stirred much less, now. She had a feeling he was paying very close attention to his lessons.

11.

Pak Clinic technicians visited their house. They examined her with instruments, some familiar and others very strange. At one point they pressed a unit to her skin very near the embedded machine and read its memory. They consulted excitedly, then packed up their tools. Only as an afterthought, one of them told Reiko her son was developing nicely. In fact, he was quite a fine specimen.

Tetsuo came home and told her that there was something new and exciting the Pak people wanted to try.

"A few fetuses, such as our son, have responded very well indeed to the lessons. Now there is something which may make all he has accomplished so far seem as nothing!"

Reiko touched his arm. "Tetsu, it is so very near the time he will be born. Only another month or so. Why push little Minoru every minute?" She smiled tentatively, making an unusual effort to contact his eyes. "After all," she pleaded, "students on the outside get occasional vacations. Can he not, as well?"

Tetsuo did not seem to hear her. His excitement was fiercely intense. "They have discovered something truly fantastic recently, Mother. Some babies actually seem to be *telepathic*. During the final weeks before birth!"

"Te...te-re-paturu?" Reiko mouthed the gairaigo word.

"But it is extremely close range in effect. Even mothers usually detect it only as a vague strengthening of their mother-child bonds. And anyway, the trauma of being born always ends it. Even the most gentle of Caesarian deliveries..."

He was rambling. Reiko lowered her eyes in defeat, knowing how impossible it would be to penetrate past the heat of his enthusiasm. Tetsuo has not changed, she realized at last. He was still the impetuous boy she had married. Still as reckless as a zoku. Only now he knew better than to express it in unpopular western eccentricities. He would choose acceptable eastern ones, instead.

When the technicians came the next day she let them work without asking any questions. They gave her a girdle of finely woven mesh to wear over her womb. After they left, she simply lay there and turned her head to the wall.

Yumi telephoned, but Reiko would not see her. Her parents she put off, claiming fatigue. Little Yukiko, sensitive as always, was told that ladies get moody late in pregnancy. She did her homework quietly and played with her computer tutor alone in her tiny room.

Tetsuo was promoted. The celebration with his comrades lasted late. When he returned home, smelling of fish, sake, and bar girls, Reiko pretended to be asleep. Actually, though, she was listening. The machine scarcely lit up anymore. It hardly made a sound. Still, she felt she could almost follow its conversations with her son.

Shapes filled her half-dreams...impossible shapes, bottles with two openings, and none. Again and again there came one particular word, "topology."

Over the following days she tried to regain some enthusiasm. There were times when she felt as she had when she had carried Yukiko...a communion with her child that ran deeper, stronger than anything the machines could tap. During such moments Reiko almost felt happy.

Year End came, and most of the husbands were out all week, weaving and bobbing in bonenkai celebrations, when so many tried to obliterate the old year in a wash of alcohol. The sake-dispensing vending machines at the train station emptied faster than the drinks companies could restock them. Wise women and children kept off the streets.

One night Tetsuo returned home drunk and ranted long about her father, knowing full well that by tradition he would not be held accountable for anything he said in this state. Nevertheless, Reiko moved her tatami into Yukiko's room. She lay there quietly, thinking about something her father had said to her once.

"Both Tetsuo and I believe in a melding of East and West," he had told Reiko. "Many people on both sides of the Pacific want to see this co-joining of strengths. But there is disagreement over how strength should be defined, Reiko.

"Tetsuo's kind sees only the power of Western scientific reductionism. They wish to combine it with our discipline, our traditional methods of competitive conformity. With this I fundamentally disagree.

"What the West really has to offer...the only thing it has to offer, my child...is honesty. Somehow, in the midst of their horrid history, the best among the gaijin learned a wonderful lesson. They learned to distrust themselves, to doubt what they were taught, and even what their egos make them yearn to see. To know that even truth must be scrutinized. It was a great discovery, almost as great as the treasure we of the East have to offer them in return, the gift of harmony."

Reiko had not understood, either then or now. But Yumi had seemed to comprehend. "It's not a question then, of whether East or West shall win, is it Father?"

"No," he had said, "There will definitely be a synthesis. The only question remaining is what type of synthesis it shall be. Will it be one of power? Or one of wisdom?"

The next day, Tetsuo apologized without words. Reiko forgave him and moved back into their bedroom.

Technicians visited them twice a week, now. Reiko wondered how they would ever pay for such attention, until Tetsuo told her that the Clinic was refunding all costs. They were special. They would make this process famous throughout the world.

At times Reiko worried that the baby would not even be recognizable when he emerged. Would he wear an expression of sage wisdom from the very start, and stare into space thinking great thoughts? Would he spill from the womb already fully forged into that intimidating, imperious creature, an adult male? Would he even need her love?

Hope also came and went in tempo with those waves of feeling deep within her. Every peak and trough of emotion left her confused and drained. She was glad that it would all be over soon.

Reiko met the other wives in the special group. Some of them were knowledgeable, more confident than her. Mrs. Sukimura, in particular, seemed so relaxed and assured. She was the farthest along. Already the Pak techs were ecstatic with the results from her child. They spoke of data transfer rates, of frequency and phase filtering, of Fournier transforms and pattern recognition.

At one point all of the women were picked up by limousines and taken downtown to MITI, the all-powerful Ministry of Trade and Industry, on Sakurada-Dor Avenue. In a great hall, technicians attached mesh girdles and gently, tenderly wheeled them close to mammoth, chilled machines.

Computers, Reiko thought. They were using powerful computers to *talk* to the fetuses!

When the Minister himself appeared, Reiko blinked in astonishment. His eminence shook Tetsuo's hand. Reiko felt faint.

12.

They were pledged to secrecy, of course. If the gaijin newspapers got hold of this too soon, there would be hell to pay. Worldwide media attention before the right preparations had been made would shame the nation, even though it was really none of the business of outsiders.

Others were already jealous of Japan in so many ways. And westerners tended to insist that theirs was the only morality. So Tetsuo and Reiko signed their chops to a document. There was talk of a leave of absence from Tetsuo's company, and an important post when he returned. He spoke to her of buying a larger house in a better neighborhood.

"One of our problems has been in the field of *software*," he explained one evening, though Reiko knew he was talking mostly to himself. "Our engineers have been very clever in practical technology, leaving most of the world far behind in many areas. But computer programming has turned out to be very hard. There seems to be no conventional way of catching up with the Americans there. Your father used to claim that it had to do with our system of education."

Tetsuo laughed derisively. "Japanese education is the finest in all the world. The toughest. The most demanding!"

"What...?" she asked. "What does this have to do with the babies?"

"They are geniuses at programming!" Tetsuo cried. "Already they have cracked problems that had stymied hundreds of our best software designers. Of course they do not understand what they are doing, but that does not seem to matter. It is all a matter of asking questions in just the right ways, and letting them innovate.

"For instance, the unborn have yet no concept of distance or motion. But that turns out to be an advantage, you see, for they have no preconceptions. They bring fresh insight, without being burdened by our worldly assumptions.

"So one of our young engineers solved a vexing problem for the Ministry of Trade, while another has developed an entirely new model of traffic control that should reduce downtown congestion by five percent!"

Tetsuo's eyes held a glow, a wild flicker that gave Reiko a chill. "Zuibun joozo desu, ne?" he said, in admiration of that accomplishment by an unborn child. "As for our son," Tetsuo went on. "He is being asked even more challenging questions about transportation systems. And I am certain he will make us proud."

So, Reiko thought. It was even worse than she had imagined. This was more than juku, more than just another form of cram-education. Her child was being put to work before he was born. And there was nothing at all she could do about it.

Guiltily, Reiko wasn't even sure she should try.

13.

A Klein Bottle...she knew the name in a dream.

It was what one called that bizarre thing—a container with two openings and none at all...whose inside was its outside.

14.

When Mrs. Sukimura's time came they only knew of it by the fact that the woman did not join the others at the computer center. Ah, well, Reiko thought. At least the respite was coming soon.

Traditionally, childbirth in Japan was done by appointment, during business hours. A woman scheduled a day with her obstetrician, when she would check into the hospital and receive the drugs to induce labor. It was all very civilized and much more predictable than the way it apparently was done in the west.

But for the women of the test group, matters were different. So important was the work the fetuses were doing that it was decided to wait as long as possible, to let the babies come as late as they wanted.

The reason given was "Birth Trauma". Apparently, emerging into the outer world robbed even the most talented fetuses of their small but potent psychic powers. After that, they would lapse to being babies again. Talented, well-tutored babies, but babies nonetheless.

The MITI technicians regretted this, but it would certainly be no "trauma" to her. To Reiko, this coming return to ignorance would be a gift from the blessed Buddha himself.

Oh, it would be strange to have a genius son. But they had promised her that he would still be a little boy. She would tickle him and make him laugh. She would hold him when he tripped and cried. She would bathe in his sweet smile and he would love her. She would see to that.

Genius did not have to mean soullessness. She knew that from having met a few of her father's students over the years. There had been one boy—her father had wanted Reiko to go out with him instead of Tetsuo, years ago. Everyone said he was brilliant, and he had a nice smile and personality.

If only he had not also had the habit of eating red meat too often. It made him smell bad, like an American.

And anyway, by then she had already fallen in love with Tetsuo.

One by one the other women dropped out of their group, to be replaced by newcomers who looked to Reiko now for advice and reassurance. Her own time would be very soon, of course. In fact, she was already more than a week overdue when she went to the hospital for another examination, and one of the doctors left his clipboard on the counter when he went to answer a telephone call.

Reiko suddenly felt daring. She reached out and turned the clipboard, hoping to see her own chart. But it was only a list of patients on the doctor's other ward.

Then she frowned. Mrs. Sukimura's name was on the list! Three weeks after her delivery, which they'd been told had been uneventful.

Reiko recognized other names. In fact, nearly all of the women who had gone into labor before her were under care on the next floor.

The baby churned in response to her racing heart. Footsteps told of the doctor's return, so Reiko put back the clipboard and sat down again with an effort to remain outwardly calm.

"If you don't begin labor by the end of the month, we will induce it," he told her upon completing his tests. "The delay was approved by your husband, of course. There is nothing to worry about."

Reiko barely heard his words. What concerned her was the plan beginning to form in her mind. For her, it would call for daring to the point of recklessness.

Fortunately, she had worn western dress for her visit to the hospital. A kimono would have been too conspicuous. At first she had considered trying to borrow a doctor's white coat to wear over her street clothes. After all, there were some female physicians here. She had seen a few.

But her protruding belly and slow waddle would have made the imposture absurd, even if she did encounter a white coat just lying around to be taken.

She did still have the gray gown they had given her to wear during the examination. This she kept balled inside her purse. In the ladies room she put the loose garment on over her street clothes. People tended to look right past patients on a ward. The uniform was a partial cloak of invisibility.

First she tried the lifts. But the elevator operator looked at her when she asked to be taken to floor eight. "May I please see your pass?" the young woman asked Reiko politely.

"I misspoke, forgive me," Reiko said, bowing to hide her fluster. "I meant floor nine."

On exiting the lift she rested against the wall for a while to catch her breath. The extra weight she carried every moment of every hour was a burden on her overstrained back, sheer torture if she did not maintain just the right erect posture. Soon it would be time to spill her child into the world. And yet, she was beginning to dread the idea with a sick, mortal fear.

A nurse asked if she needed help.

"Iie, Kekko desu," Reiko answered quickly. "Gomen nasai. Ikimashoo."

Giving her a doubtful glance, the nurse turned away. Reiko waddled slowly toward the clearly marked fire exit, looked around to make sure she wasn't being observed, and pushed her way into the stairwell.

Her shoes made soft scraping sounds on the rough, high-traction surface of the steps. Under her left hand, her womb was a center of furious activity as the baby kicked and turned. By the time she reached the eighth floor landing, the guard stationed there had already risen from his little stool.

"May I help you?" he asked perplexedly.

Certainly, honorable sir, Reiko thought sarcastically. Please be so kind as to open the door for me, and then forget that I ever came this way.

The guard frowned. Twice he began to speak then stopped. His confused expression was soon matched by Reiko's own amazement as he blinked several times, then reached back to turn the knob and pull the portal aside for her.

"Doozo...ohairi kudasai..."

"Ee, itachakimasu," Reiko answered breathlessly. She rocked through the opening in a daze until the door was closed behind her again. Then she sagged back and sighed.

For a few moments, there in the stairwell, she had felt something *fey* radiating from her womb. Her child had reached out in her time of need, and *helped* Reiko...probably without having any idea exactly what he was doing. He had helped her because of her deeply felt need.

Love. She had always believed it had power transcending all the cold metal tools men were so proud of. All the more so the love between a mother and her child.

I must find out what is going on here, she knew. I must.

Fortunately, security in the hospital seemed to have only one layer, as if the owners of this place expected a mere ribbon of courtesy to suffice. And under normal circumstances it would have been more than enough.

Reiko did not have to show great agility, or dodge quickly from room to room. The halls were nearly empty, and the few people on duty at the nurse's station were turned away in a technical discussion as she hurried out of sight.

She came to a large window, facing the hallway. Within were the familiar shapes of a neonatal unit—rows of tiny white cots, monitoring instruments, a bored male nurse reading a newspaper.

Babies.

They look healthy enough, she thought, nurturing a slender shoot of a smile. There appeared to be no monsters here, just pink newborn little boys, each of them looking very much like a tiny, chubby Buddha...or that English Prime Minister, Churchill.

Reiko's nascent smile faded, however, when she realized that the children were moving hardly at all. And then she saw that every one of them was connected by taped electrodes to a cluster of cables. The cables led to a bank of tall machines by the far wall.

Computers. And the babies, staring with open eyes, hardly moved at all.

"Wakarimasen," Reiko moaned, shaking her head. "I don't understand."

15.

The plate by the door read "Sukimura". Reiko listened, and hearing no voices, slipped inside.

"Reiko-san!"

The woman in the chair looked healthy, fully recovered. She stood up and hurried over to take Reiko's hand. "Reiko-san, what are you doing here? They told us—"

"Us? They have all of the others? Will they keep me here, too, when my time comes?"

Mrs. Sukimura nodded and looked away. "They are kind. We... we are allowed to nurse our babies while they work."

"*Work,*" Reiko measured the word. "But the birth trauma...it should return the children to innocence! They promised..."

"They found a technique to *prevent* it, Reiko-san. Our babies were all born wise. They are *engineers*, doing great work for the good of the realm. It is even said that the palace may take notice, it is so important!"

Reiko was aghast. "Do they plan to leave them hooked up to wires forever?"

"Oh no, no. The doctors say this will not harm our sons. They say they will still be all right." And yet, a hollow tone in her voice betrayed Mrs. Sukimura's true feelings.

"But then, Izumi-san," Reiko said, "what is wrong?"

"They are mistaken!" The older woman cried. "The men say we are silly, superstitious women. They say that the babies are all well, healthy...that they will lead normal lives. But, oh Reiko-san, they have no *kami*! They have no souls!"

Reiko blinked, and the spirit within her writhed in tempo to her sudden breath. *No, it cannot be true,* she thought. *I feel my baby's kami. For all he has been through, he is still human!*

Footsteps echoed in the hallway. Voices approached the door.

"At birth," Mrs. Sukimura said in a husky voice filled with horrible resignation. "At birth they...their souls were sucked away into...into *software.*"

The door opened. Reiko heard rough masculine tones. Felt hands upon her shoulders. She cried out. "Iye. Iye!" But she could not shrug them off. The hands pulled her from the room.

"Reiko-san!" she heard her friend call just before the door shut with a final click. A gurney waited. Strong hands. A needle.

Reiko wailed, but no physical resistance could overcome the insistence of those hands.

16.

The flutterings caused by inducement drugs soon became tremors, which turned into fierce contractions. Reiko cried out for Tetsuo, knowing full well that tradition would have kept him away, even if frowning officials from the Ministry did not. Spasms came with increasing rapidity now, sending the small life within her kicking and swimming in agitation.

New drugs were injected. Machines focused upon her womb, and she knew that these were the clever devices designed to prevent the cleansing fall of innocence which the doctors hatefully called "birth trauma." They were adamant about preventing it, now. They were insisting that her baby enter the world wise.

Oh, how they would discover, to their regret, what they had really done, what they had unleashed. But even were she able to speak, she knew they would not listen. They would have to find out for themselves.

In her delirium Reiko's head turned left and right, trying to track voices nobody else in the operating room seemed to hear. They came at her from all sides, whispering through the hissing aspirators, humming from the lamps, murmuring from the electric sockets.

Spirits leered and taunted her from the machines, some mere patternings of light and static, others more complex—coursing in involute electronic dissonance within the microprocessors. Ghosts floated around her—whispering kami, dressed up in raiments of software.

How foolish of men to think they can banish the world of spirits. Reiko knew with sudden certainty that the very idea was arrogant. Of course the kami would simply adapt to whatever forms the times demanded. The spirits would find a way.

They were loose in the grid, now, biding their time. And they would have revenge.

Ghosts of baby hamsters...of baby human beings...She sensed her own son, thinking now, desperately, harder than any fetus had ever been forced to think before.

Soporific numbness spread over her as the tentacle-like hands turned to other violations. The shuddering contractions made vision blur. Superimposed upon her diffracting tears were dazzling Moire' patterns and Moebius chains. How she knew the names of these things, without ever having learned them, Reiko did not bother to wonder. From her mouth came words..."Transportation...locational translation of coordinates..." she whispered, licking her dry lips. "...non-linear transformation..."

And then there was the bottle that had not one opening, but two...or none at all...the container whose inside was *outside*.

Now Reiko found herself wondering what the word "outside" really meant.

The hands did not seem to notice or care about the ghostly forms glaring down at her from the harsh flourescents. Those angry spirits mocked her agony, as they mocked the other one, the one struggling with the problem in geometry.

Another spasm of savage pressure struck Reiko, almost doubling her over. And she felt overwhelmed by a sudden swimming sensation within her...an intensifying sense of dread...desperate concentration on a single task, to turn theoretical knowledge into practical skill.

The kami in the walls and in the machines chittered derisively. The problem was too difficult! It would never be solved in time!

A container whose inside is outside...

"Desu ka ne?" One of the technicians said, shaking and tapping his monitoring headphones. He shouted again, this time in alarm.

Suddenly white coats flapped on all sides. There was no time for full anesthesia, so they sprayed on locals that numbed with bone-chilling rapidity. Nobody even bothered to set up a modesty screen as the obstetric surgeons began an emergency Caesarian section.

Reiko felt it happen then, suddenly, as a burst of pure light seemed to explode within her! For that moment she shared an overwhelming sense of wonder and elation—the joy and beauty of pure mathematics. It was the only language possible in that narrow instant of triumph. And yet it also carried love.

The surgeon cut. There came a loud pop, as if a balloon had suddenly burst. Her distended belly collapsed abruptly, like a tent all at once deprived of its supports.

The technicians stared, blinking. Trembling, the stunned surgeon reached in. Reiko felt him grope under the flaccid layers of her empty womb, seeking in bewilderment what was no longer there.

Applied Topology. She remembered the name of a text, one of the courses they had given her son, and Reiko knew it stood for shapes and their relationships. It had to do with *space* and *time*, and it could be applied to problems in transportation.

The hands did more things to her, but they could not harm her any more. Reiko ignored them.

"He has escaped you," she told them softly, and the angry, envious, mad *kami* as well. "He learned his lessons well, and has made his mother proud."

Frustrated voices filled the room, rebounding off the walls. But Reiko had already followed her heart, beyond the constraints of any chamber or any nation, far beyond the knowledge of living men, where there were no obstacles to love.

David Brin is the Hugo- and Nebula-Award-winning author of such bestsellers as The Uplift War *and* Startide Rising. *He's also a winner of the John W. Campbell award. He is a native of California and was educated as an astronomer at Caltech. David Brin is in no small part responsible for whatever success this volume may enjoy. He encouraged, suggested, and criticized early outlines.*

Truth in advertising requires me to inform you that the fine story you've just read is in print elsewhere. Pulphouse Publishing has it as one of their excellent Short Story Paperbacks. *Their flagship magazine is* Pulphouse, A Fiction Magazine. *Write for their current catalog (Pulphouse Publishing, Box 1227, Eugene, OR 97440).*

TLC

Virginia Orphant

North light, harsh light, revealing light. "I counted wrong." Myra Wilson's eyes are pinpoints, the whites luminous.

"The law's been changed," I reply.

"*Not* for me."

I continue writing out the rent receipt and it takes longer than needed for I'm deep in thought.

"It isn't like that, anyway," she dissembles. "It's just that I've started this expensive course, and Curt getting transferred...

I hand her the receipt, rake my eyes over her expensive and carefully fitted black suit and say, "The best laid plans of mice and men..."

I gaze at the window high on the north wall over my desk. For forty years it throws its cold light on one storyteller and another. I chide myself for wasting time thinking about something I can't help. I don't impose my views on others, but I wonder about Myra's sister, Margaret. Margaret is an old friend and I know how she thinks. "An unwanted child is a dead child," she says to me more than once.

Angry voices tell me the sisters are having a stormy visit. Thank goodness it's two o'clock and most of the other tenants are out. Margaret knocks on my door and without a word I sit her down to a cup of tea. She's so flushed it scares me. "You don't do anyone any good by getting so upset."

"You don't know her the way I do!"

"I don't feel I know her at all and she seems to like it that way."

Margaret sits stirring her tea, her brow furrowed and her small mouth pursed and I hope that by being quiet I can help her calm down. The two sisters both have black hair with a widow's peak and they dress their slender but well proportioned figures in expensive tailored suits. Myra, the younger one, is quite slender, her hair almost a blue-black; whereas Margaret's is somewhat gray around the temple.

At last I say, "We don't have the right to tell others what to do."
"That's easy for you to say, you don't have to take care of it."
"And you will?"
"You can say that again."
"Not unless you want to."
"As I say, you don't know better. Once she badgered our parents into getting her a puppy. For a week she spent all her time with the puppy and then she just forgot about it and who fed it and kept it from getting run over?"
"You?"
"Yes, and she has a fit when the dog takes to me and doesn't want anything to do with her."
"But couldn't you have made her take care of it? Didn't your parents put pressure on her?"
"We tried, but she's awfully good at making excuses and we couldn't let it suffer."
"But she's much older now."
"And she hasn't changed a bit. 'Poor Mother! She's so unhappy in that nursing home. We ought to set her up in her own place.' We did and do you know, Myra started making one excuse after another. Cleaning the house, getting someone to come in to sit and changing dirty linens, guess who had to do *all* of that?"
"You could have put her back in."
"I threatened to, but Sis promises to help more and she does for a while, but one day she falls asleep and can't hear Mom call for help to get to the bathroom and she tries to go alone and falls and breaks her arm and dies in the hospital."
"That could happen to anyone."
"I don't know. Sis said she's just too tired that day because a toothache keeps her awake all night. Why didn't she tell me? She knows the woman we have come on Tuesdays and Fridays is available for extra work. We could make arrangements."
"Maybe she wants to keep her promise."
"That's what she says."
There are other stormy visits but after a while I don't hear any more angry words and don't see much of either of them.
Are they avoiding me? It won't be the first time people feel they tell me too much and are embarrassed.
But no, Myra comes over one day and tells me her sister's in the hospital. "She ran that car off the road on purpose so she wouldn't have to help with the baby," wails Myra.

"You don't know if she's going to live or not and you think that!"

Eyes widen with guilt, she flees.

I grab a stack of old magazines. Now the apartment can be shown. I put the magazines on the dining room table and sit in the old rocker by the window and run my hands over the wooden arms worn smooth by many hands. It's a link with my past for I took it from my own furniture in my own apartment to be used by my tenant. My fingers cause me to relive the sorrows, triumphs, fears, hopes and joys of my past. My child-self recalls the warmth of the glowing wood fire warming my fingers as I grip the arms.

Memories of a snuggling warm bundle and smell of baby powder flood me with contentment. Concern comes later.

"He isn't gaining weight."

"I'm taking him to the doctor tomorrow."

"Don't you have to go to class?"

"I've finished. You don't have to sit any more."

"You'll be going to Chicago soon?"

"No, Curt has to come back here for a while."

"Let me know what the doctor says."

She doesn't call for two days and I resist the nosy bit. Anyway, I visit Margaret almost every day and she's the one I worry about. She doesn't seem to be trying. When I ask her what's wrong, all she says is, "I'm so tired, just so tired."

"He has a respiratory problem," Myra says when she finally calls.

"Will he have to be hospitalized?"

"No, but I'll have to take him to the hospital every other day."

"Can I help?"

"Thanks, I'll let you know. Excuse me, someone's at the door."

I finally get her after calling five or six times.

"I didn't know you'd gotten back," I say to Curt, who looks as though all the starch is washed out of him.

"I'm back for a while," he replies as he looks at me out of faded blue eyes sunk deep in their sockets.

"How's the baby?"

"All right, I suppose."

"Is he gaining weight?"

"No, he doesn't seem to be doing much of anything. I don't know what to think."

"What does the doctor say?"

"Myra doesn't want me to talk to the doctor. She doesn't even want me to hold the child."

"Well, you might be carrying some kind of infection that'd be dangerous to him."

"Could be, I don't know what to think."

A month goes by and Curt is over with the rent and a month's notice in writing.

"How's the baby?"

"He's in the hospital."

"Oh, when's that?"

"A couple of weeks ago."

"What if he isn't well enough to travel by the time you're to leave?"

"They'll stay with Margaret until he is."

"Is Margaret out of the hospital?"

"Yes, she went home yesterday. She's awful weak and doesn't feel like seeing anyone."

"Even me?"

"I hope you won't feel hurt, but she asked us to tell you she'd call when she feels well enough."

I *am* hurt. Margaret shouldn't be embarrassed that she tells me exactly how she feels. She knows I forget half of what she tells me and think she doesn't mean the other half. I can't believe she's too tired to see me.

A week goes by and I keep busy and try not to think of the Wilsons. It isn't any of my business, I tell myself.

I can't stand it any longer. I call and Curt answers the phone. He's polite but cool.

"Can I visit?"

"He's in intensive care. Even I can't see him."

"That doesn't seem right."

"I know but Myra's so hysterical, I'm afraid to say or do anything."

"It's your child too."

"I know but it's just like walking on eggs. I don't know who is worse off, Myra or the baby."

I don't want to burst out crying so I hang up.

Myra finally calls and I'm surprised at how calmly she tells me the child is dead. To me she seems relieved but what do I know?

I rock in the rocking chair, remember the warm little bundle. It snuggles and a smile flickers on the little lips. Then, Mom comes and the body stiffens and I hand it to her. Mom doesn't bring it close or cuddle it but holds the child away, stiff-armed.

Margaret knocks on the door and says, "She said I could have her magazines."

As I hand them to her, one slips to the floor and the pages flip open to an article on TENDER LOVING CARE.

"What a shame the child died," I say.

"It could have been worse."

"How?"

"It could have lived."

---

*Virginia Orphant grew up on a farm near Holden, Missouri. She taught school then went to St. Louis where she married a man in real estate and, as she says, "spent the next thirty years trying to collect rent and keep tenants happy." After her husband's death in 1976, she bought the family homestead in Holden, and since then, she's gardened, wrote, held garage sales, and dreamed. She's had a poem published in an anthology, **Dreams and Visions**, two articles in **Working Writer** and one in **Doberman World**.*

RUI-480
In the Cosmic Circus

Wendy Corrina Leadbeater

NIGHT UNFOLDS HER CLOAK OF HOLES...

The sky was dark.

The night was Jung; this was a time for Compensation & Archetypes. Better *pray* there!

The wind was cold; Sophie wrapped her cloak more tightly about herself as she approached the Limit. On the planet Lucifer.

Beyond it was Void.

The World had not been created yet—

Here at the Center of the All was the Cosmic Circus; Mind & Cosmos, proprietors. This was Sisyphus' sin: to kill his Father, Tantalus, & marry his Mother, Mind.

This was Tantalus' sin: to kill Kronos & marry Horos.

Speaking of Horos, Sophie was a Whore.

You've seen them at the vaudeville, the peep-show girls, early mourning Madonnas in the twilight. They wear their bangles of star-jewels like diamonds cast against a sable field of sky.

Horos was the Limit. W/o Horos, there's be no Void; & w/o the Void Kronos would still be devouring his children, because the Void is Death, Abyss, Chaos, & were there no Void for him to go back to he would've risen from the dead.

On Lucifer—

They say Christ rose from the Dead; but God had not yet become Incarnate (if that was even possible); & besides, God was a Clown. Every evening God would ride his little unicycle over the tightwire for the amusement of Mind & Body, who were having an affair.

Not that Cosmos wasn't also cheating on his wife; Cosmos was having an affair w/ Love & Life, who were identical twins; he was into menage a trois: One WoMan on top; the Other WoMan on his face; Spiritual Semen for everyone.

My God, an orgy of Orgasmatrons!

Sophie was a Ladytron.

The difference between an Orgasmatron & a Ladytron is that an Orgasmatron can resurrect the dead w/ a blow job; a Ladytron kills—so far, Sophie had only sucked off Death, but he was already dead, so he didn't die...not that he would rise from the dead if an Orgasmatron ate him, so he had no vested interest in Love & Life—

Sophie thought, as the cloak of holes unfurled about a river's meadow, as darkness drew the All into its tenebrous substance, I've got the very best lover—better than any other. But so far he's only asked for BJ. When will he ever want to vorkle? I think I'll let him do it bareback; I've been using rubbers cuz of AIDS, but I think...yes, I really do think—someday I'd like to be a Mother.

Soon.

They say Death is a motherfucker. They say he fucked his Mother, Night, & she gave birth to Twins: Love & Life.

What does Cosmos see in Love & Life, anyway? Why doesn't he ever come to me for a good session of sensual seduction instead of letting those hos vorkle him? I'm a *good* Whore & I'm cheap.

I think I'll look in on him—if Mind is gone for the evening, I'll try to seduce him. If I can—they say Cosmos is a swinger, but he's only interested in high-class whores.

Maybe if Mind wouldn't mind I can talk him into having a menage a trois w/ the Two of us...the only problem is, I hear Cosmos likes Love & Life to do lesbian things w/ each other, & I'm not sure I could eat Mind.

They say Kronos ate his children.

They say Oedipus Wrecks; he's the guy who backed his car into a semi the other night when he got drunk at the Corner Bar.

& so Sophie pulled back the curtains of Cosmos' tent.

Love & Life were doing lesbos douche ass.

Sophie was sure she didn't want to get into that, so she decided she'd go look up Death.

As the witching Hour approached the whore approached Death's tent.

The sands of the planet Lucifer were hot beneath her feet; & the Void was a great nothingness which consumed tourists.

It was here that she'd take her stand: a lonely (& strong) WoMan.

She was wearing a Green Shirt.

\#

SOMEBODY'S GOING TO GET IT!

...Cosmos ejaculated as he looked up from a vorkling session w/ Mind. & saw Wisdom, the Whore. Sophie Prunikos.

Sophie wondered where Love & Life were; they seemed to be just One more part of the Void of sandstorms that surrounded the Cosmic Circus; holding it back forever from the World outside—if, indeed, there *was* a World outside.

Some said you just approached Horos & there was nothing on the other side but Nothingness & more Nothingness—

But naturally if Cosmos were vorkling his wife, he wouldn't want any hos around, especially not Black Ones, especially not whores who knew that Cosmos was having an affair w/ Love & Life.

She just wondered if he was ever going to let Death bugger him. Death was bi, & had frequently expressed a desire to bugger Cosmos. He also wanted to bugger Life, if not vorkle her, but he didn't care for Love because Love was chubby compared to Life, & if there was One thing that Death couldn't stand, it was a fat woman.

Well, at least I'm on the Ultra Slim-fast Diet.

Death also couldn't stand WoMen who were too skinny, & Mind was an anorexic; Death was always commenting on how ugly Mind appeared compared to his beloved Sophie.

So Soph-kid set out to find Death.

\#

CRUCIFICTION (SIC) & CRUCIFIXATION (SIC)
in
LOVE & DEATH

When Sophie found Death he was being crucifixated (sic). Like a River of blood from the heart of the Rain; like the bloody red Sunset of a fantastic SF that hadn't come to be yet (this was all B4 the Creation, in the Pleroma, almost Heaven, west Montana; Louie says we Love you, & we dig being Stranded w/ Mother of Pearl); like the Rose of Mysterious Jungians, Death bled.

There was some heavy symbolism going down here.

Not just that, but the central Archetype of the story (besides the Androgyne, the Mother, & the Whore) was Dying.

*God is a Dyer. As the good dies die w/ the things that have been
dyed in them, so it is w/ those that God has dyed. They are immortal
thru His colors. But God dips what He dips in water:* THE GOSPEL
OF PHILIP.

Philip hadn't written his Gospel yet; Q was still a gleam in the
pre-existent Soul of Thomas, & Death was Dying.

"Death!" Soph-kid ejaculated, which was rare for a WoMan like
her. "How can U B Dying?"

Death replied, moaning in agony from the nail-bites like taloned
witch's claws, "I'm not colored like you, Soph-kid, so I am not
immortal thru my colors. Life did this to me, the little bitch—& I
thought she had a nice ass. God—& God dipped me in water—-
remember, He dips what he dips in Living Water, but I never had the
Baptism of the Spirit, or the Communion of Bread & Water, so I guess
now I have to be reincarnated as a Hindu Love god—God, I can't
stand Love! But I see the smoky orange lights, & isn't this the Bardo
we're in?"

"You've been looking at too much Dick," Sophie replied. "But
no dilettante, Philip K Fancy, beats the Plastic you!"

"I certain am flexible—as flexible as any Plastic—but even
Zarathustra could believe in me...I'm just going to miss my Mazda.
Can you climb up on the cross & vorkle me while I'm dying? I don't
care what Color I get reincarnated as; Black, White, Red, Yellow.
They're all alchemical symbols. I am the Transmutation & the Lover
of Life; no One comes to the Mother but thru me—except for the
Androgyne; She comes to the Mother thru the Father..."

Soph-kid once more ejaculated: "You're the Lover of Life? God,
& I thought *I* was a ho! You're a vorkling gigolo! But blowing somebody on a cross sounds like a good idea—& this is your Last Tempta-
tion, isn't it? I might as well give it a shot—& then go out to the
Corner Bar for a shot. I'm into peppermint schnapps."

"I'm into slow screws," Death said. "Slow gin & orange juice.
Either that or sex on a beach. Does anybody know how to make a
slippery dick?"

W/o any further hesitation, Death's dingy her destination, Sophie
climbed the cross.

Death welcomed her. "Well, strap your hands 'cross my engines
& I'll fire all of my guns at once & explode into—well...Death!"

"I couldn't slip it in sideways," Sophie commented. After trying
futilely for several minutes. "I'm going to have to give you a dingy-
homner."

& so saying, she took his dingy into her mouth & homnered it.

Spiritual Semen flowed—the impregnating power of the Holy Spirit. They say the Virgin became pregnant from the Spirit. Whoever heard of this, a woman becoming pregnant from a WoMan?

For the Spirit is Androgynous, but She's definitely a She; as a matter of fact, She's a Dykester.

Which may explain her predilection for Virgins.

But her search for perfection, her own predilection, took Sophie 'round & 'round; also, her head was reeling & rocking from tasty sweet & sour.

She ran to catch divining signs, leaving Death to Dye—

#

TANTALUS & SISYPHUS
in
THE CORNER BAR

Soph-kid wound up in the Corner Bar, which was a good place for any self-respecting ho to find johns. After using the john, she surveyed the milling throng of cyberpunks from the Invisible College & just pain nerds.

She needed a He-man Demon.

Someone to kill w/ the Sunshine of her love in this heat/night. Because she was a Ladytron. She wasn't certain if Life had really killed Death or if she had killed Death because she was a Ladytron & had given him a blow job.

Whenever I give anyone a blow job I rise from the dead, though I haven't died—& they die!

God, look at me: death has me ejaculating!

I'm a vorkling Androgyne Whore...but at least I'm not a Mother: If I had a baby I'd pull a Kronos & eat it. I just hope I'm not the Mother of Zeus—if I ever get pregnant.

If I ever get pregnant I'm getting an abortion—!

"I like your Mother of Pearl earrings," the voice of a savage vorkling he-man stud said from behind her.

She turned. It was Sisyphus.

"Like, I may be a ho, but at least I'm not into incest. Why don't you go fuck Love & Life? God, if I ever find Life I'm going to fucking kill her."

"Like Father, like Son," Sisyphus said as Tantalus approached & Soph-kid split as Jesus entered from the rear.

"God...thank God—I mean, thank you that I found you! Can you do me a favor & help me kill Life?" Sophie said to Christ.

God stared into his mystic crystal. "Life has strayed beyond the limit, Horos, the god of Whores. Hi. I see you're into lipstick & leather, wear & tear, + B&D. If you tie me up & vorkle me I'll help you find Life & kill her—fuck Love, anyway; they say that I'm Love but I always thought Love was a bitch; did you know that she's my sister? I can see it in my crystal ball that Life is in Sister Europe, which hasn't come to be yet, yet which is rapidly forming due to the void in the Void made by the absence of Life. But First—& the First shall be Last—*screw me silly!*"

"Right on!"

#

FUCKING GOD

She tied him up.

She whipped him.

Then she found out that she was out of condoms.

She could always run down to the Invisible 7-11 & get some, but Wisdom the Whore was too desperate to get revenge on Life so that she vorkled him anyway. God did it to her tied to a chair, which isn't nearly as comfortable as a waterbed, but kinkier—& boy howdy, was God ever kinky!

God does not Create.

The Creation was immanent.

Sophie dropped an RUI-480

Don't want no babies sucking my nipples dry; I'd rather feel the tongues of johns, or at least scarlet pimps! Fucking no way & if I'm gonna have a kid.

#

ROME IF U WANT TO

God & Sophie found Life in the Colosseum.

She was Rome-ing around the world.

She was going to Graceland, Memphis, TN.

"You're a Ladytron, aren't you?" God asked. "Boy howdy, am I ever glad you didn't eat me cuz otherwise what Zarathustra spake would be real & Nietzche would be right; God would be dead!"

"What does all this have to do w/ me?" Soph-kid asked.

"You're going to have to eat her."

"Ecch!" Sophie exclaimed. "& I thought you were queer."

"I'll hold her down & you eat her. One lick is all it'll take—if you can stand her scrofulous cunt."

God leaped on Life & tackled her like the Refrigerator; God was a big motherfucker for a Clown.

God pulled aside silken satin—

Silken Satan—

Sin-vitations—

One lick...

Hair—

Moisture—

A sweet taste, like marron glaced fishbones—hmm, I could even crave the flavor...

Just then the RUI-480 kicked in.

The World was made in the Labor of a Whore.

Life is Alien to the World

& THE WORLD IS SOPHIE'S ABORTION!

Wendy Corrina Leadbeater is not a woman, as you may have guessed. "Wendy" has an academic background in science fiction. He has been published in **Midnight Zoo** *and elsewhere. This piece, he tells us, is based on Gnostic mythology. The Christian Gnostics, who represent an alternative teaching to the orthodox Christian tradition, held that Wisdom (Sophie) was a Whore and the world is Sophie's abortion.*

Rabbit Hole

Ginny Sanders

"The goal is to not get pregnant before you're ready," her father said.

"If you do," her mother added, "remember we love you and we won't be angry. We'll help you find a nice adoptive family."

Andrea was two days from turning thirteen. When a child is thirteen or within ten months of becoming thirteen the great waters of wisdom rain upon them and they automatically know more about life than their prehistoric parents. Sitting at the dining room table, Andrea looked back and forth between her parents. She was too old for "the talk". They were old, but not so old that she should have been the first to inform them. *A nice adoptive family*? She thought. *Where* have they been? Rolling her eyes she announced, "If I get pregnant, I don't have to have the baby if I don't want it." They were her parents and she was responsible for them. It wouldn't have been right for another teenager to explain modern life to them.

Looking into her father's eyes, Andrea saw a swelling. He didn't blink. Her mother began mumbling under her breath. Mumble, mumble, mumble! She was crossing herself so fast her right hand looked like a propeller. Andrea hated when she did that. Mumble, cross! She was making Andrea dizzy. Shrugging, Andrea got up from the table.

Her parents were temporarily insane. The truth does that to people.

***

"You're going to Camp FuFu," her father said. He didn't look up from his breakfast. He didn't give her the wide, toothy grin or the knowing wink he usually gave when bestowing a gift on her. He mashed scrambled eggs with his fork. Her mother began crossing herself and mumbling again. Andrea didn't care. She was going to Camp FuFu!

Camp FuFu, home of the Rabbit FuFus! Andrea had been whining and begging to go since she was nine. Daddy would always say, "Nice wholesome girls with good parents don't need Camp FuFu." Her mother would start mumbling and crossing herself. Andrea wondered if this meant she wasn't a nice girl anymore, maybe her parents weren't good parents. It didn't matter; she was going to Camp FuFu.

Andrea didn't know what went on at Camp FuFu. It was a secret shared between Rabbit FuFus. At school when the girls huddled in groups to talk about their trips to the camp, Andrea was always pushed aside until they were through talking. "You wouldn't understand," they would say. Maybe she would have, maybe she wouldn't. Andrea did understand that she was the only girl in her class except for Mary Margaret Donney that hadn't been to FuFu. That was an insult. Mary Margaret had the only mom in the world that could cross herself faster than Andrea's.

"When?" Andrea asked. Her stomach felt knotted.

"Tomorrow," Daddy replied.

Her mother gasped. Andrea rolled her eyes. She wasn't going to let anything ruin the day. She was going to Camp FuFu!. She didn't know what she had done to change their minds. Maybe it was the light she had shed on life for them the night before. They may have been shocked, but they sure as hell weren't ungrateful

***

Camp FuFu sat in the middle of a pine forest. Standing at the big brass gate, Andrea felt as small as a rabbit. She waited for a counselor to escort her in. Daddy was letting her wait by herself. It was a first, but it was a FuFu rule. Andrea didn't argue.

The smells of pine needles, evergreens, and grass perfumed the air. It was a fresh, clean, annoying smell, reminding her of Mom and summer cleaning. There wasn't any tension in the air, and the gentle breeze whispered to her, *You're finally here, Camp FuFu!*

Pale blue canvas with small white streaks painted in just the right places. That's what Andrea thought the sky looked like. The sun was warming the side of her face. It was the same sun she felt at home, but for some reason it didn't seem to have the terrible rays that gave her Uncle Jim cancer and her freckles. It was a friendly sun shining on the gates of Camp FuFu. Andrea couldn't help thinking, *Heaven couldn't be more beautiful.*

Reaching out to touch a shiny spot on the gate, she heard a voice yell. "Andrea! Don't touch that!" Jerking her hand back, Andrea saw a woman on the other side of the gate rushing toward her.

"Didn't your father tell you not to touch?"

Andrea nodded. Daddy had told her not to touch the gate. But Daddy was always telling her not to touch something or other. It was impossible for Andrea to know when to listen. "It looked like gold," she said.

Smiling, the counselor showed Andrea the straightest, whitest teeth she had ever seen. Her lips were the color of rose petals. Andrea licked her own lips, wishing they were as red. A long black braid flowed down the counselor's back. The braid looked too tight. She wore khaki shorts. Andrea did too. All Rabbit FuFus wore khaki shorts.

"The gates are pretty in the sunlight. My name is Sara, welcome to Camp FuFu." Pushing a button on her watch she opened the gate, inviting Andrea to join her in paradise.

Running across black soil and trampling over thick green grass, they came to a shallow creek. The water was clear enough to see the fish. They could have walked across, but Sara quickly began stepping from stone to stone. Giggling, Andrea followed her. Sara led her to a swinging bridge. Running across, Andrea thought, *it's fun being a Rabbit FuFu.*

If this wasn't the place for nice wholesome girls, then Andrea didn't want to be nice or wholesome.

There were bunk beds! Ten of them lined up against the wall of a log cabin. Andrea had always wanted a bunk bed. Chelsa Snyder had bunk beds. She slept on the top, and when she had a friend over they could sleep on the bottom. Andrea never got to spend the night at Chelsa's, so she had never slept in a bunk bed. Chelsa wasn't wholesome and nice enough. She had kissed a boy when she was seven, and her parents let her go to Camp FuFu when she was eight.

Chelsa was a lucky dog and Andrea hated her.

Her name was on her bunk in big blue letters. Andrea's insides jumped up and down. She squealed. There was a white t-shirt lying on top of the brown wool blanket. Her Rabbit FuFu t-shirt! Picking it up, she examined the picture. A little brown rabbit lay next to a black rabbit hole. FuFu rabbit looked sick. He was skinny, not fat and soft looking like a rabbit should be. His eyes were closed, and his little paws looked like knobs of gnawed off wet fur. It was only a silk screen, but for a moment Andrea felt sad for the rabbit.

Pushing the feelings aside, she turned the shirt over. FIRST TRIP—MARCH 1996 was embroidered on the back. A surge of excitement tickled her toes. She looked at the counselor. Sara's eyes had lost their sparkle. She looked disappointed. Andrea wasn't! "Can I put it on?" she asked. Sara nodded. Ripping her own shirt over her head, Andrea put on her Camp FuFu shirt. She was definitely a Rabbit FuFu now.

"Go out and join the other girls by the campfire," Sara said. Her tone had changed. Suddenly she sounded angry and parental.

The fire danced, and the Rabbit FuFus sang. It was a perfect night for a camp fire. There was just enough chill in the air to redden the nose. The sky was dark enough to look navy blue. Andrea saw the Big Dipper and Orion's belt. Deneb was to the west, but Vega was the brightest. She wanted to reach out and touch the stars, put them in her pocket and peek at them whenever she wanted. She knew she couldn't.

Hunger pains rumbled through her stomach. Daddy had said she would eat at camp, but no one had offered her a meal. Nice wholesome girls waited for an offer. Singing and laughing and the glow from the flames kept her mind off food.

Little rabbit FuFu

It was a special song. The Camp FuFu song. Understanding the tune but not the words, Andrea hummed along while the other Rabbit FuFus sang.

Little rabbit FuFu hmmhm hmmmm hm.

A Rabbit FuFu walked toward them. Sara's arms were around the girl, holding her close. Their feet scuffled against the ground. The Rabbit FuFu looked sick and hurt. Stumbling towards the camp fire, Andrea saw her fall. The girl screamed. Andrea tried to stand up. She wanted to help. Another Rabbit FuFu grabbed her arm. "No," the Rabbit FuFu whispered, her eyes signaled a warning. Andrea looked at the other girls. They kept singing. She didn't understand why they didn't help the Rabbit.

Laying on the ground like a lump of pained flesh, the sick Rabbit kept screaming. Sara quickly lifted the girl off the ground. Holding her tight, she led the girl to the camp fire. The other rabbits kept singing. The wounded Rabbit stopped screaming.

"Happy birthday!" The Rabbit FuFus yelled. "Happy birthday!" They all turned and looked at the wounded rabbit. She almost smiled. *How awful*, Andrea thought, *to be so sick on your birthday.*

"Happy birthday," she whispered.

The sick rabbit stopped next to Andrea. Looking into her dazed eyes, Andrea saw pity, sorrow, and remorse. "Happy birthday," Andrea whispered again. Tilting her head, the girl smiled. Her lips began moving and Andrea strained to hear her words. She couldn't. The girl finished, and walked away.

***

"It's your first time here?" A voice whispered.

Turning over in her bunk, Andrea replied, "Yeah, is it yours?"

"No way! I've been coming here for three years." There was a spark of adolescent pride in the Rabbit's voice. "Tomorrow's your birthday?"

"Yes," Andrea said. "How do you know?"

Snickering, the girl said, "The first time is always the day before your birthday. It's different when you get older, they talk to you like a grown up. I think it's to make sure you don't forget what can happen. It's only your first time. The first time they show you things. To teach you."

"Teach about what?" Andrea asked, nervously. Daddy hadn't said anything about going to school while she was at Camp FuFu.

"About rabbits, silly. That's why your parents sent you here. So you can learn about being a rabbit."

"Ohh!" she replied, not understanding but not wanting to sound stupid.

The girl on the next bunk began singing, her words drifting to Andrea in the darkness. *Little Rabbit FuFu, I wouldn't want to be you.* Andrea didn't like the words. Didn't like the way they seemed to echo in the darkness, or the way they made her back itch. She put a pillow over her head. Drowning the song, Andrea welcomed the comfort of sleep.

Hands snatched the blanket.

Hands grabbed her and pulled her from the bed. She tried holding on to the bedpost, but the hands pulling her were stronger. Screaming, she felt a hand press against her mouth. Another hand pushed her stomach. Kicking and moaning, Andrea tried to free herself. Hands held her arms. Hands held her feet. Hands tied her hands and feet.

Andrea bit down as hard as she could on the hand covering her mouth. A deep voice yelled, "shit! Why do they do that?" No one answered him. Andrea could taste blood. Screaming a long frightful scream that could have summoned the dead, Andrea thought *Help me Rabbit FuFus! Help me!* None of the Rabbit FuFus helped her. Squinting, she tried to see who was grabbing her, how many hands were on her. All she could see were black silhouettes. Something whipped across her face. It wasn't a belt. *Too soft.* It felt like hair. Lots of thick heavy hair. *Sara?* She thought.

Andrea screamed louder and longer. The Rabbit FuFus ignored her. Hands dragged her toward the door by the ankles. Hands picked her up and carried her though the forest. Andrea cried. In the background she could hear a chorus of Camp FuFu Rabbits singing, *Little Rabbit FuFu, I wouldn't want to be you...*

The hands pushed her. Falling straight down through what seemed like miles of suffocating darkness, Andrea landed THUMP. Somewhere a chorus was still singing *Little Rabbit FuFu I wouldn't want to be you...*

Digging her heels in and scooting on her butt, Andrea managed to inch backwards against a wall. Turning her head slightly she stuck out her tongue. Her tongue touched the wall. Gritty. Bitter. Wet. *Mud!* She thought. *Mud, darkness, falling. Hole! Mud, darkest, falling rabbit hole. Rabbit hole! Rabbit hole! Rabbit FuFu hole!*

Andrea was trapped in a giant rabbit hole.

Panic chilled her. Tilting her head back, she screamed upwards to the stars she couldn't see. To ears that wouldn't listen. *Little Rabbit FuFu, I wouldn't want to be you.* The song seemed to seep from the wall. Every pore sang out. Every tiny grain carried the note.

"I want my Mommy," Andrea whispered. "I want Mommy!"

The rabbit hole song changed. Heavy handed bongo music vibrated from the wall. *Your mommy don't want you!* A voice taunted.

"I want my Mommy!"

Your mommy don't want you!

"Yes she does!" Andrea screamed.

She heard her own voice, or what sounded like her voice filtering into the hole. "If I was pregnant I wouldn't have the baby if I didn't want it...if I was pregnant I wouldn't have the baby if I didn't want it." The bongo music continued. Louder and louder until the clashing of a thousand angry hands crowded her ears. Whiny child voices sang.

Your mommy don't want you, your daddy don't want you! Your mommy
don't want you, your daddy don't want you!
Her ears rang. Her temples throbbed. Andrea pushed herself back
further against the wall and cried. The bongos stopped. Singing in a
low soothing whisper, an angelic voice coaxed her to sleep.

Little Rabbit FuFu,
I wouldn't want to be you.

***

CLUMP! CLICK! CLICK! CLICK! CLICK!
The sound of metal hatches rubbing together and locking woke
Andrea. There was light in her rabbit hole. Her eyes were puffy. Mud
and tear streaks stiffened her face. Andrea could see the blue bruises
on her tights. Blue wasn't her favorite color anymore. Caked blood
bordered cuts and scratches. Looking up, she saw a giant hose covering the hole. It had ridges like Mommy's vacuum hose. It was bigger.
She tried to scream, but her throat wouldn't allow the echoes of fear
to pass.
VUMMM. Andrea heard a motor. VUMMM. The hose began to
shake. Crossing herself in her mind, Andrea began mumbling under
her breath. Mental cross. Mental cross. Mumble, mumble, mumble!
The wall shook, and a chorus began singing. *Little Rabbit FuFu, I*
wouldn't want to be you. Sucked from the rabbit hole...

The suction came! Rocks, pebbles, and dirt rushed for the hose.
Andrea tried to push her weight against the hole's floor. The suction
was powerful. Pulling her hair and burning her shin it raised Andrea
from the ground, slurping her into the hose.
Flowing through the long plastic snake, her body bounced from
side to side. Rocks and dirt pounded her face. Her skin burned, her
scream couldn't be heard. Crossing herself in her mind, she was
thankful. Even in a state of shock she knew if she was a little thinner
or a little smaller the strong pull would have split her skin, ripped her
limbs from their sockets, and splattered her blood. Andrea would have
been bloody pulp with flesh chunks and crushed bones mixed in for
texture.
Andrea landed in a trash barrel. Unable to move or talk or open
her eyes, she felt hands touch her. Soft fingers pushed against her stiff

neck. "Pulse is okay," a voice said. "Take her back." *Back where?* Andrea thought. *Not back there. No! I want to go home!*
They carried her to the rabbit hole and dropped her in.
Little Rabbit FuFu, I wouldn't want to be you. Sucked from the rabbit hole...

VUMMM! She was sucked up again, and again, until she could barely hear a voice yelling, "Pulse is too weak!" They didn't take Andrea back to the hole.
Heat awakened her. The waterbed was soft under her body. Instinctively Andrea whipped the streams of sweat from her forehead. She sat up in the bed. Looking at her wrist, she smiled. *It's over!* she thought. She was untied. Moving to the edge of the bed, she lowered her feet to the floor. "Ouch!" she yelled, pulling her feet back to the bed. Leaning over, she touched the floor with a finger. The blue ceramic tiles were hot. *"No!"* she screamed. *"Please don't!"*
She looked around the room. There were no doors, no windows. Steam danced from the ceramic walls and ceiling. White clouds filled the room. Sweating and panting, Andrea wiped her red face on her arm. Her eyes were itching and sore. Watery blusters swelled before her eyes. Andrea was already dizzy by the time she heard the gurgling and bubbling from the bed. Peeling back the sheets, she saw the water in the mattress rising to a boil.
She couldn't breathe. Wheezing she pulled the covers into a little ball. They burst into blue and white flames. Andrea jumped to the floor. Her tender soles sizzled against the tiles. Smell of burning flesh made her nauseous. Convulsions attacked her stomach. Andrea's body went limp. As her mind froze she heard sweet voices sing to her.
Little Rabbit FuFu, I wouldn't want to be you. Sucked from the rabbit hole, dropped into a furnace for dead.

***

Doctors scanned Andrea's body. Repairing the little Rabbit FuFu, they placed her in a bunk. Andrea tried not to move. Even crying hurt her aching body.
"Happy birthday, Andrea," a familiar voice said.
Opening her eyes, Andrea could see a burly face smiling at her. She blinked hard, bringing the face into focus. Sara touched a bruise on Andrea's face.

Andrea tried to scream. She couldn't. She strained to speak. Shaking her head, Sara said, "Don't try to speak yet. Your voice will come back soon. Look!" She was holding a clean white t-shirt. "I have a birthday present for you!"

Andrea looked at the Camp FuFu shirt. A fat, fluffy rabbit was hopping away from the rabbit hole. His nose was bright pink. Tiny rhinestones glued to his open eyes made them sparkle. His ears stood at attention.

Andrea forced a smile. Sara helped her up and into the shirt. Touching the rabbit, Andrea whispered, "My mommy didn't have to have me."

Smiling, the counselor hugged Andrea, careful not to squeeze too hard. "But she did," Sara said, stroking Andrea's hair. "She did." Sara placed a rabbit's foot in Andrea's shaking hand.

Sara kept an arm around Andrea as they walked out of the cabin. Slowly they approached the campfire. Rabbit FuFus sat in a tight circle around the flames singing. *Little Rabbit FuFu, I wouldn't want to be you. Sucked from the rabbit hole, dropped in a furnace for dead.*

"Happy birthday!" The Rabbits yelled as Andrea approached. "Happy birthday!"

Clenching her rabbit's foot, Andrea smiled. *It is a happy birthday*, she thought. *I'm still alive.* Andrea caught sight of a girl. She was bright-eyed and filled with the same curiosity Andrea had felt when sitting around the fire humming. Andrea stepped closer. Her smile faded when she realized it was her friend Mary Margaret. Kneeling down, Andrea ignored the pain stabbing her body. She touched Mary Margaret's cheek and began to sing.

She was singing loud in her mind, but Andrea knew the words leaving her mouth were barely a whisper. Mary Margaret leaned forward wanting to hear. She couldn't hear Andrea singing, *Little Rabbit FuFu, I wouldn't want to be you.*

Ginny Sanders lives in Dallas, Texas where she works as a systems analyst. She has been actively writing science fiction and fantasy since December, 1990. A member of the Lesser North Texas Writer's Group, "Rabbit Hole" is her first professional sale.

GP Venture

L. Crittenden

The great beauty of private enterprise is that it becomes an independent source, all by itself, for exploring whatever kinds of options there are available within a society, and then making them work.

"Your scan came out positive, Ms. Carpenter," I said, keeping it friendly and neutral. I wasn't sure how she'd react, and I was a little afraid she would cry or rave. She was nineteen, and there was a note in her file that said she had been upset when she came in for the scan.

But she didn't. She just said, "Oh, damn," and looked away, biting her lip.

We were sitting in one of the elegant little consultation rooms. I was wearing my tweed pantsuit, conservative, but with a little fashionable blousing at the ankles. Some GP's are very clinical and production-oriented; but we cater to a well-to-do clientele, and so lab coats just aren't our style.

Her first name was Julie, and she had long, fine, blonde hair cut with bangs that slanted down to a point in the back. She looked very slender in jeans and a gold-studded sweater. But of course she was only about a month-and-a-half along, and it didn't show yet that she was pregnant.

I waited, sympathetically.

"I'm not one of those women that have to have a child," she said after a minute. "And I can't support one right now. I'm planning to ask for a dissolution." She sighed, a little desperately, I thought. "I was so sure a marriage would work out. My dad insisted Weston was unstable, that we didn't have enough in common to get married—but I was so sure I was in love."

"Would you like to talk to a counselor about it?" I asked, not ready to take care of emotional problems myself. But she straightened in her chair.

"No, I'm fine," she said crisply. "I'll be going back to school. Put it in vitro, please. I don't want it—now or later, either."

I was glad she seemed to be sure of herself, and mature, even if she did look so young, hardly more than a child herself. It's difficult to work with women who vacillate.

"Of course. But we don't have time for an extraction today. Could I make you an appointment?" I accessed the LAN through my wrist station. "Tuesday at two?"

"Fine," she said. "How much will it be?"

"A hundred, if there aren't any complications."

"Just a hundred? For storage, too?" She sounded surprised.

"The fee is based on the *average* storage time," I explained, "which isn't really very long."

"Oh."

"We'll have the paperwork ready for you on Tuesday. And if you can bring the father's social security number, it'll save us some trouble on the genetic history."

"Okay"

She gathered up her purse and her jacket to go, but at the door she stopped, and her hair spun a pale cascade as she turned. She hesitated. "Is it a good baby?" she asked then, carefully.

I smiled at that, glad to give her positive news. "Yes, it's fine." And she smiled too, as if it relieved her mind, and went on out, trim in the tight jeans and sweater, with an easy, graceful stride.

It was an important point that she had asked about, and she wanted to know for more than one reason. First, there are so many mutagens in the environment these days, that only about thirty percent of embryos are naturally viable at all. She would have been glad to hear she was capable of producing a healthy child. And then too, all the bad ones, the ones that can't be straightened out, go right to the tissue banks for medical use.

My partner and I run a brisk, successful little business in Manhattan. It's called a Gene Pool Storage and Matching Center, shortened, of course to GPS&M, or just GP. He's the technician and I'm the businesswoman. His name is the subject of a lot of jokes behind the scenes—it's Gene, Gene Birdzell. He's quite competent on the technical side. He manages the extractions, the storage and the incubations, but he's really poor at dealing with people. So much that sometimes I think his name should be Igor, instead. So I'm the one that handles the staff and meets the public. It takes both sides to make the business run.

The next appointment was two men, and I met them in the waiting room a little bit early. I think it makes a good impression to be prompt, like we appreciate our customers. They were black, one about middle-aged and the other young. We shook hands.

"How do you do, Ms. Polanski," said the older man. He was an executive and had white in his hair. They had been screened already by the legal department, and certified to be stable, well-off, and respectable, etc., etc. Homosex couples might still raise a few eyebrows, but it's perfectly legal now, and none of my business.

"I'm so glad to meet you," I said. "If you'll come this way, we have a station set up for you." The hallway is quiet and carpeted, with spots that highlight our art collection. It's essential for the proper atmosphere, and tax deductible, of course. There's music in the background too, soft and subliminal.

The station we had set up was recessed in golden oak paneling and featured a big, high-resolution screen. I use a touch board to operate the system from off to the side. They were looking for a little boy. I brought up the matching phenotype and scrolled through the files, giving them plenty of time to shop and think about it.

The system translates the genetic information into a portrait of what the child will look like—at birth and any other age you ask for. The little boys appear and transmute on the screen, smiling with carefully engineered seduction. I don't feel guilty about it, though. It's our business, and the children are all good.

After half an hour they had narrowed it down to only a couple of boys; and I brought up both the portraits, side-by-side, along with the genetic histories to show their potentials. I pointed out some of the good points they might not notice, taken by the smiles—and, of course, the bad ones too. Full disclosure is essential in this type of sensitive dealings. And then I kept quiet.

They discussed it in soft voices. The older man glanced up. "Ms. Polanski?"

"Yes sir?"

"We'd rather not rush into anything."

"Of course not," I said. "It's quite an important investment for you."

They got up in unison; and I rose too, leaving the portraits on the screen, smiling down.

"We are interested," he said. "If we could have a little time to think about it?"

I knew what they wanted.

"I'll print out the data for you to study," I offered. "You know it will take approximately nine months after you decide?"

"Yes, of course." Their teeth shone in the dim light, echoing the screen, and I knew we had a sale. They would have the genetic forecast checked by another lab, of course; but Gene's system just doesn't make mistakes. They took the data, and I saw them out.

That was the beginning of the week. It went downhill fast.

First, an inversion treated us to all the nasty heat and smog that New York is famous for. Even if internal combustion vehicles *are* outlawed now, and electrics mandatory; there's enough pollution in the environment to keep the air poisonous for years to come, and all it takes is a little change in the weather for us to feel it.

Then, a group of fundamentalists showed up to protest outside the building, just like we were one of those cut-rate baby mills. I couldn't believe it. But at least they stayed on the sidewalk out front, where they'd be visible but not bothersome. The police kept an eye on them; and they left the customers alone—they couldn't sort ours out from those of the other professional offices.

The haze smoldered over the skyline, everybody got cross and irritable; and then Weston Carpenter showed up.

I had caught the maglev in from Long Island Thursday morning as usual, took a taxi from the station, through the thick air, the dense streets, already sultry. Trying not to be annoyed, I excused my way through the grim line of picketers, already on the job at eight o'clock. We opened promptly; but Joanie, our receptionist, was late, so I was manning the desk myself when he came in.

I could see right away what Julie's dad meant about him being unstable. He barged in the door wearing a tailored suit but no tie, dark, wild-eyed and dramatic, wanting to see the manager. When I said I was the manager, he went into this heroic tirade about us stealing his legal issue, his son. I tried to explain his rights—that he couldn't force his wife to carry the child, that he could assume its support without legal action any time within six weeks after the extraction—but he was totally out of touch, didn't listen at all. Our first appointment came in, a well-dressed woman who looked already distressed by the picketers, and I decided to call Security. I wasn't going to tolerate a scene in front of customers. Our reputation is too valuable.

I waited the thirty seconds before Security showed up, listening to his threats, and then got the woman into the back, into the soothing atmosphere of music and control, to let the problem of Weston Carpenter fade from my own mind as well. I made a note to call our law firm though, in case he tried to take his complaint further. I don't know why some people think they have a right to children but no responsibility.

As it turned out, I should have called the police as well. Carpenter came back on Friday afternoon.

I had been hoping the week would pick up, that it would rain, or that the protest would go somewhere else. Gene kept worrying about brown-outs affecting the equipment, and was totally preoccupied, less human even, than usual. By Friday the whole staff was ready for a break.

About three o'clock we had our last appointment, the homosex couple to sign the contract for their little boy. They rose as I came into the waiting room and the older man extended his hand.

"So good to see you, Ms. Polanski," he said.

I was really glad to see them, too. I led them down the hallway to the conference room in shantung and polished parquet, where Simon had the papers ready.

We were hardly settled in the upholstered chairs, Simon just starting to go through the legalese, when I heard the disturbance up front. I was tempted to go see what it was, but Joanie is perfectly competent, as capable as calling Security as I am; so I decided against it. The noise subsided, but I heard running feet in the hall—one set, then another.

I excused myself, hoping the black couple hadn't noticed, and went to see what was going on. The steps had run towards the lab and storage area. I hurried that way, just in time to see the confrontation: Gene and Weston Carpenter, with Joanie clutching at his jacket.

I was horrified. The storage areas are off-limits to the public. They were well within earshot of the conference room. But it got worse. Carpenter had a pry bar with him, and he began smashing at the womb.

Gene screeched, grabbed at him. Joanie dragged at his coat. Praying she had called Security, I joined the fight; but none of us was big or heavy enough to stop him. He kept bashing at the equipment, the heavy bar rising and falling on the fragile sensors, the amniotic lines, the delicate heaters. Fluid sprayed my face, ran down my blouse; I clawed at him.

Then a heavier weight struck the battle. I slipped, fell on the tile, caught a glimpse. It was the older black man, the executive; and Carpenter's arm rose and fell again, trying to hit him with the bar.

Then Security was there. Confusion. Flashing alarms, screaming sensors. Gene scuttled into the equipment, disappeared. Joanie sat on the floor crying. Simon stood there, white-faced. It was over; but the remains of at least one fetus stained the tile, and our client, the polite executive, lay still on the floor. All I could think was damage control.

The paramedics took care of themselves. They carried away the injured man, and Joanie for good measure. Gene had the equipment under control. The staff looked to be organizing. But I had to deal with the police myself.

I called our law firm, our insurance company, and then went down to the precinct station to make a statement. MaryBeth met me there, our lawyer in steel lamé; and I guess it wasn't as bad as it could have been. But still it was well after dark when we were done.

"Could I give you a lift, Elinore?" asked MaryBeth, outside. But I said no.

I wanted nothing more than to go home and change my clothes, the sticky silk of my blouse; to bathe and collapse. But now, standing in the hot stillness of the night, feeling the shadows, the faceless crowd as it passed, I thought finally about Martin Dole, who had saved our machinery; and wondered how he was.

They had gone to Bellevue, and he was in surgery. It had been an emergency, and the hospital staff didn't know anything about it. I searched through the waiting rooms; finally found the right one, the younger man, waiting.

I had meant to say something warm and solicitous, to hold his hand and promise our insurance would take care of all his problems, cover all his expenses. But he glanced up as I slipped in, and somehow I didn't say anything. He looked at me, uncomfortable in my filthy clothes and ruined nails, and then away. So I only smiled, weakly, and sat down.

His name was Hart. Sitting there in his shirtsleeves, his tie loosened, it was an hour before he said anything at all. I was lost in my own mind, and it almost startled me.

"Why do people want children?" he asked softly.

I had my mouth open to say they didn't, necessarily; but then I realized he wasn't expecting an answer.

I hadn't really looked at him before, charmed as I was by the older man. The child they had chosen would look like him. He was a painter, an artist—light-colored, sloe-eyed, touched with blond. Exotic, he was a lovely, sensual boy. And, I thought suddenly, not completely aware of it.

He seemed to feel my eyes, glanced up, and away again. Time on the wall flickered, advanced.

"Martin was so casual," he said. "Let's adopt a kid."

Pause.

"That was so...unlike him this afternoon. He's not violent, or even...impetuous. I had no idea a strange fetus would mean so much to him."

He rubbed his face. He didn't quite have the middle class polish that Martin Dole had, the refinement.

"If he dies, can I still sign the contract?"

I stirred.

"I...yes, I think so." Cautious, trying to think. I wasn't really in a condition to discuss legal options. "If you..." a delicate matter, "were endowed with Mr. Dole's assets, that should be sufficient."

"Shit," he said.

I wished for our counselor.

"I thought it would be fun," he said. "A little brother. Somebody to take to the park, the shows. But Martin must feel something else. He's got some hidden passion."

"Um."

"What *is* it?" Suddenly passionate himself, his eyes sharp in the fluorescent.

I marshalled my brains, searched for the stock answers.

"The typical explanation is that children provide a kind of immortality," I said.

"Immortality? It's not my sperm that made the kid, not ours."

"It helps the human species to continue."

"Why do I even care?"

"A process of creation, to mold a child, to teach one."

"What the hell do I teach him?" he cried. "All the things I've done wrong in my life? All the things he can't have, because they're used up, or all the rotten things that can happen to him if he's not rich, or powerful, or lucky?"

He was angry at me now, for lack of anyone better. And somehow I was angry, too. "It's someone that sees the world new and bright and fresh every day," I said, "that you can love if Martin dies."

He covered his face with his hands. Perhaps he had something else to say. I was out of philosophy; but the surgeon was there, masked and gowned.

"Corey Hart?"

The boy was standing, burgundy-eyed; waiting.

"Yes?"

The surgeon hesitated.

"I don't know quite what to tell you," he said. "Mr. Dole is in the recovery room. The scan looks...favorable." He seemed uncomfortable, but perhaps it wasn't with what he had to say. "If you'd like to go in and sit with him?"

And Hart was gone.

Perhaps he wouldn't have to sign the contract alone after all.

Children are a burden to some and a joy to others, and now they're growing scarcer. They have to be allocated like any other valuable resource. A few years ago, it would have been a serious political problem; but now that the government and the moralists have gotten out of the way, it's easier. People can see it's important.

I sighed, and caught my taxi for home.

L. Crittenden is employed as an engineering specialist in corrosion and protective coatings for a contractor on Merritt Island, Florida. Her interests in writing include science fiction and fantasy. She's published several non-fiction articles, and sold a number of short stories (although only one has been published to date, in Proteus Magazine). Of all the possible futures explored in this book, Ms. Crittenden's is, in the opinion of the editor, one of the most likely to become reality.

Fetuscam

James S. Dorr

The unborn fetus shall be defined as a full human being, with all rights and protections accorded by law. Thus, the willful termination of the viability of a human fetus by any person, either through abortion or induced miscarriage, shall be a crime the equivalent of murder.
——Twenty-Ninth Amendment to the Constitution of the United States

***

Gaunt shifted his gaze from the dashboard monitor, catching his partner, Lieutenant Robbins, stifling a yawn. "You tired?" he asked.

"No—not really. Big night last night. This shouldn't take long, though."

"I hope not," Gaunt said. He felt uneasy. He wanted to talk, to get his mind off the job ahead.

"You know what, Lieutenant?" He turned to face the man sitting next to him, wondering if, perhaps, what he really was feeling was envy. Robbins was almost the same age as he was, but, dark and good-looking, could easily pass for his mid-to-late twenties. "Maybe it's time that what you should do is settle down."

"What do you mean, Gaunt?"

"Get married like me. It's all that tomcatting around you're doing that's wearing you down. Especially the kind of girls you go out with."

"So I like 'em young—nothing wrong with that. A man's got to live while he has the chance, Gaunt."

Gaunt pushed back his cap, running a hand through his thinning hair, then turned his attention back to the view on the miniature screen. It showed a dim room, slightly off focus, set up as a clinic—a long white table, a cabinet, equipment. A division surgeon, purposely dressed to look as if he was running to seed, was almost casually washing his hands. Gaunt still felt uneasy.

Gaunt had been with Feticide Division for less than a month, a transfer from Adult, and hadn't expected to take to the new routine all at once. He was used to investigating completed murders—past-tense crimes—that let a cop have some degree of righteous hatred for those who committed them. Now he couldn't quite shake the feeling that he was a part of the act himself. He remembered his law class— "entrapment" had been the term that was used before Congress made changes to tip the balance to help the enforcers—but even now it felt somehow wrong.

Still, he sat there alongside his partner. Robbins produced a cigarette—an expensive brand made with real tobacco—and the two men shared it. The night was hot and, from time to time, Gaunt glanced out the window, encountering air only slightly less stale. Across the street was the backup van, its paramedics sharing the vigil.

"Think she'll show?" he finally asked. He almost hoped that the woman wouldn't—would panic and run. "Think she really intends to go through with it?"

"Course she does, Gaunt. You get to know these people in time —know how their minds work. I don't much like all this waiting either, but you've got to admit, once it's finally over, the money's okay."

"Yeah, but still..."

The money, of course, was why he was here, staring at a tiny TV in an unmarked car. Now that his wife was going to have another child, he'd *had* to transfer. An adult victim's relatives often weren't good for the bounty—half the time they were actually glad the decedent was gone—but the Right to Life Churches always seemed to have money to spare. Plenty for bounty to augment a basic policeman's salary, with an extra bonus if the fetus was saved.

"Now," Robbins whispered, and both men watched as the subject finally appeared on the screen. The doctor seemed to be saying something—the sound on the set had long since stopped working—and moved to one side, making the woman turn to offer a better view. "Wait a minute, she's reaching for something. She's...damn!"

The monitor darkened and, even while Gaunt made a valiant effort to being up the brightness, it went out completely. "Damn!" Robbins swore again. "Damn the budget and damn City Hall for cutting equipment to keep it balanced." He opened the door on his side of the car.

"Come on, Gaunt. We'd better move in."

***

By the time the policemen burst into the clinic, the doctor was just getting back to his feet. A second door, one that led to the back of the building, was standing open.

"She was nervous, Lieutenant," the surgeon explained, gingerly rubbing the back of his head. "I mean *really* nervous. She was reaching around in her pocketbook—getting money—when..."

"Any exits to the street back there?" Robbins interrupted, gesturing toward the open door.

"Just one—to the alley. It's covered, isn't it?"

"Yeah. That's MacLehan. Hit you over the head with her purse, Doc?"

"Look here, Robbins, she must have heard you guys coming in. Why didn't you wait?"

Gaunt broke in this time. "The TV went out so we thought we'd better get here right away," he told the doctor, then turned to his partner. "What do we do now?"

"First we check with MacLehan, just in case she *did* try to go that way. Then we get the paramedics to bring the stuff from the van in here. But I think she's too smart to try the alley, so after that we make a search, room-by-room, bottom to top. You'll get the van, Gaunt—and get the rifles we left in the car."

"You think you'll need *rifles*?" the doctor protested. "She's only a kid."

"Tranquilizer bullets," Robbins replied. "Rated non-lethal—I brought them along because I figured we might have to use them—but strong enough so a single hit ought to stop her cold. If I were her, I'd go to the roof. Try to hide there—but if I was spotted I might get stupid. Like try to jump to the next building over."

"So why not just put a man on the roof over there?"

"You know why, Doc. She's pretty well into her third trimester—she gets too athletic, she might miscarry. Now let's move, Gaunt."

***

"Like I said, you get to know them," Robbins whispered. Despite his prediction, the Lieutenant had run the search by the book, thoroughly combing the first three floors until, only now, they were on the stairway that led to the roof. "Be ready for anything—once they're cornered, they act just like animals."

"Got you," Gaunt said. "But how does it happen? You heard the Doc—she's just a kid. Sure, what we're here for's to stop an abortion, but how does a kid like that get into trouble?"

"She's old enough, Gaunt—and she *is* an animal. Just remember, she came to this building to kill her own baby. And if we don't stop her, she'll go somewhere else—somewhere that isn't set up like we are to rescue the fetus."

"I guess so, Lieutenant. I guess it's not the arrest that counts as much as the life we'll be able to save. That how you see it?"

"That's it, Gaunt. Now keep it down—we're almost there. See? The door's still slightly ajar."

Gaunt held his breath while Robbins slowly pushed the door open. The roof, barely lit by the lights of the city, appeared as a maze of angles and shadows. Gaunt followed his partner out onto its surface, keeping low, his rifle ready. They took their positions and waited in silence.

Then Gaunt heard a sound, across the roof, and thought—just maybe—he saw something move. He saw the lieutenant rise to his feet. Robbins fired. Once.

"Got the bitch! Gaunt—you get downstairs and send the medics up here on the double. I'm going to make sure."

Gaunt took the stairs as fast as he could. He thought he heard at least two more shots by the time he reached the first floor landing.

***

Gaunt and Robbins were waiting in the alley when the surgeon came out, alone, to join them.

"How many shots you put into her, Robbins?" the doctor asked, his voice sounding tired. "We lost the mother."

"Enough, Doc. Enough to keep her down—but what about the fetus?"

"It's—he's—going to be fine. A perfect, Caucasian, baby boy—grow up to be a cop just like you. Want to see?"

"Sure. Gaunt, you come too. This is the kid the bitch would have wasted—the kid we saved."

The three returned to the makeshift clinic. Robbins and the surgeon crossed the room to the glassed-in cabinet that served as an incubator while Gaunt remained standing in the open doorway. He stared at the table, covered now with a stained, once-white sheet.

"Will you just look at that," he heard the Lieutenant say in an almost reverential voice. "Think there's a chance for adoption, Doc—a family with money to bring him up right?"

"You know there is, Robbins. Damn good thing, too, considering what the state homes are like."

"Just don't forget whose team gets the finder's fee."

Gaunt, not joining the conversation, moved to the long, silent table. It was too bad, he thought, about the mother. But the fetus was saved. That was the law—the system of bounties and lifesavers' fees and adoption bonuses just came with it. Besides, he wondered, what kind of woman would actually want to murder her son?

He lifted the sheet, then let it drop slowly. He took a step backwards, just as his partner came up to join him.

"Time to go, Gaunt," he heard Robbins say. "Time for us to get back to the station and fill out some papers."

Gaunt followed the Lieutenant out to the car. He unlocked the door to let him in and circled around to the driver's side

"The mother, Lieutenant," he finally said, after he'd settled into his own seat. "You used to go with her. I saw you with her at the departmental party last Christmas."

"So?" Robbins asked.

"So why the hell didn't you use some kind of protection? You're a cop—you've got connections. You could have gotten *her* something to use."

"What'd she know about stuff like that?" Robbins shot back, his voice becoming angry. "She was only sixteen—you think it's something they teach them in school?" But then he smiled, bringing his voice down to almost a whisper. "Besides, like I say, a man's got to live..."

Gaunt didn't answer. He wanted to quit, right then and there—get out of the car and just walk away—but, like Robbins said, a man had to live. So he jammed in the key and started the motor, inching the vehicle carefully around the worst of the holes in the unrepaired street.

He drove to the station in tight-lipped silence, wishing that he'd never been born.

James S. Dorr is well-known among those who work in the small press. This story was previously published in Pandora. He's had over 25 publications, mostly in the small press. Recent sales include Pulphouse, Science Fiction Review, Borderlands II (Avon Books anthology), and Alfred Hitchcock's Mystery Magazine. He's a busy man, and he writes good, too.

New Moon

Nowick Gray

i

"...and may the blessed Virgin forgive Jessie for her sin committed in ignorance, as God may forgive me for my failure to bring her wayward soul to see the truth. In Jesus' name, Amen."

Maria lies looking up at the full moon through the skylight over the bed. After a moment David speaks. "Don't you think you're being a little hard on yourself, Mar? You can only do so much."

"I know, but while there's still hope, I can't stop trying. I'll go see her again tomorrow."

He lies there silent a while longer, then says, "You still interested in this hike we've been talking about? We could go up Lightning Ridge, where we picked huckleberries last year."

Maria turns to him and places a hand on his chest, where she begins to play with the curly blond hairs. "Yes, that would be nice. Let's do that. Soon."

"Next weekend?"

"All right." David smiles; hers comes grudgingly.

In the morning Maria sets about reviewing the leaflets she's been distributing at the Williamsford Mall during Right-to-Life Week. "The Choice to Murder?", "Responsibility—God's and Yours," and "Life Begins at Conception" are topics that are all too familiar to her by now. And yet they haven't worked to convince Jessie of the error of her impending choice. Perhaps, Maria considers, it's her approach that's been wrong...

She prays again this morning—holding her head in her hands, leaning from the couch over the coffee-table strewn with leaflets and flyers. But she is not given any revelation of new strategy in this

particular crusade. She emerges from her spiritual struggle only the
more resolved to stick with it, to the end.

The phone rings. It is Jessie. Maria's heart pounds and her voice
quavers as she listens and responds to Jessie's request. Jessie wants her
to come over to talk about the baby.

Maria's hopes are high as she flies out the door and practically
runs the three blocks to Jessie's house, an old homestead cabin standing alone on a large field at the edge of the woods. As she slows to
catch her breath approaching the house, Maria readies herself one
more time, knowing that this is the time for action, for true good
works.

ii

The sun breaks over the mountain, and Jessie's eyelids flicker
open. Her first thought is the same as the last one of the night before.
The time is now; and so she begins to try to explain, in silent, inner
speech.

When it is over she sobs softly, back into a light and dreamful
sleep. When she awakes again she is still certain of her choice, and she
phones Maria before her mind changes. Then she crawls back into
bed, and closes her eyes.

Shortly there is a soft knock on the cabin door. Jessie doesn't respond. The door opens a little and Maria peeks in, hesitates, then
enters and quietly closes the door. She stands for a moment in the
kitchen space, surrounded by plywood counter, wood-burning cook-
stove, open shelves stocked with jars of grains, beans, seeds, teas.
Along the wall toward Jessie's bed are bookshelves holding paperbacks, magazines and files—worn but neat. A cabinet of rough lumber
and bricks, holding a stereo system, records and tapes. There is a
black phone sitting on a speaker. On the wall, a solidarity poster, a
Guatemalan woman and child. In the center of the room are arranged
a tattered old couch, a small low table, a rocking chair, a simple rug.

Maria walks softly across the room and settles into the rocking
chair. Her hands rest on her rounding belly. She, too, is pregnant, a
month behind Jessie.

Jessie is ready to open her eyes again.

Maria smiles gracefully. "Morning, Jess. Been sleeping well?"

"Yeah, not too bad...but oh, I can't get away from this strange
dream I had, just this morning. I saw...my baby. He was a full grown

person. I just passed him on the street. We recognized each other suddenly. He turned around again. It was the eyes. I looked at his eyes, and he told me, without even speaking, that everything would be all right. That he was all right, even though I'd, I'd..."

Jessie starts to cry. Maria goes to sit beside her and comfort her, with arm and hands around Jessie's shoulders. She cradles her with a firm hug. Finally, Jessie takes a deep breath. She sits upright, adjusting her nightgown. She looks at Maria sharply.

"You've come to try to talk me out of it again."

"Look, Jessie—"

"Haven't you?"

"You said you wanted to talk about it."

"Maria, do you really want to know what it comes down to?"

Maria is attentive but says nothing.

"Gerry. His not being here. To care for me, for the child. I don't want to do this whole trip alone, Maria; it's just not my life, what I want it to be."

"What do you want it to be?"

Jessie reflects a moment. "Well, it might have been, with Gerry...No, I'm gonna stop crying over that spilt milk. I guess it's partly the things I'm involved in, like, you know, the refugee committee, the pesticide action group...not to mention trying to make a living somehow."

"So are you morally opposed to welfare?"

"Oh, I don't know. Not on political grounds or anything. I just don't want to feel—useless."

"Useless? Caring for a new human life?"

Jessie is silent. Then—"I would have been ready to. If he had. But it's different now."

"Did Gerry love you?"

"Oh, I thought he did. I thought I'd finally found someone who could accept my faults, my imperfect beauty, my stubbornness, my tendency to doubt and cry too much, my...self. But I was wrong."

"Or maybe he did love you, but he decided that he just couldn't handle such a change in his life, as it would mean to have a baby."

"That could be. In fact that's exactly what he told me. Except that's not what I call love. At least he didn't put any blame on me. Just said he hadn't settled on a career yet, wasn't sure where he was going with the Forest Service, you know, or if he'd be staying in this area the rest of his life."

"Did he want to stay?"

"Oh, who knows. Let's forget about him."

Jessie brings her legs out from under the covers, brushes them past Maria to stand up. Maria stands and moves out of the way. Jessie runs a hand through tousled, strawberry-blonde hair cut shoulder length in back, shorter on top. Maria's hair is dark, well-shaped in a neat, wavy bob; she's wearing a navy polyester skirt to her knees, black flat-heeled shoes, a plain white blouse and yellow sweater with buttons open. Jessie feels the contrast in her rumpled nightgown, bare feet and unkempt hair. She looks at Maria's belly, down at her own, fights back a sudden, momentary spasm of tears and strides to the kitchen counter.

"You want some coffee?" she manages to ask.

"Sure, I'll have some. Do you want me to—"

"You're drinking decaf now, right?"

Maria decides to let Jessie continue the task she's started with such sudden energy. She remains where she is and answers, "Doctor's orders. Doesn't want an express train coming out, he says."

Jessie laughs now, the heartache passed. She rummages for the coffee jar while Maria goes to the couch. "Oh, there it is. Guess I'll have some of this low-octane stuff, too. I'll do yoga to wake up."

She picks out the can, puts some coffee in a filter and starts water heating in an electric kettle. Then she continues puttering, putting things away, tidying up.

"You know," she continues, "after Gerry left I didn't know what to do with myself. So I just cleaned this place spic and span. Dusted, scrubbed, I even put all these jars and stuff in alphabetical order, if you can believe it. Now they're all mixed up again. I never know where anything is."

Jessie tosses down the dishrag and steps into the space in front of the couch. She raises both hands, palms together above her head, looks straight up, takes a deep breath, then bends slowly down at the waist. As she does this she asks, "Do you believe in hell, Maria?" Her hands touch the floor.

Maria says, "I thought you'd never ask." She utters a nervous laugh. "The question every Catholic studies for. But you know, it's not like in Sunday school. The big red devil, and hot coals. It's inside, when you sin and can't get it out, and it burns and burns. That's all, really."

Jessie is slowly returning to an upright position. "'Can't get it out': How do you get rid of sin, then?" She brings one foot up to rest on the other knee, and extends her arms out and slightly up.

"Well, the Protestants believe you're stuck with it. But we believe that confession to a priest cleanses the soul, and atones for sins by repentance—and by the grace of God, through Christ's sacrifice."

Jessie switches feet. "Hmm. And that makes things all right again, does it?"

"Yes, but that doesn't mean you have a license to...commit sin, knowing it will be forgiven."

Jessie loses her balance. "Are we getting personal now, Maria?" She bends down, arms still extended, legs now spread, to touch alternate toes.

"Jessie, do you think that's really good for the baby? I mean—" but she's cut short as Jessie stands and glares at her blackly. Then she continues, "It does apply, if you're wondering about abortion. Mortal sin is not a matter to check off on a ledger because you say so many Hail-Mary's."

Jessie wraps one leg around the other, and one arm around the other. "But I wonder," she says, "if I later regretted it—or what about if I feel bad about doing something in the first place, but go ahead with it because—because it's for the best, because...it's what I have to do— oh, there's the kettle."

Jessie untangles herself and goes over to pour the water.

"So then," she says, "am I forgiven?"

"No!" exclaims Maria. "I mean, I don't know. I'm not the judge. God is."

"But you already called it a mortal sin."

Jessie brings over two coffee cups, hands one to Maria and sits next to her.

"That's true," Maria says, a little uncertainly. "The Church... well, you know it's wrong; that's why you feel bad about it. That's what counts. And it's not the regret, or even the act of confession afterwards, that makes it better. Nothing will bring the baby's life back. It's your soul at stake. The torment you'll suffer, inside yourself."

"Like now, if you want to know the truth."

Jessie sips at her coffee, burning her mouth. She puts the cup down on the table.

"Exactly," Maria continues, "because of what you're intending to do. It's the attitude of sin, not the sin itself."

"I know what you're trying to telling me, Maria, without the theological fine points on the head on the needle. I know it inside."

She sticks a finger at her own rounded belly. "But it's my life I've got to live. It's not quite the same as your life, you know."

Maria has been silently looking at Jessie and down at her feet. Now she looks up and responds: "Hey, Jess, I don't want to lose a friend over this. And I'm not trying to convert you or anything. I just want to make sure you won't do anything you'll regret; that's all. For your own sake, too, not just the child's. Because who knows, years from now your life may change and be quite different from what it is now..."

"But it's now that I've got to live my life; it's as it is now that I have to cope with it. It's now that I need to decide what to do with this baby, and if I decided to keep it I'd have to live with it from now on."

"And from now on, as well, if you decide not to keep it."

"I know it, goddammit. You keep your own child: that's for you to decide. Mine, that's for me to decide." Jessie turns abruptly away from Maria and looks over toward the bed. Then she breaks down— "Oh, Maria..." She puts an arm around Maria's shoulders and begins to cry. "If you'd just give me some credit for my own attempt to deal with this—like you did when I first got involved with that crummy man..."

"Okay, and this time I won't even tell you I told you so."

They look at one another testily; then Jessie is overcome by a little laughter. Spontaneously, they hug each other, lingering with it for a few moments. The heavy atmosphere has cleared.

Maria picks up her coffee cup, takes a sip and says brightly, "It's amazing how it works. My best friend, planning on doing something that's most against my principles, yet still she's my best friend."

Jessie smiles and responds, "I value that, Maria, I really do. And I do understand your position."

"My position...And when it's done, then, you can cry on my shoulder."

Jessie begins to cry again, stifles it. "Oh, boy, you really—"

"I mean it, Jessie. I wasn't being sarcastic. I won't moralize, when it's over and done with. It'll be too late."

"Maria, please!"

"I'm sorry, Jessie. I'm not really meaning it like it sounds to you. Maybe I'd better just go now." She puts her cup down and stands up. "Just remember through it all that somebody does care for you. I do."

Jessie remains seated, with hands folded on her lap. "Thanks, Maria. I'll try."

Then, as Maria is almost gone through the door, Jessie runs to catch it before it closes: "Maria—"
"Yes?"
"I almost forgot. The reason I called—"
"Yes?"
"What you said about best friends, and leaning on you—"
"Yes, anything, Jessie."
"Even if I decided to go through with it?"
"I would still love you."
"Could you—then could you take me to the clinic?"

iii

Maria stared at the spot of dried blood glaring up at her from between her legs on the seat of the Bronco. Was it Jessie's blood, or the dead baby's? Was the abortion a lesser sin if considered a form of suicide, self-mutilation? Was she, Maria, then less culpable as an accomplice? David glanced at her; his jaw twitched. Her face was still beautiful, though it had become, in the past couple of weeks, as pious and impassive as the Holy Virgin's. He swung his gaze back, his strong features that were marked with new lines, to his own side window, and to the rough road ahead.

Nearly a week since the abortion, and still Maria's thoughts were not free of it. She and Jessie had not spoken to one another since. Maria saw nothing out the window, when she deigned to raise her head that far, but wild waste, slash and grotesque rock.

David finally asked if Maria really wanted to be going to the ridge, if there was somewhere else she'd rather go, or something else that he could do for her, that would make her feel better. She managed a faint trace of a smile for appreciation's sake, and even looked at his eyes for a moment, but said no, this was fine. There was nowhere else to go, nothing else he could do—but this she didn't bother to say. He knew it anyway.

They passed the brown Forestry sign that read

BRUSH CONTROL AREA

with facts and figures in smaller print giving details of
the herbicide treatments planned. The year-old sign was merely a
landmark to them, signifying that they were close to their destination.

The last two kilometers of road wound along the top of the ridge, ending in a wide spot clear enough for a turnaround. David wheeled the Bronco around in a cloud of dust which settled on the collection of tire tracks. He got out and looked around, breathing deeply. The sky was a brilliant blue; a bright sun highlighted the distant white peaks which surrounded Lightning Ridge.

David walked around to the passenger side where Maria still sat, staring ahead. He opened her door for her and took her limp hand. A faint smile graced her lips. Maria stepped down onto the road with David, and they walked along the path that the road became at the end of the turnaround. David put his arm around Maria's waist; she followed suit. They looked at each other, walking quietly together. David's expression softened and a glimmer of light came into Maria's eyes.

As the clear path gradually dwindled, they chose their own path through the green brush. Where they eventually came to a space growing with soft wild grass, they kneeled. On their knees they faced each other, embraced, and kissed passionately. Maria's heart was with David now, and they both gave way to the overwhelming desire to make love, then and there, on God's earth.

The soft sound of the wind and their breathing was broken by the chattering of a helicopter that came up along the side of the ridge and then up, around and straight overhead. David and Maria, joined as one, looked up painfully and saw a broad swath of whitish mist drawn behind it—like a bridal train, thought Maria. David was not so free and easy with his imagination, but indignant, in fact outraged, as he realized what was happening. He lurched to his feet and stood with his fist in the air shouting, screaming at the departing chopper still chattering like death's teeth. And as he stood there, as she lay looking up, with her legs spread below the gentle mound of her belly, the white mist settled down upon them.

David got them moving fast—stumbling into their pants and running back to the road, hand in hand. In the ten minutes that it took to return to the Bronco, they both had succumbed to paroxysms of coughing. Maria vomited, just before getting into her seat. David was almost too dizzy to drive, but managed somehow to make it back down the twisting, rutted road to the highway, and back home without further mishap. Maria felt her skin tingling all over, but especially from the waist down, where she'd been exposed.

All this time they had not spoken. They got out of the Bronco, walked up the driveway and into the house, and stood there in the dimly lit entryway, still silent. They didn't know what to do. Finally Maria offered that maybe they should see a doctor. David agreed, but said that he was now too dizzy to drive any more, and that she'd have to take the wheel.

They covered the forty-odd kilometers to the Williamsford Regional Hospital in normal time. But to Maria it was an eternity, haunted as she was by looming visions of Lightning Ridge and the adjoining valley shrouded in fog and swirling mists: the shapes of her anxieties for David, and for her own nameless wounds. The valley she saw had an unfathomable depth. Her thoughts and feelings sank there, becoming shrouded in mystery, of unknown character or dimension.

They waited three hours to be seen in the emergency room, for the doctor on duty there had to sew up an ear that had been nearly torn off in a soccer match. And an old woman with an arm in a sling said her arm hurt and needed attending to. When finally their time came, David and Maria were interviewed and treated in short order. The doctor gave David a prescription for headache pills and told him to rest for a few days, until the dizziness went away. He gave Maria some ointment for her burning skin and told her that she, too, would improve in a couple of days. If not, they should check back with their regular doctor.

On the ride back home, David and Maria both said they seemed to be feeling a bit better, after all.

Indeed, by Tuesday David was nearly feeling like his old self again and ready to go back to work. And Maria's skin no longer tingled. But the fog lifted in the valley beside the ridge, and what she saw there filled her with horror and dread.

In the dream Maria had that night, the valley had no bottom. It was just blackness. She longed for the comfort of the fog again, or even the white mist to cover the blackness. But there was no covering that hideous void now, now that she'd seen it. And the last thing she saw before she woke up was worse, far worse: the valley filling with blood.

She screamed at the vision, and then was confronted with the reality: globs of blood and shapeless tissue had begun passing from her womb. Overhead, outside the skylight in the early dawn, rode the sickle of a waning moon.

iv

The darkest night in July has passed, giving way to a gray, blustery day. Maria lies in her bed looking up through the skylight, alone for the first time in her five years with David. She hasn't slept all night, worrying about him in the hospital with a sudden relapse after a week of apparent recovery. And then there's the feeling sorry for herself. It's too late, she's been trying to tell herself, to feel sorry for the baby.

She gets up slowly and phones the hospital, to find out how David's doing. They tell her he's still sleeping; his condition is slightly improved. She says she'll call again later.

Then, Maria knows, it's time to see Jessie again.

When she arrives at Jessie's house, it is with the hope of renewing this friendship that has been wounded by death and stretched by separate griefs. The grief is also, to be sure, a shared one—and it is in the spirit of commiseration that Jessie greets Maria at the door with a hug that is at first tentative, then quickly warm and deeply felt.

They pull away enough to smile, sadly, face-to-face.

Jessie ventures, "How are you feeling, Maria? I heard what happened."

Tears well suddenly in Maria's eyes. "Oh, I'll get over it...I hope."

Jessie pulls her closer again, but Maria resists, wanting to retreat a bit, to regain her own strength. Their smiles are gone so quickly.

Jessie drops her arms and asks, "And David. Is he all right?"

"They said he's improving, when I called this morning. It still worries me, though, after he seemed to be getting better."

Jessie turns from the doorway even as Maria speaks, and leads them into the cabin. A television set sits on the coffee table in front of the couch.

Maria takes a seat on one side of the couch.

"Does this make it easier?" she says, gesturing toward the television.

"Yes, if you can believe it; trash that it is. There's nothing else to do."

"But what about all your committees, your—"

"Right. And after all that, look what they go and do to you. To you and David. And...to your baby."

Maria listens in stunned silence. Jessie slumps into the armchair next to the couch, facing her. After a moment Maria says, "Jessie, do you still resent me for trying to talk you out of the abortion?"

"Well...no, it's not resentment." Maria waits for more of a response. She knows Jessie well enough to expect the whole truth sooner or later. Jessie obliges her:

"But goddammit was I mad at you, after it happened, after I went through with it and it was too late; I was mad at you for not talking me out of it! I guess I just wanted someone else to blame, is where that was coming from. But now you're going to ask me if I still regret doing it, and I don't. I still feel like it had to be done, for my life where it's at now and for that kid's sake, agree with me or not."

Maria is silent, absorbing the impact of Jessie's outburst. Then she says her piece. "I couldn't even talk to you afterward, after I drove you home from the hospital. When you were in there, and I was waiting, it was as if you had become, I don't know how to say it, but something less than human."

"That's funny, because that's what your pro-life leaflet accused me of thinking about my—my fetus."

"I know! I know! That occurred to me after a while. But I still didn't know how I could, could..."

"Relate to me."

"That's right. And then, all the rest...happened to me."

"It's just terrible, Maria." Jessie leans over to put her arm around Maria's shoulders. "It wasn't your choice. That's the worst part."

Maria falls silent, staring ahead at the floor, her hands together between her knees. Then tears begin to fill her eyes. "Oh, Jessie, we so wanted this child!" She turns to Jessie and clings to her, crying.

Jessie holds her, offering what comfort she can. Finally, she ventures to ask, "Maria, have you confronted Forestry yet, with what they did to you?"

"David went in and yelled at them, the next day. But they just said it was posted. With those big brown signs, that have been there for a year."

"But what about now that you've had a miscarriage?"

"Oh, we already talked about it, with the doctor. He said nothing could be proven. One case like this is no evidence at all. We're 'within the range of normal miscarriages for the population,' he said—or something like that. It's hopeless."

Still Jessie persists. "But couldn't you go to Forestry yourself and show them, firsthand, the effect of their policy?"

Maria is silent for a moment; then she turns on Jessie. "Do you know what that would be like?" She jumps up from her chair, still confronting Jessie. Jessie uncrosses her legs and backs away slightly. "It would be like you showing up on Gerry's new doorstep, wherever that might be, with your aborted baby" (she cradles her arms) "saying, 'Will you make it up to me, Gerry? Will you come back?'"

"Oh, Maria!" Jessie screams, turning her head away.

Maria drops her arms. "I'm sorry, Jessie, I shouldn't have said that to you."

Jessie purses her lips, fighting back tears. Then she blurts out— "I'd never want that bastard back. I've got my own life to live, now, without thinking about him any more."

Maria sits back down only partially, leaning on the arm of the rocker. "Interesting, isn't it, that Gerry works for Forestry. Is he involved in their spray program at all?"

"Yeah, he is. His department, anyway—silviculture. But let's just forget about him."

"All right..."

"But you, I don't want to forget about. Listen, I can see how you might not feel like knocking your head against a brick wall with Forestry. But how about just talking to a few people around here, about what happened to you? I bet we'd get a lot more support to stop those chemicals once and for all."

Maria sits still, biting her lip. "I don't know, Jessie. What do you mean, like speaking at public meetings, going door-to-door, or what? I don't think I'd be up to that sort of thing. Not about my...baby." She fights back small tears.

Jessie takes Maria's hand. "No, no," she says, "just people you know, at your church, maybe, or the prenatal group you were in. I'll help organize it if you want. You just have to be yourself—especially to let other mothers know, so their babies can have...oh, Maria—"

"Yes—say it: the right to life."

v

Maria closes her eyes. She can still feel the warmth of her hand clasped between Jessie's hands. She sees the ridge again, with sparse patches of cloud drifting around its base. Below is an immense valley, partially obscured by clouds. But farther below, on the valley floor, can be seen farms, roads, houses. The broad mountain that is Lightning Ridge now hovers as solidly as her faith, her love, her renewed sense of commitment. Above, just rising from the edge of the neighboring peaks, comes the first shining crescent of the new moon.

Nowick Gray has contributed fiction, non-fiction and poetry to a variety of periodicals. Born in Baltimore in 1950, he now lives in a small mountain community in British Columbia. Besides writing, Nowick works at homesteading, treeplanting and nonviolence education.

Feed Us

Wayne Allen Sallee

Mothers Yes! Murders, Wrong!"
The pro-lifers chanted outside the South Michigan Avenue clinic.
The doctor inside the clinic, inside one of the sterile, antiseptic rooms,
prodded carefully. The instrument he used had three prongs; gang
members were using them in the projects to castrate cop snitches. He
was using the silver instrument to poke inside a sixteen-year-old girl's
vaginal wall.

The instrument grabbed hold; the doctor gently tugged. He
thought of wadded padding in his nose, after an operation for a deviat-
ed septum years before, the image always staying with him. He told the
girl she would be taken care of. Karl if it was a boy, Sherry if it was
a girl, she had said, before breaking down in tears.

He dropped the aborted fetus into the tank at the end of the room,
wondering if the girl would be sprayed with paint by the crowd outside.
There were many others on the bottom.

An aborted fetus for every one-shot murder or serial kill, the
doctor thought. Time to dial the madhouse; he kept his thoughts this
way.

The next patient walked in, and he assured her also.

* * *

The last thing Cordell Tarves remembered before the darkness
was being given a lethal injection in the south wing of Stateville Prison
in Joliet, Illinois. The first day of summer, it had been, and he was
only the second man to be put to death, out of the 240-plus on Death
Row in the state's three correctional centers. Guys like John Wayne
Gacy were always gaining their appeals, but luck was against him, and
he was allowed his last meal of steak and eggs and introduced to what
Joliet prisoners knew as The Black Needle.

All he had done was killed some prostitutes. What the hell, they didn't care who *they* fucked; what was wrong with what he had done? Then it was the ebony, the complete and total blackness. Darker than a moonless night downstate, more imposing than the closet his daddy had locked him in the time he had put the rabbit in the weed-mulcher, thinking it was a wheelbarrow. Wanting to take it for a ride.

Blackness. He felt as if he was falling, yet floating; balancing on invisible ribbons; a tightrope comprehended only in mind. Tarves tried to lift his hands to his face; to blink, to fart, he even tried that. Nothing worked the way it should. Had something happened with the sodium pentothal and pancuronium bromide? Was he in a coma? Paralyzed with his eyes shut? But, no. He'd see gray patterns on the insides of his eyelids.

This was like being jacked on Moxodram. Tarves knew *that* feeling. He was moxed out when two cops from the Albany Park district shot him three times when they'd caught him in the act under the Wilson elevated. Lost three pints of blood and didn't feel a thing.

He stopped thinking for a moment, hearing something in the darkness. A pulsing in his ears.

Feed us. Feed us. Feed us.

Then he heard what he thought to be a scream. He couldn't tell because he didn't think anything human could ever make a sound like what he was hearing. Not even the prostitutes who weren't drunk or high when he pulled out the piano wire and sliced and sliced.

The scream faded, replaced by other murmurings. Coming from nowhere yet everywhere; faint at first, like when you doze on the bus and hear a conversation several rows back, then right on top of him; the buzzing of a million angry bees.

MOTHERLESS CURBS ALONG.

Motherless. Curbs along.

Motherless. Curbs along.

That, too, faded. Now Tarves could not even hear his heart thumping, as it had been while he was waiting for the final shot—potassium chloride—which would stop his red beating thing forever. He floated, that much he was aware of. And he was *in* the blackness, not just seeing darkness around him. He couldn't explain it, he just knew it. And it was cold.

"I sense thought."

Hearing the voice beside him, yet seeing nothing, Tarves let out an involuntary gasp.

"Is someone there? Please tell me someone's there? I didn't mean to kill her, it was all in fun. Please!" High-strung, panicky.

Tarves now realized that he could see various shades of gray floating at different levels around him, his eyes adjusting as if in a closed room

(the closet)

and then he saw that the gray were actually pulses of light. The unseen voice again came nearer.

"Please." Whining, like a whipped pup. Like the last prostitute, the one the newspapers said was really a banker's wife who had been walking to a dinner engagement.

As he adjusted to the blobs of light, he remembered more than the immediate past of his execution. Tarves thought of the *Star Trek* rerun he had watched in the Motel Tangiers the night before he had been caught, three years ago. Captain Kirk fucking some green gash.

"Hey, last one got this close, he gave me a carton of cigarettes." Trying to keep his cool. The black swirled into gray next to him, and he had this crazy thought that he was the thing lighting the area, that he was like those other blots of light.

That he was hallucinating.

He turned towards the voice. "Would you mind telling me what the purple piss is going on?" The gray flared white around him.

A blue glow appeared next to him. "Don't be angry," it said. "You're white and that means you're angry. I'm blue because I'm afraid, see?"

"The fuck..."

"I don't know how long I've been here," the blue light flickered. "I was having sex with my girl and accidentally strangled her, but she wanted it. She read a book on auto-eroticism."

Tarves didn't understand the meaning of the phrase, but he knew what strangling meant.

"I killed myself by overdosing on sleeping pills. Her sleeping pills. No one here will talk to me, they think I'm a coward."

No shit, Tarves thought, moving away. Floating away. He was in a coma, had to be. Floating away, the voice becoming distant, imploring. "My name is Calvin Sain and I live on North Winchester..."

Like he cared.

He could not tell how far or for how long he floated. Eventually he found more lights. All different colors: red, violet, the colors of the prostitutes' souls; green and brown, the colors of the prosecution's envy. One of the lights floated towards him.

"I figured you'd show up sooner of later since Gein was dragged off," it said. Tarves sensed it, really, thinking it was more of that science fiction shit his subconscious was making him dream about.

"What is this place?" Tarves asked his new companion. Adjusting further to his surroundings, he saw that, in addition to the lights, there were other things. Shapeless masses like bloodied rubbers. Some stuck to each other.

Others looked as if they had been used, discarded, and run over in the street; shapes like homeless men curled under restaurant steam vents along the Gold Coast in winter.

The light in front of Tarves flashed orange and red in small bursts. "First, tell me who you are...were."

That last part was lost on Tarves, his mind spinning, he explained everything leading up to June 23, 1992. The date of his execution. But his memory spotted in places. He could remember the fact that his second victim, back in '82 in a field near Grayslake, had huge nipples like the ends of water balloons; the slow drip of the IV as he lay on a white table in front of twenty-three people a decade later. But he couldn't remember the jailer's eyes, or his mother's name.

The orange light had said something.

"What?" Tarves reeled himself back in, concentrating the way only loners could.

"I said, 'it figures'." Some of the other lights moved closer.

"What does?"

"Why, your being executed, of course." The orange light blinked as if with surprise.

"Don't talk shit with me, man," Tarves shouted, the sound not nearly what he wanted it to be. "I'll take you out, man,"

"Oh? And how is that?" The orange light remained like a strong candle flame. "Let me back up; I'm not trying to rile you. I just didn't think you to be that stupid. It's really very simple. You *are* indeed dead."

"Dead," Tarves said flatly. "So then, this is Hell, right? Well, it don't seem so bad to me. Unless I somehows made it into Heaven..." There was always the consideration.

The orange light flickered again as it spoke. Tarves felt as if the other lights were listening, also.

"See how the others listen," the orange light boasted. "I'm the real important one here. I got the stones."

"Yeah?"

"Yeah. I used to be a guy named Starkweather."

"You mean we're all—"

"That's a positive." The light revolved towards the others, identifying them. "Unruh, Hickock and Smith, Albert DeSalvo—he said they called him The Boston Strangler and he got a hard-on seven times a day; my *ass*—Dennis Cassady, Christopher Wilder, Ted Bundy, Jack Dolenz and Reagan Andriot."

Tarves was hip enough to see that Starkweather was doing the introductions chronologically.

"But this ain't Hell," Starkweather corrected. "It's a kind of purgatory, I don't know." The light wavered. "You don't stay here long."

"This Gein guy, I know that Hitchcock made a movie based on him—"

"'Fore I got caught, there was a book out called PSYCHO, by Robert Bloch. You know that?"

Tarves didn't.

"You want to know where he went?"

"Yeah, I do."

"You happen to recall any wailin' when you first showed up here? I suspicion you do."

Tarves could only vaguely remember now.

"Aw, man. Shoot. See, when it's time for somebody new to show up, these demons kind of appear, drooling and slobbering. And they chant, 'feed us, feed us'."

Tarves did remember that much.

"Man, I tell you true, you shoulda been here when they done came for Hitler." The light vibrated in different hues of orange and red. "They done chased that Nazi fuck and dragged him kicking and screaming away. You could *feel* it in your mind, real weird-like."

Tarves felt colder than before. Maybe this wasn't such a great place, after all.

"See that dude over there," the orange light floated to the right and swiveled again. "Well, he's next to go, then maybe me. But Unruh's still here, and all his killing was done in Camden, New Jersey, back in '46. He forgot when he died, though."

"Yeah, what about him?"

"Guy won't ever tell us his name. Killed some girls named Grimes in the late 50s. Chicago, 1956, I reckon it might be. I remember it never bein' solved, and here he don't say his name or nothin'. Up and died of cancer, ended up down here. Girls were found frozen in the woods, young nipples like pepperonis. Disappeared after seein' an Elvis Presley movie. That dude still alive when you were? I never believe what Bundy tells me."

Tarves couldn't answer, his thoughts swimming. Like those shapes like discarded condoms...

"What about those?"

"The really pathetic ones show up looking like that; that one near the bottom you might know. The ones who kill when they're drunk or some shit. All of us lights here did it because we had what you call the urge." The light wavered. "Although Bundy keeps saying it was these magazines with dirty pictures in them."

"The one on the bottom there, you think I know him?"

"Yeah. That one's Richard Speck."

Made sense. When Speck killed those nurses in 1966, no one could find a true motive, though some said he was venting his anger on his ex-wife. When he died in December of 1991, he was a bloated piece of sausage. All the newspapers still showed 1967 photos of him, looking like a pock-marked James Dean, though.

"They never seem to come to life," the orange light explained. "They just sink lower and lower, the demons never come for 'em."

Tarves was starting to feel like the rabbit in his father's garage, so many years ago.

"I don't even know why some of them show up here, like that light over there. Tibbets is a hero; he shouldn't be down here, no way, nohows."

"Who's Tibbets?" Tarves thought he knew most of the serial killers, had in fact read many books about his peers in jail.

"Shit, you are dumb! That man Tibbets was the pilot of the *Enola Gay*. Dropped the A-tomic bomb on those Japs and ended the fucking war, what he did!"

"Then there should still be a hell of a lot of lights down here," Tarves said. "I went through a thing they called Viet Nam"

"Yeah," Starkweather said. "Maybe he'll get to Heaven sooner or later, get hisself congratulated after doin' his time."

There was noise.

"He—wait. Listen." The orange light looked frozen. "There's another one coming."

"How can you tell?" Tarves wanted to know.

Then he heard the chant.

Motherless curbs along motherless curbs along.

MOTHERLESS CURBS ALONG—

"You know what they're sayin'?" Starkweather asked suddenly.

"What?"

"Now, I heard this from that light over there that used to be Reagan Andriot, he killed people all over the U.S. of A. I tend to believe him more than Bundy. Least, Andriot admits that he killed people for the fun of it, not blaming it on stroke books like Teddy there."

Floating, drifting. Starkweather's voice hypnotic. Tarves easily understood how Carol Fugate could have hooked up with him. He wondered if any of these newcomers had told him that she was out of jail now.

"Andriot told me how they have these things called A-bortion clinics," Starkweather said it just like A-tomic bomb, "and a gal could go in one of these things and have the little tyke yanked right out of her. 'Course, I suspicion you have to do it right away, or it's a no go."

Tarves remembered the Wichita bombings of the clinics, of pictures in the Tribune. Placards that read MOTHERS YES! MURDERS WRONG! He then understood what the chanting meant, and of what his fate was.

"What did you do, anyways? To your victims, I mean."

"I sliced off the breasts of women with piano wire, cut a big lump of meat off, then fucked the wound. Strangled the women and got off on it." Tarves said it proud, trying to forget where they really were.

"Maybe that's why we're here like this, as punishment. No one can figure out what to do with us evil ones."

"But Tibbets ain't evil," Tarves argued. "Or that guy I met when I first showed up."

"Like I said," Starkweather replied coolly, "it ain't cut and dried. Andriot told me arguing abortion and this right-to-life thing was like arguing politics or sports teams."

He supposed Starkweather was right.

"Here they come, look now."

A distance away, a broken yellow light who had once been Cordell Tarves watched in mute terror as two unnameable things shambled from within the darkness. Their height was unimaginable; even crouched in a crawling position, their filthy knuckles making hard sounds on an unseen floor, they were taller than Tarves had once been. Their mouths moved in long-forgotten syllables, flies with rotted wings drifted out on their hot breath. Maggots the size of light bulbs fell from the demons' armpits and crotches. They glowed briefly, then were gone.

The stench was worse than anything, worse than the smell of his blood as he bit his tongue back there on the white table with twenty-three strangers watching, the rabbit's blood as it's leg was caught in the mulcher and pulled apart like a fried chicken leg, the smell of the corpse in the field near Grayslake, as he was able to fuck it for three days straight before it was discovered.

And as the lumbering demons slouched back within the swirling blackness, dragging the pleading nameless killer of those two Chicago girls along with them, Tarves realized that something that was once human could indeed make such a horrid sound. Like the one he was hearing now.

* * *

The last thing Jackson Bellens remembered before the darkness was the Fallon Ridge cop shooting him in the Severed Seven Lounge along the sin strip, minutes after himself shooting three people because White Sox security had thrown him out of Comiskey Park.

He heard chanting, off in the distance. Then he heard a scream.

Wayne Allen Sallee. What can you say about him other than the fact that he writes dark horror fiction well enough to be included in the **Year's Best Horror Fiction** *anthology (DAW Books) each year since 1986. Should I mention that he just published his first novel? (***The Holy Terror***, Mark V. Ziesing.) Or that he's hard at work on his second novel,* **Cult of Freaks**? *Or that he was a publicist for a pre-bloat Elvis Impersonator? It's probably necessary to mention that he's had fiction published—and anthologized—in a wide range of magazines and books. It's also necessary to point out that the heinous crimes mentioned in the story above are taken from real life, Mr. Sallee says. The one thing I don't think it's necessary to mention is that he was— well, I don't think it's necessary to mention it, so I won't.*

Ask Dr. Schund

Alan M. Schwartz

Dr. Schund, what essential economic keystones are derived from babies?

The baby byproduct and reclamation industry is the major industrial bulwark of a failing American economy. The frenzied carnal proclivities of our teeming lowest classes have always assured a bountiful supply of easily harvested, attractively priced raw material. Reproductive warriors smuggled past our southern border have been successful beyond expectation, requiring the constant culling of their fetal hordes. Traditional religious proscriptions of rational behavior guarantee an unending abundance of unwanted pregnancies. It is now up to the enlightened American businessmen to transform these bulging bellies into bulging bank accounts.

These, then, are the foundations of the baby byproduct and reclamation industry:

UMBILICAL CORD. Human fibroblast cell culture lines are currently an important resource for non-animal toxicity testing, the environmentalist bunny buggers and fish kissers having put sewer rats off limits to medical researchers. Because unaltered human cells will only divide a finite number of times, a continuing supply of maximally juvenile living cells must be available in bulk, and be free of the moral and ethical considerations of human donor disassembly. Human umbilical cords are ideal sources of the necessary tissue, and are sufficiently lacking in visual esthetics to assure that even the craziest pressure groups will not protest their disposal.

PLACENTA. Human placentas are an important source of pathogen-free human collagen and hyaluronic acid for use in reconstructive surgery, and as an ingredient in the finest, or at least the most expensive cosmetics. These materials also form an important biochemical resource for the academic and industrial researchers who are otherwise forbidden from obtaining human tissue by law, by culture, by religion, by ethics, and by the almost universal embalming of otherwise suitable donors. Human placentas are ideal. A walk through any supermarket will underscore the importance of placentas in human nutrition—look at all the different flavors of "Placenta Helper!"

MECONIUM. Ambergris is the scent fixative employed in the almost finest perfumes of the world. It is a digestive residue of giant squid cartilage found in sperm whales and regurgitated into tropical seas, worth many times its weight in fine gold. A secret of the royal French perfumery, known nowhere else in the world and disclosed here at the genuine risk of Dr. Schund's life, meconium is the fixative of the truly finest French perfumes. A disruption of the minute supply of Tibetan meconium from the highest Himalayan elevations during the 1790s precipitated the French revolution. The entire male cohort of the French royal house, hopelessly addicted to meconium-based perfumes worn by unscrupulous ladies of the Court, were rendered impotent within a fortnight. The House of Bourbon fell within the month. A hidden last flask of Tibetan meconium perfume was recovered in 1814, its contents carefully husbanded and cherished until the last drop was consumed in 1830. Meconium-based hyper-aphrodisiacs are still covertly manufactured today, being secretly added at a tremendous expense to the inks used on Grateful Dead album covers.

BABY OIL. Olives will liberate their oil under pressure, or can be macerated and solvent extracted to yield a less expensive but inferior product. Term babies can be hydraulically stimulated to liberate a quintessentially refined saturated oil employed in the lubrication of suitably expensive prophylactic sheaths limited in use to the finest royal Arabian brothels. Successive pressings yield the lower grade oils accessed by wealthy international industrialists through a Hong Kong cartel. A final solvent extracted residue is black marketed at astounding costs. Supermarket or pharmacy baby oil contains by law at least 0.01% real baby oil, but rarely more.

BABY POWDER. The extracted, pulverized, deproteinated residue from baby oil production is a fine white calcareous powder. Given the most limited supply of this ultra-precious resource, only the most exulted and noble distaff armpits and crotches are privy to a gentle fluffing of divine dust. The single acceptable powder puff for this sanctified indulgence is manufactured of down plucked from the breast of a passenger pigeon. Hedonistic abuse of this scarce luxury by the most recent English king lead to the abdication of the throne, the alternative being a formal ceremonial regicide.

MEDICARE BILLINGS. Government entitlement disbursements provide an unrestrained flood of folding green into any hands willing to complete the paperwork. The health care industry has realized a hundred billion dollar cash cow loudly mooing to be milked. Incubators that would stand obsolescently idle can now be filled with crack babies—viable drug-deformed lumps of metabolizing tissue—at realized revenue rates of thousands of dollars each intensive treatment day. With malpractice suits an impossibility and Medicare reimbursements a certainty, any ramshackle slum clinic with access to a Catholic priest for teenage counseling and a clever CPA to blunt the attacks of the IRS can make its owners multi-millionaires. Isn't that what America is all about?

Just as the otherwise moribund economies of highland South American countries are sustained by billions of dollars from the cocaine trade, so the long-bankrupt U.S. economy has been given vital succor by the licit and illicit trade in baby byproducts with the royal houses of Arabia, Europe and England. Were the baby presses hidden in Federal buildings and especially on the thirteenth floor of all sky-scrapers to be stopped for even a month, the hollow shell of the American economic system would collapse upon itself like the rotten house of cards that it is. Baby byproducts are not merely an economic keystone, they are our economic lifeline as industrial America progressively withers.

This is possibly the most unusual story in this anthology. The author has this to say for himself: Dr. Alan M. Schwartz is a chemist who creates human-implantable prostheses. When the moon is full and the wolfbane blooms, he unfurls a truly loathsome sense of humor and proceeds to soil the pages of Mensa publications with an attitude slightly to the right of Vlad the Impaler—more than 100 times to date. His messes ferment in the Harvard Business Review, CHEMTECH, Devachan, and The Quarterly. He lives with a lovely lady, a psychotic cat, and a custom-hacked 80486/50 in Irvine, California.

Seventh Son of A Seventh Son

T. Diane Slatton

Victor scorned modern sciences that had turned the mysticism of producing a child into something abstract. Cold like mathematics. He crushed the battered hat in his hands as the too-young doctor pointed at a shadowy ultrasound printout; and his stomach knotted at amniocentesis results that proclaimed his ninth child would be a boy. Another big, robust, *hungry* goddamned boy.

Five years ago he'd have waltzed his wife from hospital to pickup truck at such news. Five years ago, she and the crops had bloomed with equal vigor. Strange how they both began fading about the same time. Selma's eyes grew dim and tired the year tomato bugs swarmed; streaks of gray shot through her hair when the corn came up half-stalks...

Only this arid season had Victor taken up her unspoken burden, allowing thunderclouds to darken his brain as if replacing ones that had not come to bless this land. Obsession thrust him out day after sun-cursed day, drove him from creek to parched seedlings, whispered "Ir-ri-gate, ir-ri-gate" with the thump in his aching skull.

Injury crashed atop insult only three weeks after he'd bent to the will of fate and taken a job in town. Victor jerked bolt upright from a nightmare, wild-eyed when it didn't vanish with the waking. Selma's retching noises from the adjoining bathroom were a tune he knew as well as the sounds of his children at play.

"Jesus!" He pushed both hands through his hair. "Not another one. Not now. Not another one, Lord-God-*please*..."

When Selma crept back to bed smelling of mouthwash and doom, Victor slid reluctant arms around her waist and caressed her midsection to ease his own dread.

"How do you feel?"

He silently cursed himself for not asking *her* that question. "Fair enough," he said, "kinda tired." *Kinda like blowing my brains out.*

"There's no need to worry, Victor. We'll be fine. We've always been fine before."

He pressed his chest to Selma's back and clenched his teeth to keep from screaming at her soothing voice.

"No question, this isn't the best time for another child..."

I don't want it.

"...but God keeps his own schedule, Victor. Sometimes we're given more than it appears we can handle, but..."

I want you to get RID OF IT.

"...it's just one bad season. When it's over you'll be glad—"

Victor's hands jerked, an involuntary spasm that dug his calloused fingers hard into stomach flesh beneath her flannel nightgown. Selma tore from his grip and rolled to face him, her eyes flashing like lasers in the dark.

"There's the baby's eye. See?"

Victor didn't see. He *didn't see.* Sliding forward on the chair, he squinted down at the smoked-glass desk—at the tornado funnel of an ultrasound picture there that threatened to suck him into the pit where his own father had been devoured.

"I let her talk me out of vasectomy," he muttered, "because Selma's Catholic. After four years this time with no fresh kids, we thought she was finished, you understand." He swallowed rising frustration, still searching for the little bastard's eye. "I love that woman. Never loved another. But Selma's looking real sick and—"

The freckled young obstetrician loudly cleared his throat. "I'm, um...not allowed to discuss termination options, sir."

Victor's head snapped up.

"Well...abortion, you know. That's what you're asking, isn't it?"

Victor blinked, feeling salvation catch fire in his brain. "The crops are bad off," he said hopefully. "I've got eight mouths to feed besides me and Selma. She's not strong anymore—Used to take an ax to wood with a passion that put the fear of God in most men, but...You see it, don't you? That's why I brought her up here to you folks. *Tell her* she's not strong enough for—"

"Sir, I simply *cannot* discuss—"

"Six boys, two girls at home. I'm working Kirby's Slaughterhouse and *stealing meat* to feed them all because my crops are so bad off! Selma's getting gray but she doesn't cotton to birth control because her saints and priests and that HOLY CHILDLESS BASTARD IN ROME—!" Victor dropped his hat, pushed both hands through his hair, drew a shuddering breath. "You're an only child. Right, son?"

"I have a—*one* sister, sir."

Victor stood and jabbed a finger at the shadowy picture of his wife's womb. "Seventh son. The straw that breaks his daddy's back...Raggedest hand-off clothes, last scraps of food on the table, love that's worn out and dried up by the time it's passed down to the littlest. Every shitty deal *I* got is waiting out there for *him*. Now you tell me one more time we can't talk abortion!"

When the doctor's eyes fell and he looked suddenly like a little boy close to tears, Victor snatched up his hat and walked out.

Sleeping curled tight against Selma's back, he dreamed of reaching into her uterus—hand smoothly swimming the path his sperm had traveled four thousand times or more. Memory taunted him with the voice of a seventeen year-old boy whose blinding desire churned to melt the big-boned woman beneath him.

"Please get pregnant," the boy whispered. "They'll *have* to let you marry me if you have my baby."

In answer, she wrapped strong legs around his back and his roar of triumph spun through the cornfield until shattering in the starless sky.

Martin, their first son, arrived four days past Victor's eighteenth birthday. After one look at the baby's too-intense eyes, Selma's parents reluctantly gave their only child's hand to "that big, serious Baptist farm boy." Two years later, Gerald was born. Then Frank, Kent, Sadie, the twins, Bobby—two years and two years and two years, babies came with Swiss precision. Welcome all! Welcome—

Victor's dream-hand stiffened momentarily at feeling something fairly solid in Selma's liquid womb. His fingertips probed rudimentary arms, legs, a lizard spine that flowed into tadpole tail.

"You're not even *human* yet."

Working his way to the face, he felt the tiny bump of a nose and spread his fingers until—THERE! There were the blasted eyes. Victor opened his hand wide and closed it around the unformed body of his seventh son and squeezed, feeling fragile bones snap like toothpicks.

He clutched his chest, threw the covers from his wife's sleeping form, sighed relief and disappointment at seeing her slightly rounded belly unharmed. Unchanged.

Three nights later, Victor arrived home to a silent supper table where eight sets of too-intense eyes blazed accusation. Selma had obviously broken the happy news.

"Uh-oh," he joked, "pigeon stew again!" When no one except Selma smiled, Victor grunted for his eldest son to come out and help unload the new chicken-coop incubator.

"Why'd you order this?" Martin snarled as they lugged the heavy box from truck bed to garage. "You know we can't afford new equipment...can't afford *shit* thanks to you, stud!"

When the box was safely on the concrete floor, Victor snatched the overhead string to throw dim, bare-bulb light onto the enraged face of his firstborn. "Know what, boy? If I ever took that tone of voice with *my* father, he'd—"

"Blow his brains out."

"He'd kick my ass from here to Claret County. Don't *try* me."

"Measures of manhood," Martin retorted. "Keep pumping Ma full of your babies and threaten the ones already here if we're not joyful about it."

Victor tore off his hat, hurled it to the floor. "What is *hell* is your problem, Martin?"

"*My* problem?! Forget my college because we're *broke*, Daddy! Can't grow food out of rock and you're working a stinking slaughter-house and buying crap we can't afford and can't leave Ma alone—she's forty-*one* for God's sake!"

"Yeah, and I'm thirty-six and you're eighteen. If you're showing off senior year math, I'm not real impressed."

The two men glared at one another, muscular arms folded to make mirror-image similarity a twin threat of destruction.

"Supper's getting cold!" Selma called from the house.

Her voice spun Victor back to that long-ago night when boy and young woman basked in a glow of innocence that seemed eternal.

"Did you ever think about going to college?" Selma asked.

Victor smiled up at the sky and cradled her closer. "Nah. You can be the smart one. And our kids—scientists and astronauts and such. All *twenty* of them!" In the ring of Selma's laughter, the numbers sparked infinity and spun breathtaking possibility.

"Supper's getting cold!" she called again.

Victor's eyes softened on his sudden adversary. "All you kids. I brought every one of you out of your mother by myself. I was the first one to hold you and—"

"Save it, Daddy. Save it for your tombstone. I'm talking about *now!*"

Victor lunged, grabbed two handfuls of Martin's undershirt, staggered his son close. "You think your Ma is some defiled *virgin* around here, boy? Maybe if you ever get past making love to fake girls in dirty magazines, you'll see that what I've got is *real*. Find out what it means when a loving woman opens her arms to you at night and you'll *know* there's no blame!"

"Just take a look at the shitty clothes on your kids' backs, stud. *There's* your blame!"

Victor raised a fist to smash the sneering, loveless face so much like his own; but his fist froze, trembled mid-air as the truth of Martin's words crashed around him. His hands fell and he stood speechless as his son kicked the new incubator, then snatched the overhead string to leave his father in shadows.

"At least the goddamn *chickens* hatching'll be warm this winter. Huh, Daddy?"

Victor squeezed his eyes shut as storm clouds in his head broke thunder echoing like the sound of a slamming door.

"Die," he whispered to Selma's blooming middle as she slept. "I don't love you. *Die...*" His mind darkened with brutal fantasies of bleach and coat hanger and torn flesh bleeding from her body onto the sheets. How long now? Seven months? Still not too late if he did it himself.

Pulling away the covers, Victor kept his hands steady while undoing all the buttons of his wife's nightgown. Both his big hands, fingers spread, could still envelop the swollen mound that housed his seventh son. He squeezed slightly, jerked away at feeling a solid kick. The little bastard was strong now. Determined. REAL.

"I *hate* you."

Selma suddenly reached out and pulled his head to her breast and stroked his hair to sooth away wrenching sobs. Victor burrowed into her soft flesh with aching desperation—aching *need* to dissolve into his wife's body and blast his own seed into oblivion.

"Where you going, Pop?"

He slept at last—lightly, restlessly, haunted by storms of another lifetime.

"Can I go with you, Pop?"

Victor's father didn't answer. He watched the broad back retreat and his eyes fell to the hunting gun for only a second. Pop couldn't stand the sight of his seventh son. Didn't seem able to stand the sight of anything anymore, judging from the amount of time he spent away hunting.

"Can I go with you!"

His father had gotten too far away to hear. Victor returned to playing with the mongrel puppy he'd been sullenly given for Christmas and didn't look up again until he heard the explosive gunshot from the barn...Messy exit. Brains splattered everywhere and no goodbyes to anyone.

"Where are you going?"

Victor stood beside his bed, staring through the darkness into the pit where his father had disappeared.

"Victor?"

He moved to the door like a sleepwalker and said, "I'll be right back, honey" in a voice more like Pop's than his own.

"Come back to bed..."

Selma's voice faded as he was pulled down the stifling hallway in a circular route toward destiny.

"You're too big for that bottle," he said to his four-year-old. "You're not the baby anymore." When Bobby didn't stir, Victor propped his sixth son's bottle up on blankets so the tiny mouth could get a better grip on the nipple.

He moved up the line to older children, giving each a special whisper. "Sing that 'Circus Fat Lady' song to the new baby," he said to ten-year-old Sadie. "It'll make the little bastard laugh same as me. I swear it."

A chill of dread coursed through him when at last, he ascended to Martin's little attic apartment. Once inside, Victor tiptoed across the creaking wood and sat in an overstuffed junkyard chair near the bed.

He chuckled softly as moonlight through the ceiling window cast spotlight on a wild sprawl of limbs that touched all four sides of the double mattress. "How's any woman ever gonna put up with you?" he whispered.

Bending, Victor lifted a Hustler magazine from the floor and leaned into moonlight to study the centerfold. His eyebrows shot up, the corners of his mouth pulled down, he jerked a nod. "Real damned impressive, boy. You broke that little MacKenzie girl's heart because she can't measure up to this stuff, huh?" His gaze roamed pink, perfect flesh until he dropped the magazine to fix a hard stare on his eldest son. "Or maybe you like paper dolls so much because they don't make *babies*."

Victor squeezed his eyes shut and pushed hands though his hair to fight off growing, consuming blackness that screamed his name. "Funny how I remember things. Silly things that daddies tend to store away to bore their grown kids with. The memories start big when I think about you, then they get smaller on down the line with the rest. That doesn't make a bit of sense, does it?"

He was answered by a deep, rattling snore.

"What I'm saying is find somebody to love outside yourself, Martin. Grab hold of something *real* like the way I grabbed and held you when you were screaming so awful. Remember? When you fell into that pigpen at County Fair and I pulled you out and held on tight? You were six. Seven maybe...Save it for my tombstone, right?"

Victor leapt to his feet, clutched his head to hold back the storm. "God Almighty turned the word into flesh and I turned a woman's love into *you* but it's not ever enough, is it?!"

When Martin groaned and turned toward him, Victor marched from the attic apartment back to his own bedroom. The abyss bled over his brain like a tar as he slid beneath the covers and down into an illusion of plunging head-first between Selma's thighs.

Eyes wide, he squeezed into the birth canal to confront his tormentor. The top of Victor's head slammed the cervical barrier until it opened and allowed him entry to his wife's womb. Surrounded by bluish light like liquid oxygen, his breath came easily within the comfort of amniotic fluid so he waited while the infant squeezed around to have a look. The face that appeared was upside down, wizened like an old man's and its squinty eyes grew large at seeing its father.

"What'll you name me?" it asked.

Victor sneered disgust. "How about I name you 'SHIT' since that's the first word that popped to mind knowing about you?"

"That's not a real name. I thought you liked what's *real*." The baby disappeared from sight, moved around Victor's head as it talked, and was back at his face so swiftly that it took a moment or two to realize that the umbilical cord had been wrapped firmly as a noose. "But you don't really *know* what's real anymore, Daddy. You don't even know you love me."

"I can still kill you," Victor choked as the cord tightened. "My Pop missed his shot at me, but I *swear* I'll snap your goddamned neck easy as one of my chickens."

The baby blinked shock. "You *mean* that, don't you?"

"Die. Nobody wants you here...DIE!"

Victor gagged, tears of hate and asphyxiation searing his eyes until, with a banshee wail, his seventh son thrust out a tiny hand and snatched the cord from its mother's uterine wall and tugged until the noose slid snakelike from its father's throat. Fluid exploded, blasting Victor from his wife's body back into fitful sleep.

Selma's scream rode a high wind that slammed into his head with the punctuated urgency of a thunder crash. He jerked bolt upright, clutched his chest against pain that detonated there.

"Baaaaaby!" Selma wailed, the sound of it melting into happy voices of children squealing "Rain! Raaaaain!" in the hallway.

His gaze fled toward drops that pummeled the window like darts hurled by a prankster god until Selma screamed again and Victor heard a thump from the attic above and he threw the covers from his wife's body.

Lightning seared his brain with the picture of blood-drenched sheets and Victor tumbled from the bed to his knees, eyes shut in prayer against this latest nightmare.

"Let me hold the baby, Victor. Let me see—"

Thunder split the air again to swallow Selma's words while Victor's chest seized in relentless agony. Bitter irony washed over him at hearing his elder daughter singing the "Fat Lady" song in the hallway as he gripped the edge of the bed to brace for a look at the carnage.

The baby, prematurely expelled, was beautiful like the bloody Catholic statues in Selma's church. Blue. Dead. *Beautiful.* Panic and guilt tore fire through Victor's heart as he held out a gentle hand to stop Selma from rising for a look.

"Something's wrong!" she cried.

"No, honey...fine. I promise."

Seeing her face twist into a mask of agonized confusion was more than he could bear and Victor bent low to hiss rage at his seventh son. "Given me what I wanted without a fight, haven't you! Well, you're not getting away with it because—" he drew a pained breath, "because I've seen you now and I love you read bad just like *you* wanted."

"Victor? Please—what's the *matter* with him? Victor..."

Pulling himself forward, Victor affixed his mouth over the baby's mouth and nose and forced life into its lungs.

Where you going, Pop?

Lightning outside ripped echo through his chest, jolted his body as if the Puppetmaster were cutting all the strings. Victor crashed backward onto the floor as Selma and the baby wailed and the door burst open.

Can I go with you?

"Jee-zus!" Martin shouted. He threw the weight of one massive shoulder against the door, slammed it and shot the bolt before curious siblings could follow. "Gerald!" he screamed through wood to the sixteen-year-old. "Take the truck *now* and bring Doc Richards NOW!"

When his eldest turned, pushed trembling hands though thick black hair, Victor smiled recognition. "You're a real funny kid," he said. "Always were. Remember the time you were hollering for all the other kids to hush to Daddy could take a nap—hollering and yelling just like now 'till you were the only one I could hear at all."

"Victor!"

He nodded weakly to his wife up on the bed. *"You* remember that, don't you, honey?"

Selma screamed, the baby squalled, thunder crashed and no one seemed to be listening to Victor. He watched Martin rush to his mother's side, take up her hand, bend low as Selma quieted to urgent whisper. With a glance at the baby, Martin spun and fell to his knees.

"Get up, Daddy!"

"The light switch isn't working in here," Victor said. "I've been meaning to fix that, but—"

"Get up! You're scaring Ma!"

"He wants a name."

"What?"

"Your new brother. He wants a name. The boy was real clear on that point."

"Victor!" Selma called.

"Please, Daddy. Just get up on the bed 'till Doc Richards—"

"He wants a—"

"SAMUEL!" Martin roared.

Lightning flashed, bathing the room in surgical starkness for a split second—long enough for Victor to see his eldest son's face tumble in on itself and the too-intense eyes leap terror as if they beheld death, itself.

Where you going, Pop?

"Martin! What's the matter with—"

"He's okay, Ma. All the excitement's got to him is all. He says the baby can't help its screaming but he needs us to be quiet so he can take a nap, okay?"

"Yeah, you remember," Victor smiled. "Samuel...mighty fine. Go tell him so he'll shut up." When Martin glanced at his new brother and choked a sob, Victor dragged a hand to his own constricting chest and summoned a voice of strengthening calm. "Everything'll grow perfect now. Plenty insurance. I'm a sucker for those life policies. College for everybody...all the way down to Samuel."

Can I go with you?

"Go cut Samuel's cord and tie it off so he can catch a decent breath...Tell Kent, Sadie, Frank and the twins to bring that chicken-egg hatcher I couldn't afford out of the garage. Hook it up next to my easy chair and...put Samuel inside it and turn it on to keep him fresh until Doc Richards...bring hot towels for your Ma."

Victor squinted to see Selma, who rested asleep or fainted on the bed; then he turned once more to his suddenly older eldest son whose gaze softened, steadied on destiny revealed.

"He's it, right, Daddy? *Real.* That's what all the bullshit you've been talking comes down to. *I* gave the boy his name so now it's up to *me* to hold on tight and try to raise him as good as..."

Victor chuckled, closing his eyes in dire need of sleep. Selma called his name from somewhere in the universe and her love echoed in the voice of a man who issued quiet instructions to children in the hallway.

"That's real good," Victor sighed peacefully. "Cut the cord, son."

Diane Slatton says, "I'm a wife, mother, decorated former U.S. Army sergeant who caused a familial scandal two years ago by quitting my 'real' job as a secretary to teach myself to write." Last year, she won an Illinois Arts Council grant, and she placed 23rd out of 2,000 entrants in Writer's Digest annual short story competition. I think this is just the beginning. I think Ms. Slatton made the right decision to quit her 'real' job. She concludes: "Somewhere between the chicken-egg hatcher and the slaughterhouse lies an answer to the abortion question. Victor and I are still searching..."

Order of the Virgin Mothers

Lois June Wickstrom

The dark green UPS van just ahead of her blew a tire and toppled, spewing an avalanche of packages into the street. Patricia Turner had been following too closely to stop. She bounced her sports car up over the curb, onto the grass. Then one of those adrenalin moments she lived for happened. Her fear left and she was transformed into her alter-ego—the *Bugle's* police reporter. She firmly believed *accidents do not happen—only opportunities.*

Tatters of the driver's shirt flapped across his arm and the right leg of his pants clung in a patch of red. But he did not go to the phone booth across the street. Instead, he crouched on all fours like a child in a pile of leaves, rummaging in the mountain of boxes, oblivious to cars honking and swerving about him. *Jewels, government documents, steaks?* wondered Patricia. *What could be more important than calling a doctor?* Then the driver stood, smiling proudly and clutching a box labelled:

> Dry Ice
> Freeze Promptly
> Fresh Frozen Fetuses

The return address printed in bold red: "WomanCare Labs."

Drops of condensation fell from the box, leaving a trail of water spots on the sidewalk. Patricia found herself thinking *bread crumbs.* Then she noticed a second trail—drops of blood from the delivery man's leg. Despite his condition, Patricia found it difficult to keep up with the delivery man in her high heels. She remained a discreet distance behind, but the delivery man noticed her and asked, "Why are you following me?"

As long as her cover was blown, Patricia decided to be friendly. "Where are you going? Where are you taking the fetuses? And don't you want me to call a doctor for your leg?"

The delivery man only scowled at her. He did not look back again.

When he arrived at the stone mansion, he didn't stop to ring the bell. He pushed his way past children playing jump rope, barged through the heavy wooden door, turned down the hall, and then, changing demeanor entirely, stepped reverently into an office where a pregnant woman in a red, yellow, and blue religious habit was kneeling on the wooden floor below a picture of Christ. Patricia followed him, swearing under her breath. Throughout the house, she could hear the sounds of babies crying, toddlers toddling, and older children reciting their lessons.

The pregnant supplicant prayed, "And please, God, bring us more implants. Sister Beth is almost ready to deliver her triplets, and Sister Helen is in labor now with twins. Give them both healthy births, and quick recoveries so they will soon be ready for more implants. With faith, I await your Second Coming. I know you have already made your decision, but please God, let it be a girl this time. It would only be fair..."

The delivery man interrupted her. "Fresh frozen fetuses, from WomanCare Labs. Sorry they're late, and a bit soggy. The truck broke down. The doc said they were important, so I got here as fast as I could with this nosy reporter nagging at me all the way." He put the damp box down on the wooden desk between two glasses of water and a tower-cased microcomputer. Patricia noted that the brass nameplate on the desk read, "Sister Carmen."

The delivery man asked, "May I borrow your phone to call a doctor? I'm bleeding."

Sister Carmen said, "Of course. And sit in my chair."

The man sank in Sister Carmen's leather office chair. Sister Carmen knelt beside him and rolled up his bloody pants leg. Blood still trickled down his leg. Sister Carmen took a handkerchief from her pocket, dipped it into the nearest glass of water and pressed it against the wound.

While the man spoke on the phone, Patricia squatted beside Sister Carmen. "I'm Patricia Turner, police reporter for the *Bugle*," she said. "I heard the message on the police report—truck broken down, carrying frozen fetuses. For our readers, can you tell me what this is about?"

Sister Carmen did not look up from tending the wound. "I've seen you on television. You're the reporter who broke that story about water being added to children's milk in the schools..." Fresh wails started from two stories above them. Jumprope chants droned like bees nesting under the window. And the delivery man shouted into the telephone, "that's right...the orphanage at 16th and Race."

"I'm glad you liked the story," Patricia said.

"I didn't say I liked it," said Sister Carmen. "I said I recognized you." She began to pray, "Dear God, help..."

"I'm bleeding. I don't have time to answer your survey!" The delivery man dug his fingers into the seam of the cardboard box. The side ripped off in his hand. Chunks of dry ice squeaked and bounced onto the desk and floor. Several pieces hit Patricia's leg. "Ow!" she shouted (*ow* being the only word she could think of as acceptable in this company). "That burns!" A chorus of children marched below the window singing, "When the saints..."

Patricia thought, *if it doesn't quiet down here soon, I'm going to walk out on this story.* Then she looked at the contents of the mysterious box she had followed here. In the midst of this bedlam was a frost-covered insulated red bucket. The delivery man breathed a sigh of relief. "They're still cold." Sister Carmen began another prayer. The delivery man interrupted, pride obvious in his voice, "These are the latest, fresh frozen from the clinic. Where should I put them?"

Sister Carmen stood and faced the delivery man. "You aren't moving anywhere except into an ambulance."

"What about the fetuses?" persisted the delivery man.

"They're just what I was praying for. And your timing is perfect. Now, you tell the clinic—no more for a few weeks. Tell them to keep them in the deep freeze until we have an empty womb. Sister Gloria won't be ready until next week, and she can only take two because her pelvis is narrow. And the rest of us are still pregnant."

"Did I hear you say triplets and twins, when you were praying?" asked Patricia. "And why do you call yourself *sister*?"

Sister Carmen turned to give Patricia a better view of her belly. "Multiple births are more efficient," she said. "And *Sister* comes from the women's movement, of which our Order is an outgrowth."

Patricia walked over to the insulated bucket. "Are these the frozen aborted fetuses?"

The delivery man answered. "Yes, Ma'am. And they really need to be put into a minus 80 freezer soon."

Patricia turned her attention to Sister Carmen. "As I was saying, the police report said the truck was carrying frozen fetuses, and I've followed this man here. *Have you ever tried to run in high heels?* Now please tell me what this is about!"

Sister Carmen grabbed the insulated bucket protectively. "You know, some people think that just because this is an orphanage, that the children here are public property. And that everything we do here is public information." She paused and checked the delivery man's leg. It was still bleeding.

Sister Carmen picked up the phone.

Patricia persisted as Sister Carmen dialed, "I expected you'd want to set the record straight. And, an interview would be a big step toward clarifying your position in the public mind."

"That so?" Sister Carmen said, pushing the last few buttons.

Patricia used her most officious voice. "Surely your orphanage depends on the generous donations of the reading public for its continuing existence. And you must admit, frozen fetuses sounds peculiar."

The crying from the room next door increased by about ten decibels.

Sister Carmen laughed gently. "We don't mind that the public sees us as religious nuts. It is much easier to be thought an eccentric than to be understood..."

The delivery man pulled out a clipboard from under his jacket. "Sister, would you please sign for the delivery, so I can be on my way?"

"You're not going anywhere," said Sister Carmen. "You need an ambulance. I'm calling to see where it is."

Patricia continued trying to interview her. "I think I understand you all right. You are a religious order, and you're doing something secretive with frozen fetuses. If you won't talk, I'll go to the delivery company, the doctors, the mothers of these frozen popsicles. This will be the exposé of the decade, and your donations will plummet."

The delivery man handed Sister Carmen his clipboard.

Sister Carmen signed the form. But before she could return it, Patricia stepped between her and the delivery man.

"You certainly are rude," said Sister Carmen. "You get in the way of a simple business transaction, as if you were the only person who matters. And you say you are a reporter, yet you don't know about the Order of the Virgin Mothers. A teenaged girl with an unplanned pregnancy puts more preparation into her work than you do."

Sister Carmen leaned around Patricia and gave the clipboard to the delivery man. Then she spoke into the phone. "That's right—it's an emergency at the orphanage—one of God's children."

"No, I don't know about the Order of the Virgin Mothers," Patricia persisted. "Are you new in town?"

Sister Carmen began speaking as if to a potential donor. "We're a right-to-life organization. We've been implanting aborted fetuses for over a decade. We have a special court order authorizing us to implant any unclaimed aborted fetus. This order makes implantation equivalent to adoption in the eyes of the law."

Patricia jotted down notes. "But once the babies are born, you give them up for adoption, right?"

"Oh, no! We keep *all* of them." Sister Carmen was indignant. The crying next door stopped, and several women's voices could be heard singing, "Hush little baby..."

Patricia's mouth hung briefly with surprise. "What? With all the demand for babies to adopt? I thought right-to-lifers were mainly opposed to abortion because they wanted the babies to be adopted instead of aborted. How do you justify keeping them?"

Sister Carmen continued her donor's spiel. "It is a tenet of our Order that one of these children will be the Second Coming of Christ. We are keeping them, so we can discover which child He is."

"How are you going to tell which one He is? He wouldn't be born with stigmata on His hands and feet, would He?" asked Patricia.

Sister Carmen patted the frosted bucket as she spoke. "No, we aren't expecting anything like that. In fact, I'm hoping that this time, *He* will be a *She*."

"So, how will you recognize Him, or Her?"

Sister Carmen offered one of the glasses of water on her desk to the delivery man. He waved a hand in refusal. Then she said, "We have just begun the Search. We are looking for a child who can perform the miracles He performed last time."

"What if you don't find a child who can perform miracles?"

"All the Sisters will continue to love the children we have, and we will continue to accept more implants." Sister Carmen patted her protruding belly.

"Then, if you do find the Christ Child, you'll stop taking implants?" asked Patricia.

"Never!" Sister Carmen raised her fist in salute. "As long as I am able, I will use my womb to rescue aborted babies! And so will all the other Sisters. We have pledged our lives to this."

"I think you're being too optimistic. I'm a reporter. I've seen human nature."

"Uh huh," replied Sister Carmen, losing interest in the conversation. "I think I hear an ambulance. Let's help this poor man to the door."

"Let's let the professionals lift him," said Patricia, making no move to help. She continued the debate. "This organization will fall apart the instant you declare that you have found the Christ Child. If you really want to save all the aborted fetuses, you'll make sure you *never* find Him."

Patricia followed Sister Carmen as she walked down the hall and opened the front door. Sister Carmen said, "You, dear, obviously do not know the religious mind. Finding the Christ is a bonus in the cause of Life."

Two ambulance attendants brought a stretcher up the steps.

One of the medics asked Sister Carmen, "Where is the injured child?"

Sister Carmen led them to the delivery man and said, "Here he is."

The medics looked puzzled. One said, "I thought you said you had an injured child."

"This is God's child," said Sister Carmen.

"I like the little ones better," the medic said. Then the attendants helped the delivery man onto the stretcher and carried him to the waiting ambulance.

"Suppose, for example," Patricia asked, "that one or two children can perform miracles, say healings—lots of people claim to be healers—that wouldn't necessarily make the children Christs, would it?"

Sister Carmen dismissed the argument, and in the same gesture reached for the insulated bucket of fetuses on her desk. "You're a fine skeptic, and that's good. God told us to question all things. For example..."

Patricia's curiosity got the better of her. "May I see them? I've never seen a frozen fetus before."

Sister Carmen lifted the lid, and allowed Patricia to peer inside. "I always like to check them out myself. Aren't they just adorable?"

Patricia pulled back squeamishly. "Not really. They remind me of the frogs I had to dissect in biology. The women who have abortions...do they come to you, and ask you to continue their pregnancies?"

"Sometimes. But more often, they sign a consent form at the doctor's when they have their abortions."

Patricia felt the inkling of a story, but only said, "Uh huh."

Sister Carmen continued. "Ours is a right-to-life organization. We believe in putting our bodies where our mouths are. We want all fetuses to be born, so we give aborted fetuses the wombs they need."

She replaced the lid on the bucket.

Patricia decided on a new tack for the interview. "Do you save all the abortions?"

"Unfortunately no," said Sister Carmen. "Some of the fetuses come out damaged—the doctors say they look as if they were about to miscarry naturally."

"Uh huh," Patricia said. More pieces of her story were coming together. Here was an inconsistency.

"If we ever have a surplus of Sisters, I'd like to try implanting some of them, but we do save all the fetuses the doctors say are viable, even the retarded and deformed."

Patricia decided she'd heard enough gory details. She tried one of her conversation stopping lines. "I see."

Sister Carmen misinterpreted Patricia's response as an invitation to go into a more technical explanation. "Thanks to the new wider cannula that came into use fifteen years ago, almost all babies aborted before 10 weeks can be saved and implanted."

Patricia tried again to end this topic, while her brain searched wildly for another. "Thank you for the clarification."

"You're welcome." Sister Carmen smiled.

"Do these mothers know that you think one of their children will be the Second Coming of...?" Patricia couldn't bring herself to say the word.

Two children came to her rescue. A boy and a girl dashed screaming into the office. The girl's arm jostled the frosted bucket of fetuses in Carmen's arms as she ran by. She had obviously been hugging a paper cup of Kool Aid so tightly to her chest that she had smashed the cup against her blouse, and a river of red now ran down her front like a wound. The boy was holding another cup of Kool Aid, still intact.

The boy shouted, "Reen's been giving the kids Kool Aid, and Sister Paula says we're not supposed to drink sugary stuff."

The girl didn't sound defensive at all. If anything, her voice carried amazement. "I can't help it. I was just using the drinking fountain, and the water just turned to Kool Aid."

"Drinking fountains don't make Kool Aid!" the boy insisted. he flailed his arms as he spoke, further jostling the bucket of fetuses.

Sister Carmen hugged the insulated bucket to her chest, and spoke sharply to the children. "Those are your brothers and sisters in there. You must be careful."

Then remembering her manners, she turned to Patricia. "These are two of our older children, Reen and Izzy."

"I'm older than Reen," Izzy said, "and I'm in charge on the playground. I stop the little kids when they break the rules."

Sister Carmen shook her head. "Izzy, dear, you're supposed to watch out for the children's safety—not report to me about every broken rule."

"Aren't you going to punish her?" demanded Izzy.

"Aren't you going to put the babies in the minus 80 freezer in the kitchen?" asked Reen.

"Don't let her out of your sight—she's getting that Kool Aid from somewhere," insisted Izzy.

"I'll take the bucket to the kitchen," offered Reen. "I know right where they go—in the freezer next to the great big oven—the one big enough to cook a witch in like in *Hansel and Gretel.*"

"That won't be necessary, Reen. They're in liquid nitrogen, so they'll keep for several hours." Sister Carmen seated herself at the desk.

"Ask her where she's getting the Kool Aid. And tell her to stop it!" said Izzy.

"I didn't do it on purpose," repeated Reen, amazement still in her voice.

"Both of you, stop arguing," said Sister Carmen, calmly. "Reen, you say you just turned on the fountain, and out came Kool Aid?"

"Yes Ma'am," said Reen.

"Cherry Kool Aid, I hope. That was always my favorite," said Sister Carmen, allowing herself a slight smile.

"Yes, Ma'am," said Reen. "It's cherry."

"Aren't you going to punish her?" demanded Izzy.

"Our Lord asks us to prove all things, Izzy," said Sister Carmen. "So now we'll do an experiment. Here's a glass of water." She offered Reen a glass of water from her desk. "Can you turn this into Kool Aid? Cherry Kool Aid?"

Reen stepped toward Sister Carmen. "I didn't do it on purpose."
Izzy leaned over Reen and sneered, "You little faker. Go ahead,
show Sister Carmen how Kool Aid *just happens.*"
Reen looked straight at him. "I'll show you," she said. She
reached toward the glass. Suddenly, light flashed and they all heard a
ping like a spoon hitting a crystal bowl. The liquid in the glass turned
red.

Sister Carmen picked up the glass and sipped. "This is good.
Better than I remembered Kool Aid as a child. Be polite now, make
another glass for our guest," she told Reen.

Reen touched the second glass, again light flashed, something
pinged, and the water in the second glass turned red.

Patricia tasted the liquid. "This *is* good," she said. "Is this the
kind of miracle you were looking for?"

Izzy's face was almost as red as the Kool Aid. "Aren't you going
to punish her?" he demanded.

Sister Carmen ignored his question. "Izzy, you are needed on the
playground. Go outside and resume guarding the children."

Izzy walked to the door, turned to Reen and stage-whispered,
"You're going to get it!" Then he strutted importantly out to the
playground.

Sister Carmen calmly asked, "Reen, has anything like this ever
happened before?"

Reen paused thoughtfully, and then said, "Last week, I found a
hurt puppy in the street. I picked him up and carried him to the grass,
and when I put him down he was all better."

"That was a good thing to do, a Christlike thing to do," said
Sister Carmen, encouragingly.

Reen smiled. "You and the other Sisters are always telling us to
act Christlike."

Sister Carmen agreed. "Yes, we are." She looked at Patricia, and
then asked Reen, "Do you remember why we want you to act Christlike?"

Reen answered promptly, "Because one of us children is the
Second Coming of Christ."

Patricia quickly masked her horror. She kneeled down to be eye-
level with Reen, and asked, "Aren't you a bit young to be Christ? He
was twelve last time before He did anything special."

Reen stood stiffly, as if for a spelling bee, and answered, "Girls
mature more quickly than boys, and I'm ten already."

Patricia smiled briefly, but kept herself from laughing. Then she turned to Sister Carmen, and pointing to the glass of Kool Aid, she asked again, "Is this the sort of miracle you were hoping for?"

Sister Carmen paused, not wanting to hurt Reen's feelings, or say anything that could be misinterpreted by the press. "Not exactly."

Patricia persisted, "If she'd made wine instead of Kool Aid, would you like that better?"

"No, this is a perfectly good miracle," said Sister Carmen, as if she saw miracles every day, and was used to judging them.

Reen, still unsure if she would be punished, asked, "Can I go outside and finish my hopscotch now?"

Sister Carmen got up from her chair, walked (or waddled) over to Reen, and hugged her. "Honey, you've performed a miracle! Of course you may finish your hopscotch."

Reen ran to the door, and then stopped, and bravely asked, "And can I have some more Kool Aid?"

"Of course—you must never waste a miracle." Carmen gaily waved her away.

"Thank you," said Reen, giving a slight curtsey. Then she ran away before Sister Carmen could change her mind and perhaps say something about not ruining her appetite.

As soon as Reen was out of sight, and presumably hearing, Patricia asked Sister Carmen, "If she had been lying—if she'd sneaked Kool Aid powder into her glass, how would you have punished her?"

Sister Carmen leaned forward, put the container of fetuses down on her desk, and looked Patricia in the eyes. "We never punish the children. None of the Sisters wants to be the first one to spank Christ."

Patricia took another sip of the Kool Aid. *This is going to be an interesting story.* "Her Kool Aid is really good. By the way—what Reen said about the puppy—do you suppose she's a healer, too?"

Sister Carmen hesitated. "That would be a Christlike miracle." She paused. "I wonder if any of the other children can heal?"

* * *

When Patricia arrived at the park, a long line of sick people had already assembled under a banner: "Healings Here." And half-a-dozen pregnant women in red, yellow, and blue habits were corralling what looked like a hundred children who ranged in age from three to fourteen. Patricia glanced back at the orphanage, and thought, *they must sleep in shifts—there can't be enough beds in that building for all those children to lie down at once.* The cries of babies wafted from the orphanage.

Sister Carmen walked over to the only woman in a habit who didn't seem to be pregnant, and said, "Sister Gloria, I hope this doesn't take long. It sounds like they need help in the nursery."

Sister Gloria had clearly heard, but did not respond.

Sister Carmen asked, "Sister Gloria, did you hear me?"

"She can't answer you," Reen said, tugging on Sister Carmen's habit, "She's having a day of silence."

Sister Carmen patted Sister Gloria on the shoulder. "God bless you, dear." Then she turned to Reen and said, "Get ready now, say your prayer, and heal the next sick person."

Patricia inspected the line of sick and injured people and jotted down notes for her article. One woman looked like someone had spilled vegetable soup on her, and the vegetables had stuck. A man, wearing a biker's jacket, had a gash down the right side of his face. The sight made Patricia step back. Then she saw Reen, standing up from her prayer, approach the line.

"That's horrible," Patricia said to Reen. "Do you actually have to touch these people?"

Sister Carmen stepped between Reen and Patricia. "Don't bother the children. Of course they have to touch the sick people. How else can they heal them?"

Reen curtseyed to the gray man with a bad head cold, and said, "Dear God, please heal this man." She touched the man, but did not look at him. He sniffed wetly, and she pulled back her hand.

Sister Carmen tapped Reen's shoulder and said, "Say a prayer, and heal the next man in line."

The next man was the biker with the gash. Patricia noted a "Wheels from Hell" tattoo on his shoulder as he removed his jacket.

"God, I am..." said Reen.

The biker grabbed Reen. "Get on with it! Heal me!" As soon as his hand touched Reen, Patricia heard a ping—the sound of a spoon hitting a crystal bowl—and a flash of light temporarily blinded her. When she could see again, the man's gash was gone.

"Oh baby, baby!" shouted the biker, pulling Reen to his chest, kissing her on both cheeks.

"Help! Help!" shouted Reen.

"I'm healed! Hallelujah! Oh, baby!" shouted the biker. Sister Carmen stepped up to him and freed Reen from his grasp.

Half a dozen of the orphans, ranging in age from about seven to ten, formed a cheering squad and began chanting.

"Healing is what women know!

"Go, Reen! Go! Go! Go!"

Sister Carmen led Reen to the next sick person in line. "Reen, it's time for you to heal another one," she said.

The cheerleaders waved home-made pom pons and skipped in line as they chanted again.

"Healing is what women know!

"Go Reen! Go! Go! Go!"

Reen touched a purple woman. Nothing happened. No ping. No flash of light. And the purple color remained unchanged.

Sister Carmen asked, "Are you healed?"

The woman said nothing.

Sister Carmen hugged Reen.

Reen stepped back and faced Sister Carmen. "I tried. I really did!"

Sister Carmen hugged her again. "I know you did."

Izzy stepped up to the purple woman, hands on his hips. He turned and faced the crowd. "I'll show you how it's done." He then faced the woman and said, "Prepare to be healed."

He touched the woman's forehead, and the purple coloring disappeared.

Then Izzy raised his hands together over his head and pumped them several times in a fighter's victory pose. "She is healed. Praise the Lord!" shouted Izzy. "Bring on the next one."

Sister Carmen announced, "After your healing, we have chicken soup ready for you at the table over by the pond. Sister Gloria will serve you." She paused, and added softly, "Reen, you go have some soup, too."

The next woman Izzy touched threw down her cane and shouted, "Praise the Lord. I am healed!" Then she walked away.

A group of boys grabbed the pom pons from the girl's cheerleading team and began shouting.

"Seven, eight, nine, ten! Who is Christ come again? Izzy! Izzy! Yeah, Izzy!"

Patricia approached the biker, who was slurping his soup straight from the bowl.

"What was your problem?" she asked.

"A stab wound—I got in a street fight." He pointed to his cheek. "Look—not even a scar! I'm healed!"

Patricia leaned close to his face to get a better look, but the man's breath caused her to back up. "Thank you for showing me that," she said, "But since I didn't inspect your wound before Reen touched you, how can I believe?"

The biker spoke with a preacher's voice. "It is a sick generation that asks for a sign." Then more calmly he added, "Hey, doubt if you want. But this is for real!"

The biker sucked the last dregs of his soup from the bowl and walked away.

Patricia sat down beside Reen. "How does it feel to heal a man like that?"

"I wish he wouldn't grab me, and he smells bad," she said.

"You're right about the smell," said Patricia.

Izzy set his bowl of soup down opposite them, splashing Reen with the hot broth. Patricia patted Reen with her napkin.

"I won the healing contest," said Izzy. "I healed five. But I'll give you two out of three contests. Now let's see who can walk on water the longest. Sister Gloria can be the judge." He turned to Sister Gloria. "You get in the pond and check."

Obediently, Sister Gloria stepped into the pond, her skirts dragging on the water's surface.

Izzy whispered to Reen, "Don't you just want to step on her toes on her silent day; to see if she'll scream?"

Reen whispered back, "Yeah! But not in front of the sickies. They might not donate if they hear her scream."

"She won't scream," Izzy said, "She's tough. Come on!"

"We'd better not," Reen whispered back.

"Spoil sport," said Izzy. "Well, here we are. You first." He led her to the edge of the pond.

"No," said Reen. "You healed five—you go first."

"You just want to see how it's done, so you can copy me. You have to find your own way to do it." Izzy stepped toward the water. Then he commanded Sister Gloria, "Make sure you watch carefully now!" The growing crowd of sick people eating soup stepped closer to watch. Sister Gloria's skirt had now sunk into the pond, and water wicked up past her knees. She positioned herself in the middle of the deepest spot, and nodded to show she was ready.

Izzy stepped into the water. Not only did his feet sink to the bottom—the bottom acted like quicksand and pulled him deeper. The soup eaters groaned. Then the formerly purple woman said, "Let the girl try now!"

Sister Carmen approached the crowd. "What's going on here?"
"We're trying to walk on water," Reen explained. "Sister Gloria
is the judge."

Then before Sister Carmen could stop her, Reen stepped into the
water, slipped and splashed full-length. The splash soaked the front of
Sister Gloria's habit.

Izzy pointed and said loudly, "Hey, look at that! Sister Gloria
looks like a real lady under all those clothes."

Then he bent down, scooped water into his hands, and threw it at
Sister Gloria, soaking her further. She didn't make a sound.

Sister Carmen lifted Reen out of the water. Izzy was too far from
the edge for her to grab. "Izzy, Reen, I'd like to see you in my office,
at once."

She pulled Reen, while Izzy followed at a short distance, shouting
for all the sick people to hear, "You can't punish us. We're the top
two Christ Child contenders."

Patricia followed them to Sister Carmen's office.

When the children were seated, Sister Carmen said, "I'm truly
disappointed in both of you—you are both blessed by God with the gift
of healing, and even as you use that gift, you make a mockery of our
religious order! I expect apologies from both of you, and I expect
better behavior in the future."

Izzy stood and stepped boldly toward Sister Carmen. "I'm better
at walking on water than she is. And I healed more people."

Sister Carmen ignored Izzy, and tapped on the computer keyboard in front of her. She turned the monitor so it faced the children.
"I've been reviewing the files on both our healers. And I found something unusual about Reen's." She pressed a button to create a printout
of Reen's records. Reen stuck her tongue out at Izzy.

Sister Carmen tore off the printout and held it up to read aloud.
"According to our records, Reen's mother was not a virgin." Izzy
stuck his tongue out at Reen.

"So I'm the Christ Child, right?" Izzy said.

"Not so fast," answered Sister Carmen.

Before she could continue, Reen spoke up. "You've always said
that all us orphans were rescued abortions, who were grown in virgin
Sisters—kind of like a fine wine." She paused and her voice took on
shocked tones as if talking about a taboo. "Am I just born of a bio-
mother?"

Sister Carmen ran her index finger over the paper again.

Izzy jumped to his feet and said proudly, "if she's not an abortion, then I am!"

Sister Carmen soothed the children. "No, Izzy. You are both abortions. The whole idea of the Order of Virgin Mothers is that Christ is the stone rejected by the builders, and you are the babies rejected by your bio-mothers, who are the true builders of our society. In fact, Reen is a double reject." Then addressing Reen, she added, "The embryo you grew from was rejected by the Sisterhood implant program."

Izzy put his thumbs in his ears and wiggled his fingers at Reen. "Nyah! Nyah!"

Sister Carmen continued, still facing Reen, "Our doctors thought you wouldn't grow normally, that you had been damaged in the extraction process, and might die or miscarry if you were implanted. Your birth-mother, Anna, had you illegally implanted after you were rejected by our program. So you're a *double reject.*"

Izzy sang out, "Reen is a reject! Reen is a reject!"

Sister Carmen ignored him, and continued. "Since Anna, your birth-mother, was separated from her husband, she couldn't have a legal implant. Only virgin Sisters, and married women whose husbands give permission, are allowed to have implants. God brought your birth-mother, Anna, to our doorstep when she was in labor, and we took her in."

Reen seemed relieved. "Well that wasn't as dirty as I thought it might be. Do you still think I might be the Christ Child?"

"I don't know what to think," Sister Carmen said.

Patricia reached for the printout. "I'd like to see the files."

Sister Carmen ignored her, and punched in some more commands at the keyboard.

Izzy stood up again and leaned over Sister Carmen's desk. "I think it's obvious. You've been wasting my time with this contest. Christ wouldn't break the law, so He can't possibly be Reen!"

Sister Carmen turned the monitor back so she could read the screen. Then she said, "This isn't a contest, it's a search. We all win when we find the Christ Child." She paused and added sadly, "Oh, Izzy!"

Izzy responded, "Don't take my name in vain, you know!"

Patricia had been pondering the meaning of Sister Carmen's announcement, and now she asked the question that had been forming in her mind, "Do you mean that you have *no* records on Reen's natural parents?"

Sister Carmen answered, "Just her birth-mother, Anna's statement, that she was an illegal implant. But remember, the first time,
Christ was an implant, too. Neither Joseph, nor Mary were his biological parents. Mary was his birth-mother. We are following in her
tradition."

Patricia couldn't help it. She blurted, "You mean you are a bunch
of women with a Virgin Mary complex?"

* * *

Sister Gloria entered Sister Carmen's office. Sister Carmen was
staring excitedly at her computer screen, and one single page protruded
from the printer. Sister Gloria apologized. "I'm the only one who
could get free from the nursery. Sister Beth is delivering her triplets,
babies are crying, the older children are having their lessons...So
what's happening?"

Sister Carmen pointed to the computer screen. "This is it! The
computer says we now have sufficient data to determine which of
the children is the Christ Child."

Sister Gloria frowned slightly. "Computers make mistakes.
Remember our phone bill?"

Sister Carmen persisted in her enthusiasm. "The programmer
who wrote this for us has considered both miracle quantity and miracle
quality. The data bank includes every recorded miracle in the Bible.
And there is a supplementary file listing Jesus' undocumented miracles. Each of our children has been compared to the entire data bank.
The computer is ready. Shall we pray?"

Sister Gloria and Sister Carmen fell to their knees simultaneously,
and from years of practice, recited their prayer in unison. "Hallelujah!
Unto us a child is born! Christ is returned!"

When they finished, Sister Gloria stood rapidly and asked, "Are
you sure you want to push that button?"

"Why in heaven's name wouldn't I want to push it?" asked Sister
Carmen.

"Because, once we name the Christ Child," warned Sister Gloria,
"young girls will see no reason to preserve their virginity and join our
order."

Sister Carmen dismissed her worries, waving her hand. "We're
supposed to forgive sinners, you know. Please let's not argue. This is
a blessed moment. Our Savior is here!"

Sister Gloria persisted in her doubts. "I wish to go on record, stating that this is a mistake."

Sister Carmen tapped some computer keys, and said, "So noted. Are there any other comments before I push the button?"

"Yes Carmen," said Sister Gloria, changing the subject and pointing at Carmen's large belly. "I've been meaning to ask—how many do you have in there this time? You look really huge!"

"Four," answered Sister Carmen, a trace of pride sneaking into her voice. She paused while Gloria's jaw dropped. "I'm forty-six. This may be my last pregnancy. I wanted to go out with a bang."

"What zeal!" said Sister Gloria. "But if we do have the Christ Child, aren't you stressing your body for nothing?"

Sister Carmen chided her gently. "These are four rescued souls. Christ would not say these souls are nothing. But, I want to get on with this momentous event. I want to push the button!"

"Remember what 'push the button' meant in the '70's!" said Sister Gloria. "This is just as dangerous as a bomb. How can we single out one of our children as better than all the rest? We've worked so hard at treating them all equally."

"There is nothing to fear," said Sister Carmen. "We give gifted education to the gifted and remedial education to the ones who need remediation. Now we will give religious training to the One who will rule over us all. To deny the Christ Child extra attention would be like denying the Christ Child Himself!"

"And to name a false Christ would endanger our souls!" added Sister Gloria.

"We won't name a false Christ," said Sister Carmen. "We aren't depending on the fallibility of men—we're depending on an impartial computer."

"I suppose the computer has successfully picked a Christ Child before?" asked Sister Gloria.

"The doubters too shall enter into heaven. I want to thank God that I have lived to see this day!" Sister Carmen raised her hands to the heavens.

"I hope we can protect this one—so He won't be crucified!" said Sister Gloria, resignedly.

Sister Carmen poised her hands over the keyboard and said, "Sister Gloria, have you anything else to add?"

"God bless us one and all!" Sister Gloria positioned herself beside the printer, where she could watch the screen.

"I'm so excited! In the name of Christ, I push this button!" Sister Carmen smiled ecstatically as the printer's pins hit the paper.

Sister Gloria grabbed the paper. "He's a girl! Amen!"

"Amen!" seconded Sister Carmen.

Patricia pulled up to the orphanage in her car, still talking into her car phone.

"Yes, I'll remember," said Patricia. Then she hung up. Hurriedly, she undid her seatbelt and ran into Sister Carmen's office, forgetting to lock the car door. She arrived just as Sisters Carmen and Gloria finished their cheering.

"Yeah! Yeah! Healing is what women know!
Go Reen! Go! Go! Go!"

Sister Carmen added,

"Seven, eight, nine, ten
Who is Christ born again?
Reen! Reen! Yeah, Reen!
One, two, three...
Yeah, Reen!"

Sister Gloria fell silent and Sister Carmen looked meaningfully at her.

Half-heartedly Gloria said, "Yeah, Reen."

Patricia cleared her throat to gain the Sisters' attention.

"Ah, our reporter," said Sister Carmen, sounding glad to see her. "You're just in time—our computer has selected the Christ Child."

Patricia's face fell, obviously taken aback. "Oh, I thought... but...Yes, that is a good story."

Sister Gloria said, "Let's go tell Reen!"

Sister Carmen turned her attention to Patricia. "You came here for a different reason? We've got the story of the millennium, and you are interested in something else? What could be more important?"

Patricia allowed anger to enter her voice. "I'm still researching my story on your orphanage as a fraud and rip-off."

Sister Carmen smiled. She'd dealt with angry reporters before. "Often, if we look at what we don't like—what we really get angry and upset about—that's really an aspect of ourselves that we haven't yet accepted. I knew when you came here that you did not approve of our Christ Child Search. But your anger told me this search was important to you—that it would benefit you in some way."

While she listened, Patricia regained her composure.

Sounding more businesslike, but slightly distracted, Patricia said, "Look, I think this Christ Child contest is wrong. Possibly the most terrible thing you have done. Your other frauds have taken money from gullible sick people. You've conned healthy young women into becoming mindless brood-sows in some kind of religious cult. But at least you were fooling adults. This contest—this Christ Child Search as you call it—hurts the children—the ones you say you are trying to save!"

Knowing that self-righteousness is always a front, Sister Carmen said, "That's not what is really bothering you. You were going to say something else."

"Yes," admitted Patricia. She paused. "I still have a question."

Sister Carmen thought *I've got the Christ Child here, and I've got a reporter. But the reporter wants to talk about something else. God must be trying to teach me patience.* She took a deep breath and said, "Yes?"

Patricia said, "...about Reen..."

Impatience showing, Sister Carmen again said, "Yes?"

Patricia said, "Her birth-mother must have had real guts!"

"I like to think that all mothers have real guts. Why hers in particular?" asked Sister Carmen.

Patricia continued, "You said Reen was rejected by your Order because the doctors thought she would miscarry or die if she were implanted."

"Yes," said Sister Carmen.

"Well, when I was ten," said Patricia. "My parents brought my sister Emily home from the hospital. My sister had spina bifida, a hereditary disease. For three years, they told me she was okay, she was getting better. Then she died. Ever since then, I've been afraid to have a baby. There is a fifty-percent chance that I carry the gene that killed Emily." She paused. "And Reen's birth-mother wanted to have Reen even though *she* was almost sure to have something wrong with her."

"I see what you mean," said Sister Carmen. "That is a special kind of guts. But Anna was a very spiritual lady. She might have had a vision about Reen—a vision can often provide the guts for very brave deeds."

"Was?" asked Patricia. "She's dead?"

"Our Order is forbidden to ever reveal the name of the living birth-mother to any child under eighteen years old," said Sister Carmen.

"How did she die?" asked Patricia.

"She died in childbirth. I talked to Dr. Miller, the doctor who did the implant. He said he warned her she could die, but she was determined." Sister Carmen hoped some of Anna's inspiration would make it into Patricia's story.

"Tell me," said Patricia. "Since your doctor does illegal implants—does he ever implant fetuses from mothers who did not sign consent forms?"

"No consent form is needed," said Sister Carmen, matter-of-factly. She was not going to let the story of the Christ Child turn into a muckraking scandal. Patricia appeared upset, even angry.

"Of course it's needed," Patricia insisted. "Why else do they offer the forms to women who get abortions at the clinics?"

This interview was getting off the subject. Sister Carmen decided it was time for a history lesson. "We take the consent-form fetuses first, but we usually have room for more, so then we take the others. We brought a lawsuit, claiming guardianship of all aborted fetuses, and now all aborted fetuses are considered wards of the state. The implantation process is equivalent to adoption. So, members of our Order may request implantation without the bio-mother's consent."

"And then, do you tell the mother—the woman who had the abortion—that her fetus has been implanted?" asked Patricia.

"Absolutely not!" said Sister Carmen, indignantly.

"There's a lot of guilt that goes with an abortion," said Patricia.

"If they are going to feel guilty—that's their problem," Sister Carmen ran her fingers over the computer printout impatiently.

"Knowing her baby was all right might help a woman feel better," Patricia persisted.

"We don't want bio-mothers coming around here checking on *their* children. They gave up all rights to those children when they had their abortions." Sister Carmen did her best to sound sympathetic, so Patricia's article wouldn't portray her as unfeeling.

Patricia looked slightly sick and changed the subject. "Ooh." She paused. "Reen's birth-mother was definitely one gutsy lady." She paused again. "And, I know this sounds strange coming from me, but maybe she was right about Reen. I don't mean Reen is the Second Coming—I don't believe in that sort of thing. But Reen is a really special kid."

"They all are," said Sister Carmen, proudly. "But for an outsider—noticing one is an excellent start. Our computer has selected Reen as well. She is the second coming of Christ."

Patricia gasped and her face turned red. "You can't! You can't make her the Christ Child!"

Puzzled by this outburst, Sister Carmen asked, "Why do you think you can make this decision better than our computer?"

Patricia burrowed into her chair like a frightened child. "Uh. This is kind of hard to say."

"Go on," said Sister Carmen.

"A child tried to come to me eleven years ago," Patricia began. Then she paused.

"Go on," said Sister Carmen again.

"But I had an abortion," said Patricia, the last word barely audible.

"Uh huh," said Sister Carmen. She'd heard it all before. The guilt. The tears...

Patricia continued. "And when you said that some of your implants are from bio-mothers who didn't sign consent forms—well, I thought that the child who tried to come to me might be Reen, and here she was trying again."

"So you're here to take her away. That's the story you're really after—you're not interested in our Christ Child Search at all. You're not even interested in your fraud story. You're just trying to make up for guilt." Sister Carmen sat back sternly in her chair.

"Isn't that what religion is about—helping people deal with guilt? When did you turn from being a religious Sister into an avenging monster?" Tears dripped down Patricia's face.

"You're the one who had the abortion—not me!" Carmen let out a deep breath.

"And you think it was wrong to have an abortion!" Patricia persisted.

"You can have all the abortions you want. Just don't come crying to me to get the babies back again when you change your mind." Sister Carmen turned back to her computer, indicating that the conversation was over.

Patricia stood up and leaned over the desk. "That's a monstrous thing to say!"

"So now I'm a monster—because I won't just give you a child you've taken a fancy to? Is that what you think my faith and my life have been about? Depriving mothers of their children?" Sister Carmen was bored. She'd heard all this many times before. Eventually the guilty woman would give up and go away. They were all alike.

"I don't want to turn her away a second time. I mean, she's the right age, and everything. Dr. Miller *was* the one who did my abortion..." Patricia's voice cracked as she choked back the tears.

Sister Carmen decided to try a mild joke. "So, you think finding Reen is kind of your own personal Second Coming?"

"Yeah, kind of," said Patricia relaxing, then tensing.

Sister Carmen keyed in some notes onto the screen. "You're just the first of many. Now that she's the Christ Child, hundreds of women who've had abortions, and even some who haven't will be here trying to claim her."

"If she is my child, would you let me adopt her? I mean keep her? After all, I didn't sign a consent form, and her birth mother is dead. Your legal claim on her is weak. And I've heard her say she *never* wanted to be the Christ Child." Patricia's voice reminded Sister Carmen of a child who hasn't done her homework.

"How long was *never* when you were ten years old?" she asked.

Patricia hesitated. Then she said, "I see what you mean—*never* just meant not now, not soon." Her voice took on a desperate tone. "But being the Christ Child is different!"

"And when you had your abortion, you were saying that you didn't want that child—not ever—never," reminded Sister Carmen. "Was your never the same as a ten-year-old's never?"

"When my sister Emily died—I vowed that I would never have a baby—never let a child die like that! It was horrible! And when I got pregnant, I kept seeing Emily dying over and over again in my dreams," tears streamed down Patricia's face.

"Uh huh," said Sister Carmen, bored again.

"It took my sister three years to die. She was so sick, and in such pain. I didn't sign a consent form because I didn't want anyone to go through watching my baby die." Patricia tried to sound reasonable.

Sister Carmen tried one of her best closing arguments. "So, why are you changing your mind? Reen could catch a terrible disease and die slowly with pain. None of us have any guarantees. Reen's birthmother died giving birth to her."

"It's just that I've met Reen," said Patricia.

"And you're still feeling guilty about your abortion? And you think somehow, through Reen, you can make it all better?" Sister Carmen finished for her.

"Yes!" said Patricia, relieved that Sister Carmen seemed to understand. "I'm here to demand a blood test to prove that she's mine. No child of mine is going to be the Christ Child!"

"When did you stop being a hard-hitting reporter and turn into a silly goose crying over an aborted baby?" Sister Carmen wondered aloud.

While Patricia was thinking of a suitable comeback, Reen dashed into the office carrying a basket of rolls. Sister Gloria followed close behind. All conversation stopped. Reen handed rolls to Sister Carmen, Sister Gloria, and Patricia. Each time she reached into the basket, crystal bells rang from no discernible source, and the room light glowed warmly. The basket remained full. Sister Carmen took a bite from her roll, but Patricia just held hers and stared.

"Why is she doing vaudeville tricks?" Patricia asked. "This is no way to raise a child!"

Sister Carmen ignored Patricia and put an arm around Reen's shoulders. "This is even better than the Kool Aid. May I see your basket?"

Reen handed her the basket. Sister Carmen carefully removed each roll and placed them on the table. Then she felt around in the basket for a false bottom. Finally satisfied, she said, "there are only five rolls in this basket, and it's full. But you just gave us each a roll. How did you do it?"

"I picked them up with my hands and I gave them to you. I don't know why the basket is still full," said Reen.

Patricia walked slowly over to Reen as if approaching a frightened puppy. "Reen, do you want to be the Christ Child?"

Reen answered promptly, "I want to be an astronaut."

Patricia turned to Sister Carmen, "See, she doesn't want to be the Christ Child."

"Neither did the last one. I don't think anybody wants to be the Christ Child," replied Sister Carmen.

Patricia put her arm around Reen's shoulders again and asked, "Reen, would you like to come live with me and be my daughter?"

"I like it here with my friends," said Reen.

"See, she doesn't want to go live with you," said Sister Carmen, aware that she sounded like a school girl having a got-you-last argument.

Reen addressed both the women, "Why are you talking about me as if I'm not here?"

Patricia laughed at the humor of the situation, and with a twinge of self-deprecation, answered, "Because we're adults."

Sister Carmen responded stiffly, "Nowhere in the Bible does it say that we are *adults* of God."

"Just what I need—platitudes when I'm fighting for my daughter's life." Patricia stepped between Reen and Sister Carmen.

"There is a lot of truth in platitudes," said Sister Carmen.

"The issue here is the kind of life Reen will lead. I want to take her home with me and raise her as my daughter," said Patricia as calmly as possible.

"And I want to prepare her for her role in the coming millennium," said Sister Carmen. Then she addressed Reen, "Reen, the computer has determined that you are the Second Coming of Christ. Have you been keeping up with your prayers?"

"I did pray for a miracle on the history test. But it didn't work," said Reen.

"Of course not, dear," said Patricia sympathetically. "Only studying will help you pass a test."

"I was hoping you would pray about the Christ Child," said Sister Carmen. She beckoned Reen to her side. "Come on! Pray with me, now. We mustn't keep God waiting."

"Why?" asked Reen.

"We are celebrating!" answered Sister Carmen.

"Okay," said Reen.

Reen and Sister Carmen kneeled beside each other on the floor under the picture on the wall. "Thank you God for all your blessings."

After she stood up, Sister Carmen asked, "Now, tell me Reen, how do you feel?"

"Fine. But it's not going to help me with tomorrow's spelling test. And I'll never make it if I have to do more healings tonight," said Reen, heading for the door as she spoke.

"The healings will continue only if you want them to, on whatever schedule you say, Lord," said Sister Carmen.

"Don't talk to her like that! You'll give her a swelled head," said Patricia.

Reen paused in the doorway, as it registered on her that she had been called *Lord*, and she looked questioningly at Sister Carmen. Then seeing that the adults looked like they were about to start arguing again, she said, "Good. I need to catch up on my studies." She stood in the doorway waiting to be formally dismissed.

"I agree," said Sister Carmen. "You need a break."

"Aren't you excited about being the Christ Child?" asked Sister Gloria.

"What for?" asked Reen. "The Christ Child has to study religion all the time and do healings on gross yucky sick people."

"See what I mean?" said Patricia. "That's no way to raise a child!"

"I'll make sure you have time to play and be a normal child," promised Sister Gloria.

"Can I go outside and play jump rope, right now?" asked Reen. She didn't want to be around when the adult arguing got fierce, and she could see it was coming.

"Yes, you may go play right now," said Sister Carmen. "But be back in time for dinner. And be sure You study tonight. I expect You to get an A on your spelling test tomorrow—not by a miracle—but because You learned the words."

"Yes, Ma'am," said Reen. She ran out the door and onto the playground before the women could change their minds. She took the basket with her and continued to hand out rolls to children on the playground. Still the basket remained full, and bells kept ringing from nowhere.

Reen ran past children who were playing jacks and jumping rope. Some of the girls chanted: "Teddy bear, teddy bear, go upstairs. Teddy Bear, teddy bear, say your prayers." Reen joined the line to jump to the rhyme.

Meanwhile, back in Sister Carmen's office, Patricia shouted at Sister Carmen. "This is an outrage! My child is doing vaudeville magic tricks and you all act like it's a miracle."

Sister Gloria clapped her hands loudly, and said, "The rolls in the basket are another Christlike miracle. Be sure you log it into the computer!"

Sister Carmen tapped briefly on the keyboard.

Patricia calmed herself and said to nobody in particular, "The sooner we have the blood test the sooner we can end this charade. I don't want my daughter touching all those sick people at your healings. I don't want her handing out bread or Kool Aid, as if the world were a big feeding line. She deserves a normal life."

Sister Carmen looked up from the keyboard and asked, "Is that why you had her aborted?"

Patricia put her hands on Sister Carmen's desk and leaned over to look directly in her eyes. "I've already explained to you why I had her aborted! Let's get beyond the past, and look at the future—Reen's future!"

Before Sister Carmen could respond, Izzy entered the office, carrying an even bigger basket of rolls than Reen had had. He reached deep into his basket and handed a roll to each Sister and one to Patricia. His basket, too, remained full.

Then he said, "Look, I can make bread—just like Reen. And my rolls are bigger."

"May I see your basket?" asked Sister Carmen. She grabbed the basket from Izzy and probed its depths with her hand. Then she turned sadly to the boy and said, "Izzy dear, the computer has determined that Reen is the Christ Child. You didn't have to waste your time putting a false bottom in this basket to hide the extra rolls. You can go back to being a normal child, now."

"The rolls may be fake," said Izzy. "But the healings were real! I healed more sick people than Reen did! The computer isn't fair! I demand to check its programming!"

Izzy walked around to stand beside Sister Carmen and looked at the computer screen.

"What's that on the screen?" he asked.

"Those are the files we keep on each of you—your grades, your miracles, your biological history..." explained Sister Carmen. She clicked a few keys. "See, you have a very impressive list of miracles—all recorded in the computer."

"The computer is prejudiced, 'cause I'm a boy," said Izzy. "I'll bet my list is longer than Reen's."

Sister Carmen blanked the screen, and said, "The computer's decision is final."

Izzy ran angrily out to the playground. As soon as he passed through the doorway, the delivery man arrived with another frost-covered bucket of fetuses.

Izzy greeted the delivery man, "The contest is over—lousy little Reen is it—she's ruined it for all of us! They probably won't want to see you any more either." Then he threw down his basket, and stomped the rolls as they spilled onto the ground.

When he looked up, he saw Reen jumping rope with easy shallow swings. Reen was reciting, "Blue bells, cockle shells, eevie, ivy, over." After a few more swings, she changed the chant to "Mabel, Mabel, set the table. Salt, Vinegar, Silverware...don't forget the Red Hot Peppers!" The swingers spun the rope faster and faster until she tripped and was out.

Izzy scoffed, "Some Christ Child—can't even do red hot peppers! I'm a better healer than you are, too. You cheated somehow." As Reen was standing up to face him, he hit her, knocking her back to the ground. Then he shouted loudly, "You ruined it for all of us! You're not even born of a virgin!"

Reen wiped pebbles from her bloody knees and stared at him dumbfounded. The other children grouped around Izzy, and joined in his chant, "Not born of a virgin, not born of a virgin."

The children formed a line and paraded around Reen, pointing at her and poking at her. Izzy tore off her sweater, in imitation of steal ing Christ's robe.

The delivery man entered Sister Carmen's office, put the frost covered bucket on her desk and said, "Here's some more—fresh frozen from the WomanCare lab." Then he presented the clipboard for her to sign.

Sister Carmen took the clipboard, and pen poised, said, "We still haven't placed the last batch you brought us. Can't you ask them to hold these until we have some empty wombs?"

"I just deliver 'em," said the delivery man.

"Don't worry," said Sister Gloria. "We should have lots of new recruits soon. We just found the Christ Child. Everybody wants to join a winner." She turned to Patricia. "We're going to have a big story in the papers, aren't we?"

Patricia interrupted, "I demand a blood test. If she's my child, I won't let her be the Christ Child."

Sister Carmen signed the line. "Okay. Take them to the kitchen and put them in the freezer."

"Which way is the kitchen?" asked the delivery man.

"I'll show him," offered Sister Gloria.

"Don't any of you leave now," said Sister Carmen. To the delivery man, she said, "Just put them on the desk." He put the bucket on the desktop, and walked rapidly out of the orphanage.

The children on the playground began chanting "One potato, two potato, three potato, four...five potato, six potato, seven potato, more..."

Sister Carmen picked up the lid on the bucket of fetuses and peered inside. "They're just adorable." Sister Gloria and Patricia leaned in to get a closer look.

Patricia spoke first. "There's a whole army of them in there this time!"

"Think of the publicity!" said Sister Gloria. "Everybody wants to join a winner!"

Her curiosity about the fetuses satisfied, Patricia returned to her earlier topic. "I demand a blood test to prove that Reen is my child.

I've made an appointment at the clinic for 4 p.m. tomorrow. I expect
her to be there. She is my child, and the blood test will prove it."

Trying to sound reasonable, Sister Carmen asked, "What if I
allow the blood test, and she isn't your child? Will you still want her?
Will you still try to rescue her from what you see as the terrible fate
of being the Christ Child?"

Patricia's voice showed that she was having doubts. "Would you
let me have her if the tests say she isn't mine?"

"Let me tell you a story," said Sister Carmen.

"What have I got to lose?" asked Patricia, sitting down on one of
the hard oak chairs.

Sister Carmen cleared her throat to get attention, and then began,
"I have noticed that cause and effect are not always simple to figure
out. For the first two weeks, when I was in fifth grade, the lights went
out whenever I left the classroom. I was one of the heaviest children
in the class. I tried walking to the left of the doorway and then to the
right. I tried jumping over the tiles, so I couldn't trigger the light
switch. I even tried going out the back door of the classroom. But still
the lights went out whenever I left the room. Then, one day, I looked
over at the teacher, as I approached the door. There he was, standing
by the switch, ready to push it. Ever since, I've looked for the man by
the light switch. None of us are as powerful as we think we are."

"Is the point of that story that you don't think Reen is my child?"
asked Patricia.

"I leave her parentage in God's hands, where it has always been.
I do not think he will take the Christ Child from us," said Sister
Carmen.

Sister Gloria looked out the window, and saw Izzy pummelling
Reen, cheered on by the other children, who were adding kicks and
pokes of their own. She opened the window, and heard the children
shouting as if at a sporting event, "Hit her again, hit her again, harder,
harder." Reen was crying.

Patricia shouted, "They're beating her up! Help her!"

Sister Gloria ran out the door first, closely followed by Patricia
and Sister Carmen. She stood in full view of the rowdy children and
stared. Without her saying a word, the children dispersed. Patricia ran
to help Reen up. The sisters helped to dust her off.

Now that the women were out of the way, Izzy sneaked back into
Sister Carmen's office and began scanning the files on the computer.

The women led Reen to a washroom and bathed her gently with
warm washcloths. Patricia spoke soothing words to her. Sister Gloria

said excitedly, "Isn't this amazing, they tried to crucify her, just like last time!

"People don't change, do they?" said Sister Carmen. "But this time we can stop them."

As she sponged off the child's badly scraped elbow, Sister Gloria said, "Reen is truly the Christ Child! I can't wait for the millennium! Everything will be so wonderful!"

"All thanks to Reen!" said Sister Carmen.

Some of the children who had been chanting now gathered at the bathroom door. Sister Gloria turned to them and said, "Now children, the Christ Child is just that—a child. We have to take special care of her, so she will grow up and rule the world..."

The children ran off again before the sisters could begin one of their maudlin speeches.

Izzy, clutching a stack of computer printouts, called from the playground, "Come and get it! I've got the names and phone numbers of your biomothers!" As the children approached him, he handed each one a sheet of paper.

One of the boys shouted, "Oh, Goody! I've dreamed of finding my bio-mother. I'll make her pay for aborting me! I'll make her suffer!"

A girl said, "I just want to know what mine is like. What she was doing that was more important than taking care of me."

Another boy said, "Maybe mine is nice. Maybe she'd give me money."

And another girl said, "Let's call them and invite them over. After we meet them we can decide what to do to them!"

Izzy hopped into Patricia's car with his printout and dialed the phone. "Remember that abortion you had twelve years ago? Well it's me!"

The woman on the other end of the phone said, "You nasty little boy. You should be ashamed of yourself, playing pranks with the telephone."

"I'm not a prank. I'm real, and I'm really yours!" said Izzy.

"Wait a minute," the voice took on a hopeful tone. "Are you calling from the Order of Virgin Mothers? Are you all right?"

A sick person came up to the car and tapped Izzy on the shoulder. "I've come to worship you, Izzy! I've brought gold and jewels, fit for a king," he said.

Izzy answered the woman on the phone. "Yes, I am!"

"Oh," said the woman. "I've been praying you'd call!"

* * *

On the playground, Sister Gloria pulled Reen in a wagon, lined with a manger-shaped papier-maché sculpture. Children headed the parade singing "When the Saints Come Marching In."

Meanwhile, in the office, Sister Carmen explained the results of her blood test to Patricia, who had again left her car on the playground.

"According to the lab, you and Reen share most of the major histocompatibility complexes, and several minor ones as well. But the data are not conclusive. You both have very common blood types."

"So?" asked Patricia.

Sister Carmen paused, then said, "There is a fifty percent chance that you are Reen's mother."

"That's good enough for me," said Patricia. "I'll take her home this afternoon."

"The Christ Child is not up for adoption," reminded Sister Carmen.

"My child is no Christ Child! And, I will not let my child be sacrificed to your religion!" Patricia said.

Calmly, Sister Carmen answered, "You made that choice eleven years ago when you had your abortion."

Patricia stood to give her words impact. "That's ridiculous! Give me my child!"

"If we were to give any of our children to their bio-mothers, we would become nothing more than the brood-sows you accused us of being in your newspaper article," said Sister Carmen. "If you have your way, we might as well hang out a sign—Is Your Pregnancy Inconvenient? Let a Virgin Sister grow your baby for you—and then —when it is convenient—if you like your child—come and get him or her any time you like." She paused. "That would be ridiculous!"

The parade outside suddenly fell silent, but Sister Carmen and Patricia continued talking.

"I didn't tell you to start your religion. You didn't even ask my opinion," said Patricia. "And I don't see why it would be ridiculous to offer the service you suggested. I'll bet there are lots of women who'd love it. They might even pay you for it."

"Of course I didn't ask your opinion before starting the Order of the Virgin Mothers. And if I had, your child would not exist, and we wouldn't be here arguing. So, what is it you really want?" Sister Carmen leaned back in her chair.

Sister Gloria entered the office. "Sisters Beth and Helen just spoke with me. If you declare Reen to be the Christ Child, they see no reason to stay in the Order of Virgin Mothers."

"Why is that?" asked Sister Carmen.

"We're asking you to choose," said Sister Gloria. "Which do you want more: The Order or the Christ Child. You cannot have both! The Order existed to find the Christ Child. If she has been found, we don't need to live here and remain virgins any longer."

"We have all worked for the Coming of the Christ Child. The Christ Child and the Order are one," said Sister Carmen.

"But, if Reen truly is the Christ Child," said Sister Gloria, "why should I maintain my virginity? Why should I not marry and have children of my own?"

"You swore your life to Christ—it is not up to me to choose for you. My conscience impels me to choose the truth! I cannot deny the Second Coming of Christ! If you leave, I will find others to help me raise the children." Sister Carmen placed her hands behind her neck, and did her best to look relaxed.

"But, consider if you are wrong," persisted Sister Gloria. "If Reen is not the Christ Child. Reen is truly a miraculous child, but she isn't as good a healer as Izzy. She makes Kool Aid instead of wine, and rolls instead of bread. I don't think she is the Christ. If you choose her over the Order, and then discover you are wrong, you will have lost all chance of finding Him in your lifetime. Do you want to take such a risk?"

"I am sorry your faith is so weak," said Sister Carmen. "If I deny my Savior, just to keep my Order together, I am no better than Judas."

"You could wait," said Sister Gloria. "You could give Reen to this reporter, here. Let her grow up in a normal life, like Jesus did. And then, when she is an adult, if she continues to behave like Christ, there will be plenty of time to acknowledge her. And, meanwhile, we can continue accepting implants, and continue our Search."

Patricia tried to stifle her smile.

"I have found the Christ Child," repeated Sister Carmen. "Do what you will. But, ask God's Guidance before you act."

"You are a foolish vain old woman!" said Sister Gloria, and she turned to leave the office.

Before she could leave, a large man barged into the office pushing her back inside.

"I won't have my child worshiping that scrawny wimp in the basket! What sort of joint do you run here?"

"This *joint*," said Sister Carmen, "is the religious establishment of the Order of the Virgin Mothers, and we..."

"The contest was a fraud," said the man. "Anyone can see that my Izzy, who is my son, is more wonderful than that Reen girl! I demand a recount!"

"I'm sure this can all be settled reasonably," said Sister Carmen.

Patricia turned to Izzy's bio-father. "Watch what you say about my child!"

"She's your child?" said the man. "Then this is all your fault!"

"Who are you, and why are you in my office, criticizing my children?" asked Sister Carmen.

Patricia's alter-ego, the reporter, took over again. She pulled her notepad from her purse and began writing. She asked the man, "Please spell your name so I'll have it right for my story."

"You never asked if he wants to be in the newspaper," said Sister Carmen.

"It can't hurt," said the man. "Public outrage will help us get our children out of this dump."

"Many of the bio-mothers never told anyone they had abortions. They might not want their stories told," said Sister Carmen.

"Oh, grow up!" said Izzy's bio-father.

"Nowhere is it written that we are grown-ups of God," said Sister Carmen.

Not again, thought Patricia. *Does she say that to all the parents?*

"Just what we need—platitudes when we are trying to get our children back!" said Izzy's bio-father.

"You gave up your rights to these children when you had them aborted. I have your consent forms on file in our safety deposit box. I can arrange an appointment for you with our lawyer, so you can see them, if you have forgotten," said Sister Carmen.

"You don't have my consent form on file—because I never signed one," said Patricia.

"My wife signed under duress—she was pregnant and scared," said Izzy's bio-father. "I was a kid. That agreement can't be valid in a court of law."

Sister Carmen keyed something into her computer.

"The children belong to their birth-mothers—who saved them from certain death," interrupted Sister Gloria. "Give the Sisters the birth certificates and computer records of their children."

"What about my child?" persisted Patricia. "What about Reen?"
"The children belong to their bio-parents," insisted Izzy's bio-
father. "Give *us* their birth certificates and their computer records."

The delivery man interrupted the argument by knocking on the
door jamb. "Here's some more, fresh-frozen from the lab."

"I still haven't placed the last batch. Couldn't the clinic hold them
until I have some wombs ready?" asked Sister Carmen.

"I just deliver them. Sign here," said the delivery man. He
offered the clipboard to Sister Carmen, reaching between Sister Gloria
and Patricia. Sister Carmen signed as Izzy's bio-father reached for the
bucket.

"May I see them? I've never seen an aborted fetus, said Izzy's
bio-father.

"If you look, you have to take one," said Sister Carmen.

No one moved toward the bucket. Then Izzy's bio-father said,
"They can't just sit out here on your desk. Where should I put them?"

Before Sister Carmen could answer, Sister Gloria said, "Put them
back in their bio-mothers. I've got ten children already, and two more
on the way. I don't want any more."

Reen entered the room apparently walking on air, her feet definitely off the ground. She held a magician's hat, out of which she
pulled doves at random intervals. Crystal bells rang, and a light
glowed warmly around the child. The adults fell silent and turned their
attention to Reen.

Sister Carmen spoke first. "I realize that Christ was in his thirties
last time before he was called on to make difficult moral choices, but
I need your advice now."

Reen seemed to have developed a great deal of poise since her
crying episode on the playground. Her carriage and voice tones were
now those of a self-confident child. "I'll try to help if I can," she said.

"Discovering that you are the Christ Child has caused a great deal
of anger," began Sister Carmen. "Bio-parents want their children
back. Some of the Sisters want to leave the Order and take the children
they have borne with them. We need your advice on the future of our
Order." Sister Carmen patted what was left of her lap, inviting Reen
to climb in for a cuddle.

Sister Gloria stepped between Reen and Sister Carmen, and
addressing Sister Carmen she said, "The Order has no future if you
insist that *she* is the Christ Child!"

"I certainly don't agree that she is *my Lord*. She is a child, and
should be treated like a child," added Patricia.

Abortion Stories

"I say she's a child—and a naughty one at that. If she were mine, I'd spank her!" said Izzy's bio-father.

Patricia stepped in between Reen and Izzy's bio-father. Then she said, "Sister Carmen, surely you don't mean to trust all our fates to this ten-year-old child? This should be handled in a court of law."

Sister Carmen smiled beatifically. "For me, and my Order, God's law is beyond man's law. Reen is God, and I will abide by her decree, even if it lands me in jail. I know that you and your unbelieving multitudes will take this to court if you do not like Reen's decision, and if you don't like the first judge's opinion, you'll appeal that, too. For me there is only one judge. And all I ask is that we hear Her out."

"Okay," said Patricia. "I'll listen—but I'm not expecting any Solomon."

"Why are you women all such softies for children? I won't listen to anything this wimp has to say!" said Izzy's bio-father.

"Sisters, are we agreed that we will do the bidding of our Lord?" asked Sister Carmen.

"Perhaps I was hasty. I will abide by my Lord's wishes. Forgive me, Reen," said Sister Gloria.

"Let us pray together," said Reen.

The Sisters and Reen kneeled together on the floor. When their backs were turned, a rabbit jumped out of the magician's hat, but neither Patricia nor Izzy's bio-father dared to giggle.

"Thank you God for all your blessings," said the Sisters and Reen together.

Then Reen said, "Sister Carmen, you taught me that the Order was created to find the Christ Child. You did it. Now it's time for the Sisters to resume normal lives."

"That's what I said!" said Sister Gloria.

"Does it surprise you to hear your judgment confirmed by the Christ Child?" said Sister Carmen, still recovering from Reen's pronouncement.

Sister Gloria hesitated, then said defensively, "No. I knew I was right." Then she asked Reen, "May we take our children with us," she paused, "Lord?"

Reen's voice carried unusual confidence for one so young. She stood facing Sister Gloria and said, "The children you have borne are yours—that is the law of the land. The Order has served its purpose—it has saved the Christ Child. So, you and your children can live where ever you want. Your vows are fulfilled." Then she added with wisdom beyond her years, "But I do not know how you will like life without a cause controlling every minute."

"What about us?" asked Izzy's bio-father. "Must we watch our flesh and blood be sacrificed to religious nuts whose only purpose was to find you?"

Reen faced Izzy's bio-father. "The Sisters taught us that you sacrificed your children to God when you had your abortions. And now, thanks to Izzy and the computer, you have been given an extra blessing. You know your children survived their abortions and are loved. Perhaps, if God is willing, the Sisters will let you visit them."

Izzy's bio-father's hands balled into fists as he faced the young girl. "You're no Christ Child. You're just doing what the Sisters taught you. You're a puppet—nothing more! You can't stop me from taking Izzy home this very day!"

"That's true," said Reen. "I cannot stop you from breaking the law. The Sisters taught me that the freedom to break the law is as important as the freedom to keep it. Without that freedom, we are all enslaved."

Izzy's father picked up the frozen fetus bucket, and then having second thoughts said, "Will somebody take this bucket? Before I throw it at her?"

Sister Carmen held out her hands for the bucket, "I'll take it. And, if no one will help me, I'll grow them all myself."

Patricia asked, "Reen, will you come to live with me and be my daughter? The blood tests say there is a fifty percent chance you are my flesh and blood."

"Last time, Christ was raised by his birth-mother," said Reen. "He was an implant, too, you know. My birth-mother is dead. Sister Carmen is the closest thing I have to a birth-mother. I'll stay with her." Reen looked up at Sister Carmen and hugged her. Sister Carmen returned the hug.

"I can sue for her in a court of law," Patricia said to Sister Carmen.

Reen answered, "If you go to court, the judge will ask what I want before he decides. And I'll tell him I want to stay with Sister Carmen."

"If the judge said you had to live with me, would you do so?" asked Patricia.

"I trust God will not make me make that choice," said Reen.

"But you are my child," said Patricia. "I want you to be part of my life."

"You can come visit me in my new home," said Reen, snuggling into Sister Carmen's lap.

Sister Carmen lifted the lid on the frozen fetus bucket and displayed the contents to Patricia and Izzy's bio-father. As if offering hors d'oeuvres, she asked, "Would you like one of these?"

Patricia looked at the fetuses, over at Reen, and back at the fetuses.

"Take one," said Reen. "They are my flesh and blood."

Lois June Wickstrom is a '79 Clarion graduate, with publications in **The Berkeley Showcase,** *the 1983* **Clarion Anthology, Owlflight, Fantasy Book,** *and the* **Tampa Tribune.** *She founded and edited the magazine* **Pandora** *for eight years. She's the author of* **Oliver,** *a children's book on adoption (Our Child Press), and her Amana-Mini-Health-Mysteries appeared in* **Jack and Jill** *for most of the '80s. She's also the creator of an award-winning series of videos that teach chemistry as a situation comedy called "It's Chemical". Lately, she's taken up firewalking.*

Miscarriage

New York to Desmoines,
no spare cash.
The bus was cheapest.
He found it good
sitting by this Iowa
girl; tense, chatty, midwestern kind. Sharing
potato chips. Nibbling her
nails. When the Greyhound
pulled into Chicago, this Italian-American
kid gave him lotsa dope
on the Mafia. Not that she knew
any more than he did.
But it was nice to lounge, holding hands
and other places under
his overcoat. Gave him the inside
story.
In fact, many inside stories.

He felt nervous

but flattered. The girl's tale

trembled as she told

how her sacramental family

saddened at the miscarriage. Or was it

he wondered an abortion?

Anyway, it was a downer.

She sobbed gently

and he slid his hand from under her

breast and held her wired head

against his tired shoulder.

The bus bumped them gently

out of Moline going West.

---

*A.M. Friedson, Emeritus Professor of English at the University of Hawaii, is Media editor of **Biography**. He is also editor-at-large for **Kaimana: Literary Arts Hawaii**, official quarterly of the Hawaii Arts Council. He has chaired the creative writing departments of the departments of English at the University of Hawaii and the University of British Columbia. His books include **Literature Through the Ages** and **New Directions in Biography**. His poems have recently been published in **Chaminade Literary Review, Festival, Hawaii Review, Last Issue, Northwest Poetry, Poetry Hawaii** and **Seaweeds and Constructions**.*

About the Cover Artist

Michael Taylor

Designs Unleashed
P.O. Box 11742
Prescott, AZ 86304

Michael Taylor is slowly moving into the SF-Fantasy-Horror arena with recent illustrations for **Midnight Zoo, Gauntlet, Gothic Light,** a cover for **Aberations,** and the cover of this book. He's good enough to support his family with freelance art. Most of what he's done previously has been illustrating children's books, drawing maps for books that need maps, and T-shirts. His illustrations have appeared in the John Muir Publications series **22 days in...**(i.e. France, New Zealand, India, etc.). He's done some political cartooning and illustrations for newspapers, and cartoon strips. For this book, Michael was given a pretty much impossible task: An illustration that at once evoked controversy, yet without falling too far into the pro-choice or pro-life camps. I think he did an equitable job, and I predict the SF-H-F world will soon "discover" Michael Taylor, and you'll be seeing a lot more of his work.

About the Editor

Rick Lawler

This is the first book Rick Lawler has edited (although he edited newspapers for five years in the late 70s and early 80s). He is the author of **How to Write to World Leaders** (AVON 1992) and **Valley Fire** (Blair Publications, 1991). He has published numerous articles and short stories in a wide variety of publications. He belongs to the Authors Guild, the National Writers Club and Small Press Writers and Artists Organization. He lives in Sacramento with his wife, Alice, and daughter, Sara.